Leslie
Weelant
2014

Evie & the ElemMates

Leslie Wallant

ISBN 978-0-9916465-0-0

for Alan, Jon and Ed

Contents

Chapter 1
The Weird Carved Box

Evie was still fuming mad at Liz.

Sure, Liz joined her at the wastebasket, concern showing in her deep, brown eyes while Evie tearfully tore up her first science quiz of the school year. She failed royally. Liz hugged her friend and walked down the hall with her trying to comfort her.

"Hey let's take our secret shortcut past the back of the toy store. Maybe there's a consolation gift in their dumpster for you. We've found some good stuff in there, remember?" Liz suggested, trying to distract her.

They walked to the back of the school to the dirt path through woods. Students knew the shortcut led to the back of a small strip mall in the center of their coastal New England town. Liz bushwhacked through thorny brambles, holding back branches for her sorrowing friend. The fresh September air was a relief after the sweaty smelling school halls. These little back woods seemed a secret garden with goldenrod, dahlias and little blue flowers. "Aw, cheer up, kid, it was just a science quiz."

"Easy for you to say, who never fails a thing. Ms. Melillo says this counts. I can't remember all those Chemistry formulas." Evie stank in Science. She sucked at just about everything except art. The walk and anticipation of new found dumpster treasure did take her mind off school a bit.

"OK, next quiz we'll study together. Wow, look there!

6

The Dumpster is overflowing." Upon a closer look, the bin was only full of discarded packing boxes. Liz being taller than Evie looked in and grabbed the only two discarded items holding onto the brand new game CDs and tossing Evie the brown case. Evie missed of course. They both knew she would. She grabbed it and ran after Liz. Usually kids grabbed and ran in case the owners came out though everyone knew the owners didn't care. As they rounded the next block Evie noticed the words "Chemistry Set" written on the top. Damn, was this a nasty joke? Some best friend. Tears whet her rage. She almost flung it aside in disgust.

Instead of following Liz toward home, Evie dashed across the street into the town's park following the path down to the seaside promenade. She ducked under the iron railing and settled down on her favorite boulder. This spot was always her remedy for bad moods. The sound of crashing waves soothed her. The ocean sprayed foaming water into pools in the boulder's crevices. Mellow afternoon light warmed the stone. Evie admitted to herself that Liz had tried to help. Perhaps Liz hadn't noticed the words on the case. Still Liz had just grabbed all the CDs for herself.

Lately Liz had been drifting away from her into new activities and friends. She had grown tall this past year of Middle School and now in seventh grade had joined several sports teams. She hung out with kids Evie didn't know. Liz included her at lunch and occasional gatherings with her new friends, but Evie never really could relax with them. Liz's rare sympathy today, now so quickly retracted made her feel the loss of her friend even more sharply.

Best friends since kindergarten Evie remembered all their adventures both real and imaginary. In summer the girls made forts and secret hideouts in the raspberry bushes behind her house. They created their own worlds building furniture from sticks and crates, acting out little dramas with their dolls. They hung out high up in her crab apple tree's branches hidden in its pink blossoms in spring and crimson leaves in fall. Both girls were happy making up Adventure Stories, starting one to let the other finish. Fantasy or realistic, the stories fueled the girls' forays into the local woods, dips in hidden water holes and hikes up the cliff that edged the town. But while Evie was content to relax and take in the atmosphere, Liz was non-stop action. Evie sat dreaming while Liz scampered around throwing acorns at tree trunks.

Now Liz was a rising star on her teams and seemed to have lost interest in their private adventures.

So Evie felt disconnected with everyone, and not just Liz. Old friendships faded as classmates found new interests. She did not share their interests in fashion, movie stars and gossip. Nor was she interested in the highbrow literary Magazine or Tech clubs. Although she went to some of the art club meetings, so far she had made no new friends. Online gaming gave her some connection with kids through their avatars. She never met anyone in person.

So she had no one to share her passion for fantasy. Her bookshelves were full of beautifully illustrated fairytale books. She enjoyed building fantasy worlds in online games more than battling and winning points. Wandering on nature trails with her sketchbook, she drew fairies and mythical creatures hiding among the wildflowers. Only her Dad joined her in writing fantasy stories, mapping out imaginary lands and constructing them with clay and junk. Truth was, as Liz grew tall and developed, Evie at 13 was smaller than average and couldn't seem to fill out her scrawny body. She hated her dirty blond hair. It was neither fashionably straight nor luxuriantly wavy.

"What a klutz I am, wimpy, dumb and boring," she lamented to the empty air. "And yes, I admit it," she said aloud to the ocean spray, "I am lonely, really lonely. Still, Liz isn't the only one who wants action. I gotta do something. Get out of my rut. Make a change. I'm ready for anything, anyone, anywhere."

Evie wrenched herself out of her musings to focus on the box in front of her. Evie didn't care what the stupid box said. She was going to do whatever she wanted. She'd have fun no matter what. Who cares anyway!

Rummaging through the beat-up case, she assured herself she wouldn't follow those ridiculous scientific procedures in the little booklet inside. Funny it seemed to have tripled in size. It was no mere plastic case. Pretty cool actually. Looking closer she noticed polished woodcarvings. Miniature figures nestled in each curve: a unicorn, a knight, a flying horse and other characters with stars circling their heads. A latch made of tiny metal rings seemed awfully fancy for things usually sold at the store. A gentle prod easily sprang it open. Evie gasped. It was not what she expected a chemistry set to look like. It was more like a treasure chest. Inside lay over a fifty ornate cut glass vials filled with bright colored powders. The liquids were arranged in neat rows and layers in thick velvet compartments. Excitedly she lifted out each layer examining each flask. The stoppers were chiseled into jewel like flowers and animals. Each bottle had a different shape with crazy designs. Neatly written numbers and letters labeled each in codes she didn't understand.

"Hey, not too shabby. This looks like the perfect find, custom-made for me." She murmured.

Rummaging through the box Evie picked out bottles of

colored liquids and crystals. She uncapped them, pouring and mixing the liquids into the rock's puddles. "Wow! Beautiful. Look at that purple. Here's a brilliant blue to take away the blues," she chuckled. "I'm either an artist or a pretty lame kid." She always felt good playing with colors. "Now add some drops of magenta; now drop in a bit of orange. Cool how they swirl together. Here's a little yellow. Drat, why did it turn clear? How boring is that?"

In her growing excitement Evie forgot this was a Chemistry Set, that the paints she played with were chemicals. She added a pinch of emerald crystals. "Wow, it turns red…Hmm, interesting why it's bubbling". The bubbles began to boil, then steam, then rose into multi-colored clouds and burst into flame. Evie wasn't worried. She knew rocks don't burn. She knelt close watching the flickering colors on the warming rocks. Soon the flames rose higher, so she stood up and backed away. Great green flames flickered above her head. Strange, she thought she saw letters J..U…M…P repeated over and over again. Jump, jump, jump. Lots of numbers and symbols floated around more strange words she couldn't make out. So weird, nothing she recognized from the Science quiz for sure. The air and earth hummed and vibrated into a choir of voices. The boulders began to rumble under her now burning feet. She kept backing up hopping from one foot to the other as the rumbling turned to shaking. Then the boulders cracked. Her foot felt air. She reached for the ledge as she fell backwards towards the water. Missing it, flailing, free falling, burning pain then icy water. She gasped for air only swallowing water. Sinking weightless.

Chapter 2
Welcome to Atom City

Evie breathed easily. At first when she opened her eyes all she saw was bright, white light. Then she realized she was immersed in a crowd of beings. They crowded around her yet the air was fresh. At first glance they were almost transparent, light-blue, wispy glowing figures filled with tiny flitting sparks. She felt light as air as they leaned against her. Soon she could make out individual faces.

"OK, we've got her. She's all right," said a voice near her. "Hey everyone, give the stranger some air". The beings pressed closer, her lungs filled with pure fresh oxygen. Through her half opened eyes, Evie could make out a faint set of eyes, a round nose and full rounded pale lips. "How are you feeling?" a blue figure in a fluttering aqua dress asked gently.

"Never saw anything like it. A human made so small," another faint face mouthed.

"Where is my fear?" Evie thought, surprised she could understand the being's speech. These creatures seemed friendly, and they spoke English. She was glad to be alive and feeling so well. "What happened to me? Where am I?"

"You fell into the water." The faces and rounded figure became clearer.

"But where am I now? I'm not even wet and I can breathe. Did you pull me out?"

"No, you are still in the water." Several voices chorused.

"I don't see any. I'm not so stupid. Yes, I see I'm rescued. I

11

thank you all for that. Now I must be on an underwater vessel. Great! I love travel and I'm up for some excitement…." Her voice trailed off when she realized she was hemmed in, a prisoner. "Whoa…wait a minute. Hey what's the story here?" She panicked. When she attempted to back out of the group she couldn't catch her breath. "You guys had better tell me where I am and who you are." She attempted to stand up and keep her voice steady.

"Their soothing voices said, "You are immersed among us. We are oxygen surrounding you."

"Oh, sure. Come on," Evie muttered. Now she was scared. The figures pressing tightly against her seemed to be filled with flitting sparks.

"Shh, shh, relax." the first figure said in a voice sounding like a breath of air, "Let me explain. You see we are ElemMates, each of us is an atom of an element. We are citizens of Atom City, citizens where 118 kinds of ElemMates families live together. I am just one in my trillions member Oxygen family. Glad to meet you," she said politely tilting her head of windblown blue hair toward to her. "I am Octavia Oxygen, Tavia if you like. And the reason you can breathe is you are surrounded by members of my Oxygen family. When we bond that is join together with Hydrogens we form water. That's the crowd behind us filling the pool you landed in. Take a look behind our Oxygen group here to see our close friends, the Hydrogens. Alone they are a very wild kind of light gas."

Sure enough beyond the little group surrounding her with fresh air were different looking figures of flickering orange and green flames, their hair spiky red.

"Yes, you are definitely in salty sea water," she continued.

"Just look behind the Hydrogens at the white-skinned Sodium ElemMates and their chartreuse-green Chlorine friends. When they hang out together they are salt. This is our city's salt water pond."

"Whoa, this is too weird. I should be dead or something. Is this real or some fantasy story 'cause I bumped my head in that explosion? "

Tavia backed away indignantly. "Fantasy! Why my electrons! There is nothing more real than ElemMates! Believe me, we're real enough to feel the blast you caused. You sure created some strange reaction to compress yourself to our atom size. Truthfully I can't explain why as dense as you have become we are still able to keep you afloat. Nor can I explain why and how this happened to you. We will take you to our research center and hospital to find out more.

Evie was flabbergasted. "Hey, I'm not even that clear on what atoms are. And come on. That chemistry set was just a cheap toy full of bottles of colored water." The ElemMates stood quietly. "So what are atoms really?"

"Just, the smallest particle of an element that can exist on its own," A single red haired ElemMate stepped up. "Hi, Heidi here. Small as we are, we are big hearted," she said pointing to the two joined spheres visible through her translucent body. Always loud, Heidi's voice echoed. "Look closely. Our hearts are made up of protons and neutrons. I only have one of each. Our Hydrogen Family is the smallest of the ElemMates. Instead of blood, our electrons orbiting our bodies give us our energy. Every ElemMate family has a different number of protons, neutrons and electrons."

"So now I'm the size of an atom? Oh, no. I was already too small. I always hated being the smallest. This is all I need. Please, I have to get my size back, and you have to help me. Oh, this is the worst." Evie felt very sorry for herself.

"Don't worry," said Octavia firmly in a calming voice. "You seem fine, just highly concentrated like soup stock, a more powerful, even super powerful you. But please, don't insult our size. We are proud to be nano size, the smaller the better. Without tiny there can be no big. We are the building blocks of everything."

"Oh, so sorry for my outburst. Soup stock, huh, well this is all a lot to digest." Her own joke released some of her tension. "So you say I may have great powers. Does that mean I'm a Super Hero? What can I do? Wait 'til I tell my parents and my friends." Then worry crept into her voice. "Super Heroes can go home, right? They aren't stuck in Atom City forever are they?"

Tavia's breathy voice added, "To tell you the truth I really don't know much more than you do. Maybe your powers will be great, and you will learn what you can do with them. Being a Hero is up to you. Yet there is no question you are special. You are the first to ever appear in this form."

"The first? That's amazing. Was it the Chemistry Set? Was it the chemicals I mixed? Was I just in the right place at the right time? Fate? Or did someone set me up?" No one answered.

Evie noticed Tavia's frothy lace trimmed a gauzy blue and green gown. As she moved, more tiny bubbles glistened like pearls between the wavy folds of her clothes, around her neck and through her wavy blue hair. Her calmness put Evie at ease.

"Let's go to the WISE Center, at Radon Hospital where maybe our scientists can explain more. Come, we'll float to the Center further down in Atom City. Stay close so you can breathe easily until you get used to our atmosphere. Enjoy yourself. We'll float you like a bubble." At that Tavia laughed. Evie smiled too, glad they both enjoyed humor. She would have fun with Tavia. Trusting her, Evie leaned on Tavia, a floating air mattress.

Heidi joined them as they floated up away from the pool and the park into the air. Held securely in Tavia's arms, Evie looked down from where they hovered above the Oxygen's 500-floor bubble towers set on green lawns.

She reveled at this amazing ride. Flying higher the view below, the city's shape rang a bell and the word Periodic Table came to mind..."Oh, yeah," she mused, breathing deeply, "that chart in the science book that lists all the elements. That's one thing for sure, I always remember the pictures.

Atom City looked beautiful from the air. Sure enough, it was laid out just like the table of elements in her science book. Where the table showed a colored square for each element, Atom City had a different neighborhood with structures made with that element. Amazing skyscrapers, mansions and apartments divided into a grid by tree-lined streets came into view. Green parks filled the blanks of the periodic table. Smaller parks bordered the edges of the city. As they floated south, she saw a great river edged by large buildings and open green plazas splitting the city. Floating lower she saw the leaves sparkled like gems, and flowers looked like rock crystal. They hovered over a gold castle, then a silver one and a huge stadium. Further on Evie could see a beach by the river with cabanas and colorful boats.

Well, now I'm psyched up and ready for anything. This is real enough for me though I feel like one of the characters in Dad's crazy stories. Wish Dad was here now to share this adventure".

Suddenly Evie was too sleepy to move. She felt herself slipping away from Tavia. Tavia dipped and pulled her back. The setting sun reflected orange, then purple over the city.

"You know it's getting late. Let's just go back and spend the night in our neighborhood and go to the center tomorrow. Sometimes the ElemMates get a bit wild at night downtown." Tavia turned in a graceful arc and headed back north to her Oxygen Neighborhood. They touched down in a grassy field near a complex of bubble shaped glass spheres.

Her ElemMate oxygen tank escorted her through the wide doorway. As the sky darkened the electrons orbiting their bodies stood out brightly. Breathing all that pure oxygen made her feel light-headed. She snuggled with Tavia and her friendly relatives and fell asleep.

Chapter 3
Super Hero Powers

Evie found herself stretched on the most comfortable bed—all air, no-mattress. Then she realized this was no dream because she was famished. Surrounding her now were sleeping Oxygen ElemMates, their light blue bodies pulsing gently in Octavia's apartment. Despite the calm environment her mind raced. "What do these ElemMates eat? What are they really?"

Opening her eyes, Tavia divined her thoughts. "Don't worry, we'll get you something to eat. We don't eat much here, but everyone enjoys hanging out at cafés and restaurants. Can you wait a bit for the others to wake up? Arranging food for you will be a group project."

"No, I'm fine. I always eat breakfast late anyway." Evie was not just being polite. She was geared up for the adventure to continue.

The ElemMates stirred. Octavia smoothed her windblown waves. "First, let's get you something to drink. We need Heidi and her sister to help. I can send a thought message and have them meet us back in the park where you landed. The Hydrogens live all the way across town and a block north, so the park is in the middle." Tavia closed her eyes. Her eight electrons orbited faster, then flashed. "Done. Message sent and received. They'll meet us at the Main Quark Park fountain."

They slipped down from the 500th floor onto blue-green

crystal grass studded with dewdrops. "Careful stepping on it, those crystals can be sharp," Tavia warned as they turned left through the Oxygen family complex. They crossed to the next block on the same street. Here the architecture formed transluscent, cloud-like towers painted bright red, yellow and orange surrounded by a meadow of the same colored flowers. "This is the Nitrogen neighborhood. You'll meet my friend Nyla later."

They turned right one block and re-entered Atom City's largest and most northern park. Crystal flowers and groves of strange looking trees bordered glittering paths. The curving walkway led them to an open plaza with a huge round pool and a gushing fountain at its center. At the far northern part was an outdoor café.

"Hey, what's up?" A bouncing fireball ElemMate with a ruddy face and wild red hair raced over. "I'm Heidi Hydrogen. Remember me from last night? Word is out about you. Everyone is talking." She was followed by another ElemMate with the same spiky hair barreled right into Evie and knocked her over. "Oops, so sorry. You OK? Great to meet you. I'm Heidi's sister," she said, tugging Evie back to her feet.

"Please be careful. Evie is weak with thirst. OK, can you two calm down for a minute," Tavia said in an even tone. Tavia, Heidi and her sister began spinning in a circular ring-around-the-rosy at higher and higher speed. A low musical hum scaled into high, then higher notes.

"What are they doing?" Evie said backing away from the spinning bodies. They were whirling so fast she couldn't distinguish their different faces. Their flickering electron sparks enlarged into balls of fireworks. Evie was blown gasping into a café chair as they disappeared into a grey mist. The mist dissolved leaving an ice cube on the café table. Evie stared at it in shock.

A second later Tavia and the Hydrogen siblings reappeared. "There you go, Evie, something to quench your thirst." Tavia said handing her the cube to suck.

"What was that all about?" Evie sucked thirstily on the melting cube.

"Everyone knows that when Oxygen joins with two Hydrogens you get water. I mean our electrons join, and that's what you just saw when we held hands and spun around. That's how we connected. We bonded," explained Tavia.

Meanwhile Heidi panted, "I sure needed that exercise, gets rid of all that extra energy inside me."

Thirst almost satisfied, Evie tried to take all the shocking events in stride. Nonchalantly she thanked them, but still curious. "Wasn't that a lot of work for just one ice cube? There's a fountain spewing lots of water right over there. Would it have been easier if we just took a cup of it?"

"Good point. Guess we could have. But you never know what else is in the water. We made you the purest water there is. Besides, we wanted to show you our bonding dance. In any case now we need to get you some real food."

"We need Carl Carbon for that" said Heidi, much calmer after their exertion. "We could get some in town.

"Let's go get the others. I'm still energized, and up for a bit of more bonding myself," Tavia said giggling. "Better to give her the fresh, home made version. She won't need much; glucose is powerful stuff. Let's just hope the Carbons are home. They have a perfect place for Bonding."

The four walked arm in arm out of the Park back towards the Oxygen neighborhood.

Evie felt more comfortable with them. She realized the Hydrogens' outbursts were just part of their fiery personalities.

"How do you guys know so much about me? How come you guys know more about what happened to me than I do?" Evie asked.

"Actually, I am a journalist. It's my job to find stuff out. I had some leads about a visitor arriving," Tavia said.

Was all this crazy information making her dizzy, or was it her hunger?

The group crossed out of the park and walked back toward the Oxygen Neighborhood one city block to the east. They walked on powdery black paths up to the lacy coal black structure studded with millions of dazzling diamond windowpanes.

"Carl, whoo-hoo, we're here!" shouted Heidi. Her hyper energy restored.

At first Evie saw a glint of light zigzagging down the dark path. Closer up the glimmer became a dark, sharp-jawed guy with curly black hair. His eyes and teeth twinkled like diamonds. Carl also knew her story and their immediate plans.

"Hello, there, Evie. I'm Carl." He held out his hand to her. "Well, then, let's get together for some fine, sweet Bonding. We'll make it simple." He spoke in a rich, warm voice.

"We're all gonna get together and make sparks," giggled Heidi.

"Yup, we're gonna bond for some fine, fine sugar for you, babe," laughed Carl, winking at both Evie and Heidi. "You do know about atoms and molecules, don't you?"

Evie's face was blank with embarrassment. "Not too much, really. Could you maybe run it by me again."

Heidi stepped in. " Don't worry about it. You saw how an Oxygen ElemMate and two of us hydrogens made that ice cube for you. Now, look closely at my electron." Heidi held out her hand to reveal a tiny sparking light, and began spinning and waving her hands in a delightful dance. "It's so much fun whirling around like this."

Carl continued," Each family has a special number of those electrons. Heidi has one. Tavia has eight and I have six. He pointed to his whirling sparks. Bottom line, kid, is we connect by our electrons. It's a party. A bunch of us, my cousins, a dozen of Heidi's cousins, and six Oxygens dance around, and voila you get a great piece of candy to fill your belly."

Actually she was getting it: the ice cube thing with just more dancing ElemMates. She hoped it would fill her growling stomach.

They turned up one of the black paths and entered one of the Carbon family's buildings. The ElemMates flew Evie up hundreds of stories to Carl's apartment on the top floor.

"Okay, everyone, let's set up for dancing." Soon 24 ElemMates filled Carl's spacious living room. Amid all the socializing and laughter, Carl raised his voice for quiet. "Okay, are we ready?"

Heidi directed Evie to a chair carved completely out of yellow colored diamonds. Evie noticed all the furniture was a matched set of yellow diamonds. The blankets and fabrics were soft, velvety black.

The ElemMates hugged each other and grabbed each other's hands. Heidi kept giggling and turned to wink at Evie.

The group began their circle dance, turning faster and faster, bouncing, swaying, moving in and backing out. Their electrons flashed, crackled and began to orbit faster and faster around their bodies. They moved so fast they became a blur. Evie could only see their electrons smashing into each other. Finally after a blinding light her new friends reappeared. On the floor next to them lay a long green crystal. "Whew," they sighed collapsing on Carl's couches and chairs. "This should keep you going for awhile. Help yourself."

Three second rule, Evie thought picking up the crystal from the floor. One lick on the sweet green "candy cane" filled her up completely.

"Come on guys, now let's show her the City and get over to the Wise Center," urged Heidi, taking Evie's hand and heading toward the door.

Once outside they continued straight south. Now, feeling full and more relaxed, Evie was able to take in the scenery. "What a lovely park. Can we go explore?"

"You'll have lots of time. Now they are waiting for us at the Center." Carl said taking her gently by the arm.

Curving, silvery structures lined the avenue going south. "Wow, look at all this silver. This looks like the Chrysler building, my favorite New York City skyscraper multiplied. Beats Frank Gehry, my favorite architect."

"Well, my girl. You certainly know about architecture. None of these buildings are actually silver. We'll take you to the west later to the Silver and Platinum Palaces. You can visit our Titanium building further west south of Quark Park. Lot's of Gehry's buildings use titanium. You know your Chrysler Building is actually clad in steel which is iron with a bit of carbon. Truth is we love so much of your human architecture we copy it in our own materials," said Carl admiring the architecture as much as Evie.

"Well, these have such crazy shapes. Even bigger and wilder than the ones they've been building in the Middle East and Asia.

I love this city. Not too many of my friends are interested in talking about architecture with me," Evie said catching Carl smiling at her.

It wasn't just the buildings that awed her. Everything was set in lush landscaping. Water sprayed from sculpted fountains surrounded by jewel-like vegetation. Trees sprouted huge leaves and blossoms only seen in fantasy. No picture book nor tropical paradise grew such huge, colorful, wildly shaped flowers. The most exotic orchids couldn't compare; Evie's passionate gardener mother had shown her plenty. "My Mom would go bonkers here. She'd examine each plant and never get anywhere."

"Sorry to disappoint you, but most of these plants are mineral. Crystals and stone." Carl said picking a small yellow one for her. The fourth block, Bismuth Street, had the most beautiful multi-colored crystal foliage of them all. It seemed to merge with its prism-like buildings. Turning left put them on a wide boulevard crowded with chattering ElemMates of every shape, color and description.

After walking a few more blocks the wide avenue ended at a silvery building. ElemMates poured in and out. Huge white marble pillars set on a rose-colored granite base soared around wide glass doors. Evie felt a bit dizzy.

"Here we are at the Wise Center. It is connected to our city Hospital...Are you ok, Evie? The Center gets its power from the Radon on which it is built. Mild compared to more radioactive neighborhoods, the power is used for our health clinic and ElemMate rehabilitation as well as for our scientific research areas. There are masks at the welcome desk for visitors not accustomed to the atmosphere."

After Carl placed a mask over Evie's nose, she immediately

felt better. The others caught up with them. "This kind of looks like a factory…more than a hospital. I love watching assembly lines," Evie observed. Sure enough rows of complex machinery reached so high she couldn't see where they ended.

"We do have lots of factories all over the city. Here it's purely Medical and Creation. It's where ElemMates and connected ElemMates, called Molecules, get healed. No one ever dies here," said Carl. "The power for all the machines in this neighborhood generates from the ground and is piped up. This place works like an automated, bigger version of what we did to make you the ice cube and sugar."

"I do research on power sources and new bonding on the 200th floor," said Heidi heading for the elevator. "I'm off to work. Let me know how it goes."

Carl said, "We're going to the top to meet the top honcho, Mayor of the City and head of this whole Center, Dr. Plutarch Plutonium. You know why don't you, Evie? Cause you are something special." The group headed to the central elevator bank.

Perhaps the mask was making it difficult to breathe or the bad air, but Evie was becoming nervous. Where were they taking her? Who were these weird creatures? Why was she just following orders like some cow? She couldn't get those questions of why this was happening to her out of her mind.

Just as she began to panic Tavia leaned close to her and whispered, "Remember, you are very special and powerful. We are watching out for you. There is nothing to worry about."

They walked down an endless hallway. Crowds of ElemMates entered wide doorways opening off both sides. Bright lights flashed from the rooms within. The crowds diminished the farther they walked. By the time they reached the massive door at the end of the hallway, they were the only ones there.

Tavia waved her hand over a screen and the elevator doors opened. It whisked them up so high and fast Evie's ears popped. In no time at all the doors opened onto a room lined with computers and monitors.

A large raised platform under a huge crystal dome dominated the center of the room. Computer stations ringed the room. In front of each monitor sat the largest ElemMates Evie had yet seen. Clouds of sparking electrons revolved around their huge silvery gray bodies. Seated at the central platform a metallic ElemMate dwarfed the others. His cloud of grey hair gave him a distinguished, scientist-like look. His flashing electrons stood out brilliantly when he turned to them with a welcoming smile.

"Honored to finally meet you, Evie. We have been awaiting you. I'm Dr. Plutarch Plutonium, Director of Research and Development and Mayor of Atom City. Let me show you around. Because we ElemMates are forever transforming and reconfiguring from different states and into different molecules, exposed to wear, tear and sometimes utter destruction, we periodically need some rejuvenation and repair. The patient steps up onto this platform. We push some buttons and ZAP! The universe's electromagnetic forces put electrons back in shape or strengthen bonds. We use gravity, solar energy and some controlled radiation to work for us. In our research and fabrication departments we study and make new materials, breaking apart old molecules and bringing them together in novel ways. Like breaking apart a chair to make a table, so we change carbon into oil then into diamonds.

We coordinate with the other health facilities, power producers and factories around the city. Our gardens full of living plants are little power factories turning the sun's energy into food.

Although we regularly break apart molecules, we rarely break apart an ElemMate. Avoid open-heart surgery so to speak." Dr. Plutonium pointed to his heart visible beneath his sparkling electrons and purple skin. "Merging two hearts together or take one apart can cause dangerous explosions. Basically we really do follow the age-old laws. Little changes at a time. We don't do wild experiments the way your scientists do. When I heard you'd arrived I wanted to meet you to find out more about how your scientists work."

"Oh, but, sir, I don't know anything. I don't even like Science. You've got the wrong girl," Evie said looking down at her feet. Embarrassed she wasn't the great scientist whose brain she thought he wanted to pick.

Dr. Plutonium had spoken looking straight into Evie's eyes. Though his eyes flashed purples, fuchsia and reds, they didn't frighten her and surprisingly she had understood all the science stuff he told her. He suddenly turned serious. "With human advanced intelligence creating computers almost like ours and quickly surpassing them, human beings are one of the universe's greatest forces. You are experimenting creating new molecules, and even new elements. We welcome new citizens in Atom City, as long as they obey the rules and behave with others. But perhaps you humans have gone too far manipulating our citizens. Now the earth is reacting. We are seeing many more sick ElemMates here.

And you, Evie, could be the most powerful of humans. The trillions of atoms and molecules in your body have become condensed and concentrated, giving you incredible physical and mental powers. Our computers cannot describe you." Dr. Plutonium spoke with reverence.

Evie was overwhelmed. "Whoa, wait a minute, are you sure you're talking about me, little ol' Evie, the shortest, dumbest kid on the block? Me powerful? I can hardly lift my science book."

"Now you are transformed," said Dr. Plutonium respectfully. "Come. Look at the screen. Here are the chemical reactions you created up on those cliffs. Correct me if this is wrong."

"Correct you? I was just fooling around with those cool crystals and colored liquids in the bottles. I have no idea what I did." On the screen complex chemical symbols and Formulas were less decipherable to her than the Egyptian hieroglyphics she'd seen at the museum. "All I remember is mixing a blue and magenta to get a purple. Then I just added orange, yellow and a little green. Yeah, that's it. I do always remember colors. It should have turned a muddy brown." The whole memory returned. Again she saw the strange writing amid the words "jump". She recalled the haunting tones. Her arms trembled, then her legs burned as she relived those flames on the cliff. Suddenly as if a blind had opened, the screen was no longer full of gibberish. She could understand it as clearly as the alphabet. "Hey, what's going on! It's all as simple as pie. It's as clear as a comic book."

Dr. Plutonium answered calmly, "So, now you begin to see. You are a concentrated human. Your brain cells are so compact, so fortified that your mere thoughts make things happen. No human mind is as sharp and powerful as yours."

"So," Evie took a deep breath, realizing she'd been breathing fine without the mask. The tingling in her arms and legs felt wonderful. "I AM a Super Hero!"

"You could be. You are certainly a super human being. It is up to you to realize and develop your powers to become a Hero. There is plenty for you to do. Actually I have many ideas…" said the huge grey ElemMate.

Evie cut in, "Sure, sure. Right now I'm a bit flipped out. It's also so wild. Am I dreaming?"

"What do you think? Fact is the elements are real. You know we are elements. You are certainly seeing us in a very unique way. We make up all the matter or material of the earth, of the universe. But we cannot control it. Humans know how to manipulate us. They learn more every day. Although we have highly complex computers, ours are all preset and programmed by the forces of nature."

He continued, "We need a Creative Coordinator, someone to help us communicate with your world and your knowledge. We need someone to take action to solve problems, change us into new materials and to seek new horizons to help solve the world's great tragedies, both yours and ours. I have such ideas for you."

Hooked, ideas percolated in Evie's mind. "You ask a lot. But I agree. I hadn't thought about all this before. Yes, there's so much to do. What about droughts in the desert? Amassing Hydrogen and Oxygens to migrate from flooded places to dry. Maybe transform the molecule to make it last longer...." Evie surprised herself at her newfound environmentalism.

Plutarch now spoke to everyone. "Actually there is a danger now. Earth is protected from harmful rays by the Ozone Layer, Oxygen threesomes. The Fluorines and Chlorines are bonding with those Oxygens, enticing them to abandon their guard posts which caused holes appear in the protective Earth shield." Dr. Plutarch turned to Evie.

"Perhaps your scientists know how to solve this problem. You could help us communicate with your scientists. We want to know their new laboratory discoveries. Perhaps then we can replicate them on a grand earth wide scale. We can work together."

Evie was all keyed up. "This sure isn't the boring science I'm used to. I'm pumped!" She knew her own electrons were probably exploding inside her. "But I don't know any scientist that would listen to an ordinary kid like me. Not sure I can help you…"

Suddenly the power went out. In the dark ElemMates' electrons crackled in fear. Tiny invisible impacts brushed into everyone. To Evie it felt like a gentle tickle. Someone screamed "Neutrino shower warning. Cosmic Ray alert! Cosmic Ray Alert!" ElemMates raced around the room in panic, their electrons in disarray. Some electrons broke free and bombarded their neighbors.

When Evie focused, she could make out the tracks of this invisible shower coming from above, passing through windows, seeping right through everything, coming out the other sides of objects as if they did not exist.

"Calling Leads! Calling Leads!" echoed through the building from loud speakers. "Cosmic Ray Attack! Gamma Ray Attack! Go to the Lead Shelters!"

The doctor rushed to gather everyone into rooms reinforced and guarded by the Lead ElemMates. "Hurry, hurry. The Neutrino showers usually give us fair warning of Cosmic Ray attacks. Only the Leads can protect us!"

Too late huge black rays crashed into the room. Most ElemMates couldn't make it to the shelters in time. The result was devastation. Electrons were knocked off their bodies. Some were pierced right through their hearts, splitting their nucleus releasing powerful life force energy into other ElemMates. Energy and radiation released in the havoc supercharged the air in chain reactions causing shocks, fire and poisonous toxins. Computers exploded. Screams filled the room.

"What to do! What to do!" Evie's mind raced, as she stood helpless for some reason unscathed. "Some Hero I am. Some Super Being. Super...Super...That's it! Play Superman. What would he do?"

Without thinking she leaped up, and to her amazement, shot through the air toward the ceiling as easily as the fabled Super hero. She flattened herself against the ceiling. "If I'm so concentrated, maybe these big rays won't get through my body." Sure enough as she shot back and forth around the room, her body successfully blocked and repelled every ray. The energy forces from her movements formed a shield repelling the rest of the rays. The bombardment stopped. "Hooray! Hooray!" Everyone cheered. Heidi, Carl and Octavia rushed to her side, lifting her above the crowd in celebration. Evie was relieved her new friends were fine.

Dr. Plutarch Plutonium approached, reaching up to shake her hand. "Thank you. That was an unusual attack. You have saved us. Not only do we usually have more warning from the Neutrinos, but the Cosmic Rays don't contain so many and such huge Gamma Rays. Indeed you are finding your powers so rapidly. Your body is so dense even the Neutrinos could not penetrate. And while Neutrinos usually pass right through most everything, the other rays are not so harmless. You stood up to one of our most feared enemies."

"How often do they attack?" Evie asked.

"Too often. It depends upon the sun. It sends the Neutrinos and the Cosmic Rays in solar storms. We cannot predict their attacks except the short pre-warning of the Neutrino shower. We have no defense against them. The attacks are becoming more frequent and more intense. The percent of Gamma Rays in the mix seems to be increasing," he said nodding sadly.

"Here's an idea." Evie's mind was racing. "What if we replicate the protective force that protected me from the rays, and enlarge it to shield the whole city? Take a small piece of my hair since it's part of me. Put it in your replicating chamber to create a thin force field. It should be as strong a shield as I was to block the Gamma Rays."

Before Evie said another word Dr. Plutonium plucked one of Evie's hairs from her head and a few threads from her shirt, dashed to the one computer restored to power and furiously tapped on the keyboard. Huge rolls of a gossamer clear fabric began folding off the platform. ElemMates rushed to attach the first section to the ceiling.

"Amazing, my powers transfer into fibers that can be woven into powerful fabric. I love it. That's really Fashion Power. Maybe I can train myself to produce the cloth myself," Evie said thinking of all the possible ways to use the cloth.

A smaller assistant approached. "Sir may I volunteer to work on this project. We'll need tons to cover the city. Yet we want access to the sky. I'll work on some engineering for it if I may, and direct workers."

She was flushed with pride and excitement. "Wow! Little ol' Evie with hair stronger than Samson. Wait 'til I tell Mom and Dad. They'll be so thrilled. They won't believe their little loser has so many untapped talents." Suddenly she lost her verve. The fact that she was stranded in this nano world or dream world deflated her. No one would ever know. If this were a dream, she'd wake up the same old under achiever.

"Hey, lighten up, girl," piped up Carl Carbon. "What's with

the sad face?"

Tavia placed her arm around Evie's shoulder. They sensed her feelings. "You aren't lost here. Remember you are now our connection with the human world. You found out you have great powers. Those powers will carry over to new powers at your human size as well, perhaps different, but there for you to discover. I think we all want our friendship to continue..."

"Yes, but how do I get home?" Evie almost whined, still in fact a tired, homesick kid.

Dr. Plutonium sat down at the now working computer. The Formulas he had shown her before on the monitor, the numbers and symbols from her experiment reappeared on the screen. "First and most important, you must memorize this Formula. As you probably realized during the attack, one of your powers is that all you need to do is think something to make it happen. So if you want to come to us all you do is think this Formula, recite it to yourself. You must protect it though. While I have seen it, only you can memorize it, and only you can know it."

"Fine, fine," she interrupted impatiently eyes tearing, "But I want to go home."

"Simple. Just think the Formula in reverse. That may have been difficult for the old you, but you'll find it quite easy now," the doctor said gently.

"Easy? In reverse? I may now have some alleged physical properties and powers and I now do understand a lot of this science. But I can't memorize stuff. I can't even memorize my friends' phone numbers. I confess I don't even have the multiplication tables down pat. It takes me days of agonizing study to memorize anything serious."

"Come, just try." Plutarch made room for her in front of the monitor. She focused on the screen. As if she'd just opened closed eyes she realized she really did know the Formula. Backwards and forwards like the fingers on her hand. "I got it! It's a cinch. I sure hope this memory improvement thing works when I'm normal size." She was thrilled by her new found smarts. "Speaking of normal size, you realize I'm pretty small for my age at home. You think my powers could make me bigger than I was?"

"I think you will look the same, Evie. If you are a relatively small human, you should be proud that your power is a result of miniaturization like the smaller and smaller microchips packing more and more information. The smaller you are, the more powerful. Now at your compressed atomic size you are at the height of your powers," responded Plutarch in a fatherly tone.

"OK, OK, whatever, fine, now let me go home." She shut her eyes to concentrate on thinking The Formula in reverse to go home…

"Wait!" yelled Heidi and Carl. "You will come back to help us won't you? You want to use your great super powers and enjoy our city and help the world with us won't you?"

Evie almost let the voices fade then opened an eye and smiled. "I sure do". Her new friends gathered close around her. "This has been a great adventure. You've been great. I certainly hope all this is real and I'll see you again…and do what needs to be done." She closed her eyes seeing her new friends in her mind. Then she thought the Formula in reverse and pictured home.

Chapter 4
The Ozone Hole

CRASH!

The sudden sound interrupted Evie from completing the Formula. She opened her eyes still in the Atom City Medical Center.

Havoc! The shield had failed. Evie sprang into action once again as the rays bombarded in full force.

Plutarch shouted, "It's happening. The rays are coming through the ozone hole. We need everyone's help. Evie, we need you too. Stay. Go with Octavia. Octavia Oxygen's family will join you since the Ozones are cousins. You, too, Carl. And try to rally your family to join also. The hole needs to be closed NOW. You need to head directly to the upper atmosphere. The Fluorines and Chlorines will be there to lend a hand as well."

"I don't know. What can I do? Me, fix it? I dunno. That's more than anyone can do, super hero or not. Not sure I'm actually a super hero. I'm no superman who stops floods and earthquakes and spins the world around. That's all fantasy."

"Those ultraviolet rays destroy us ElemMates. It will cause much cancer for humans and animals. Do what you can. Octavia needs some support." The doctor insisted.

Tavia reached out her hand. "Let's go Evie. This is it."

Taking Evie's hand Tavia lifted off in the face of the oncoming rays. Evie felt her own strength. She let go of Tavia's hand and flew on her own.

Facing the city she concentrated on every fiber in her hair and clothing to make her hair and the threads of her clothes stretch into long shimmering multi-colored strands that wove themselves into cloth. She focused on her fabric so it stretched to patch the city where the rays had torn through the first shield. Satisfied the City was safe for now, she followed Tavia into the sky.

"Wait, where is this hole? How am I supposed to get up miles into the atmosphere? Isn't it miles up and freezing cold there?"

"As you have undoubtedly heard in your newscasts, it is directly overhead. You must go way, way up through the troposphere to the border of the stratosphere. That is where the Ozones form a shield against the sun's dangerous radiation rays. Ozone molecules, my fellow oxygen cousins, prefer to live as triplets, three bonded together. Air conditioning and spray cans send dangerous chemicals called Chlorofluorocarbons, a bad mixed up gang causing trouble to the Ozones. They smash the triplet Ozones apart and brutally bond with them. This has happened before. Diplomacy worked the last time.

We thought we had solved the problem, but now they have forgotten their promises and more holes are appearing in other areas of the atmosphere. Perhaps your presence and powers will help," Tavia shouted.

Evie was not sure where they were going. She had not tuned in to all that atmospheric stuff in the news and at school. But the doctor's words sank in. "Super hero, okay, I'm game." She shot up, feeling the air cool on her arms and soared into a blinding azure sky. The air became fresher as she swooped higher and higher, then turned icy cold. She looped on the air currents. Up, up, up on the warm air, then a cooler current took her down. Tilting and banking to this side and that, she perfected her piloting technique. "It sure helps to have special powers." She was bursting with joy. "I'm flying, really flying," she shouted.

Gleefully she practiced her skills. Glide, dive, swoop and fly. She could do a stomach dropping dip, float on her back then twist and launch upwards. While she could never manage to jump from a diving board, leaping up into the sky, riding air currents was a breeze...ha, ha, she chuckled. Flying up she noticed the temperature change. "Oh, I thought it was supposed to be cold up here, but it feels warmer here. And where did the air current go?" She had reached the troposphere layer. She found she could balance in this spot, letting the warm lower level buoy her up.

Suddenly she choked on the most awful stench. Her nose and throat burned. Sickly greenish-yellow ElemMates surrounded her. Their eyes flashed green. Yellow-green mucous dripped from their long bony noses. Fwop! Evie leaped up knocking some of them over. She saw Tavia surrounded by another group of the monsters. Two of them had her friend locked in a tight embrace. Desperately Evie rushed over using all her strength to break them apart. In a spray of electrons they unbonded. Grabbing the Oxygen ElemMate as best she could, she took off into the air.

"Oh, thank you, Evie...I'm fine...I'm fine," Octavia panted, breathing deeply, slowly until her racing off kilter electrons regained their proper even rotation. Her skin returned from colorless to healthy pale blue.

"Whew, I wasn't ready for that. What is going on?" Evie panted also trying to catch her breath.

"It's them, the Chlorofluorocarbons, CFCs. It's when normally pretty nice Chlorines, Fluorines and Carbons bond becoming monsters. They don't listen to anyone, even their Fluorine and Chlorine cousins. They attack our Ozone cousins; maybe they like the triplets because they are also a threesome," said Tavia.

Evie helped the almost recovered Oxygen up to the safer stratosphere. The view was a beautiful carpet of pale blue Ozones as far as the eye could see except directly below where the slimy green hole grew, and dark space showed through.

"I guess I'd better get down there and give diplomacy a try. It worked a bit last time this happened, but with you, Evie, perhaps everyone will really listen," said Tavia. As Evie and Tavia turned to swoop down, they caught sight of Carl Carbon in a stranglehold with a Chlorine and Fluorine. Instantly Evie was upon them. She smashed their bond and ripped them off her friend.

"Wait! Wait!" screamed Carl.

"Hey, Evie, we are fine." Carl gently pushed her away comforting the fallen adversary. Evie stepped back confused.

"These guys are with us.," Carl explained. The Chlorine's yellow-green complexion matched his camouflage uniform. The smaller Fluorine's pale yellow skin and wavy blond hair blended with his khaki uniform.

The larger Chlorine soldier said, "Boy, you pack a mean punch there. We're glad to have the famous Evie on our side. We're both here to help out. We're all a bit shaken up about this situation, too."

"Oh, I'm so sorry. I don't know my own strength, yet. I guess I should be a bit more cautious. Can't let my brawn outweigh my brains." They all smiled at her attempt at humor. "I'm so glad we have a good team here."

Together they flew to the gaping hole's edge where troubled Ozones struggled. The stench was even stronger than before. She swallowed to stop the nausea. Her eyes stung painfully. Like a fiery blob of spilled mustard, attacking CFCs bee-lined to engulf their victims, the helpless Ozones. The air vibrated with the death crackles of amputated electrons. Desperate the Ozones failed to escape the passionate assaults.

Evie was knocked down. She sank below the ozone level to confront a more shocking, frightening sight. Her courage faltered as millions of huge green-yellow, ElemMates bound together as triple sized warriors arose from the earth marching toward her like a three-headed monster.

Evie rallied and stood her ground. Thinking herself as a shield, "Stop" she shouted at the hoard. "What do you think you are doing?"

The front line of CFCs stopped abruptly causing the back lines to topple into them. "Hey, what's going on," came the shouts from the back. "Halt, halt!" the front row shouted. The great green-yellow army of hooligans stood still.

Evie's firm, quiet voice resonated back to the CFCs. "Control your impulses. Your passions will destroy us all. The Ozones you molest shield all of us from the sun's poison rays."

Their leader retorted, "You Humans created our army. We can't help our passions; they are part of our chemical make-up. Our great numbers are your doing."

"So, are you fated to your so called properties?" Evie countered, hands on hips. "That 'I am what I am and can't change myself' thinking. Well, I don't cotton to that. Sure you are right. Humans cause your release in huge masses, creating this marauding band. Humans are attempting to end this behavior. But for now what are you going to do? Continue your rampage blindly disrupting and destroying your families and friends, or disband these gangland bonds. Think for a bit. It's your choice," she finished firmly.

The words barely out of her mouth, screams arose through the green-yellow mass. Turning around she saw huge black arrows raining through the hole opened to dark space, piercing the CFCs. The CFCs fell burning and writhing under this deluge. "Radiation Rays!" Everyone tried to escape the killing radiation shooting through the hole in the Ozone Shield. Many rushed right into the arrows in panic. Others fled desperately straight up through the hole into the stratosphere, lost forever in outer space.

Evie took command of the crisis. "Ozones! Release your bonds with the CFCs. Rejoin your threesome family bonds. Quick move back in together! Block that hole! Only you can stop this Radiation Ray onslaught." She raced among the newly released Oxygens guiding them back to bond with two other family members. Her body for the second time blocked the powerful rays. She grasped the huge arrows in her bare hands and hurled them back into space. Ozones rallied to her call moving back together into newly formed threesomes. In turn they joined with other Ozones, knitting together from the edges into the middle to darn the hole. Soon the quivering net struggled to close the hole.

Then an amazing thing happened. Surviving newly single Fluorines, Chlorines and Carbons gently filled in not yet mended spaces until more Ozones could fill in without attempting to bond with the reunited Ozones. Apologies were extended to the Ozones. " Uh, we'll stay until you get more Ozone reinforcements, ok?" they asked meekly.

The Hole mended. The bombardment stopped. "Hooray! Hooray!" everyone cheered. "Everyone did great!" Evie was glad all her friends were ok.

Wounded ElemMates were rushed to the Wise Center at Radon Hospital for care. Evie and her friends stopped off at the Wise Center to debrief the doctor.

Tavia announced they were invited one block north to the Xenon's photo studio for some shots to go with her news article. Afterward Carl suggested it was time to party. Neon is having a great party a couple of blocks up. A huge crowd trooped over to the best city club. Krypton, a neighbor, contributed to the party's light show with colorful twisted glass tube lights. The Hydrogens, Carbons and Oxygens mixed up some bubbling soda with glucose flavoring. "A toast. A toast."

Dr. Plutonium, Mayor of Atom City, did the honors. "It was wonderful how so many of you rallied for the good of us all. The CFC Gang has disbanded and will self police to try to keep the rogues from reorganizing. Thanks to Evie we remember we are not slaves to our properties, our impulses or fate. We can take control of ourselves. The Ozones realize how important they are way up there to shield us.

Finally, a toast to Evie. You are learning more and more about your strengths and abilities. You find you can grow physically, mentally and emotionally."

Evie replied, "I want to thank everyone for welcoming me in this wonderful land, for allowing me to help you when you needed me, for…being my friends."

It was so pleasant sitting in the garden of the club with her new friends snacking on the special green treats. She hoped Tavia felt as she did about their new friendship. Tavia was so easy to open up to. Evie found herself talking about her life at home, her school and artwork. Tavia shared her interests in writing and her work on the newspaper. She confessed she was upset about the invading radioactivity rays and the simmering trouble with the Radioactive ElemMates. Evie was learning about politics.

"Oh, Tavia, you have so many concerns and interests. You're a good influence on me. I realize I waste too much time worrying about silly, selfish things. You've inspired me. I'm going to work harder on my artwork and try to concentrate on my other classes more. As I said to Dr. Plutonium, I've opened my mind to act beyond my own little interests. While I'm not sure what that Chemistry Set is all about, it has certainly inspired me to strive for much more, to improve myself and take advantage of new possibilities."

"OK. Enough talk. Let's relax. Join me in my favorite way to relax?" Tavia took Evie's hand and floated up above the café. High above the city Tavia lay on her back, her hands clasped behind her head. Evie did the same. They lay peacefully looking into the brilliant blue sky, breathing deep, slow, calm breaths. Tavia feeling the gentle vibrations of her eight electrons orbiting her body, Evie feeling relaxed and calm.

Chapter 5
Problems in Paradise

A hot air current disrupted Tavia's and Evie's airborne nap as Heidi Hydrogen's flaming red hair came into view. "Tavia, come quick. Dubni's son is fighting with his Polonium friend at the Dubnium Café."

"Well, why do you need me? Can't they work it out?" said Tavia irritably.

"Oh, come on, you know everyone listens to you. You somehow calm everyone down. Besides all the other customers are upset," insisted Heidi.

"Posh, you guys…" Nevertheless Tavia straightened up and gracefully dove toward downtown where the sidewalk café drew ElemMates from the Main Street shops and Mall. She flipped and spun creating air currents. Taking her time she enjoyed the sun casting glittering rainbow colors through the city's crystal foliage and flowers. Evie followed. Banking left they landed at the café.

Heidi waited impatiently having rocketed down to the ground instantly. "Tavia, no emergency seems to shake you from your enjoying yourself."

"Aw, come on. This is no emergency. Dubni Dubnium should just watch his kid better. Anyway, I could use another one of his cool energy drinks, right Evie?"

Mr. Dubnium usually kept everything under control, kept

a firm hand on his children and had channeled the energy into building and running one of the best most popular cafés in town.

A glass smashed near Tavia's foot. Overturned tables and chairs festooned with food and broken dishes were strewn all over the sidewalk as two ElemMates slugged it out. These were big guys. The Dubniums were some of the biggest ElemMates in town. One weighed in at 262 versus Tavia's mere 16. His buddy weighed a bit less, a hefty 209. These guys were high energy and edgy. The young Dubnium had a tight grip on the Polonium, son of a beach side Café and boat club owner. Electrons sizzled and snapped around the entwined silvery bodies.

Heidi's anger ignited an explosion jarring the two boys apart. "I've had enough of this," she shouted.

Tavia quietly approached creating a cool, calming breeze. The two, spent, seemed relieved. "What's the problem with you two? I thought you guys were on the same team. Why don't you guys go work it off at the stadium and practice for the Smash Tournament tonight…But first you both had better clean up this mess. And where's your father?"

The Dubnium youth hung his huge head, "They are all off boating on the Primordial River. Dad figured I could handle the café for the day. My friend came to help." Neither knew what started the tussle.

Forgiven, everyone helped the boys clean up. Then the two of them graciously served drinks for all on the house.

As they sipped Tavia said, "I'm still unnerved by the boys' unusual behavior. I'm feeling lots of electrical energy in the air. Anyway, Evie, hope you'll join us for the Smash Tournaments tonight. It's our City Sport, Collider. Everyone goes."

Evie was getting tired and a bit overwhelmed by everything:

the arrival, the tour, the gamma rays, the Ozone hole and now this fight. But the drink revived her a bit and how could she say no to her new friends. Her sense of adventure overcame her tiredness.

As evening approached, shops closed and everyone headed east down Main Street, past the shops, the library, and museums. The crowd strolled down flower-bordered paths in the public gardens. Water from the fountains glistened and refracted off the delicate crystal blossoms.

All the paths converged onto a great open plaza in front of the entrance to Darm Stadium. Built of gleaming aluminum pipes with intervals of red, blue and orange magnets all around the circumference, the Darm Stadium Family powered the great Collider track, keeping the magnets that propelled the players at the proper cool temperature. The Collider track consisted of two separate loops that connected at the goal posts: Players on each team sped on the tracks, coming in contact at the goals where they smashed into each other. Instruments at the goals calculated the number of particles created by each team. The team with highest particle count wins the Collision. Three out of four Collisions wins the game.

The whole city came out for these games. It was a social time for different ElemMate families to get together. The teams were made of ElemMates from all the different families so everyone was involved. Evie, Heidi and Tavia joined Carl Carbon in the high bleacher seats. Air born, Tavia's light blue skin and wispy form looked like she would blow away in a breeze. In contrast Carl Carbon was earth bound and solid. They were all warm, life loving friends.

Though hard to see clearly from their seats high in the

bleachers, as the players raced around at almost the speed of light, everyone could see the the slower moving Leads easily routed. The whole arena shook when the teams collided. Millions of particles showered into the air in a multi-colored fireworks display. The spectators ooed and ahhed, and cheered for their teams. Then everyone waited in silence for the Refs to do their official counts.

Usually each heat sped up with the same energy, but now the crowd noticed the second heat went much faster, the Smash much more explosive and the Particle display larger and longer. Intensity increased even more on the third heat. Spectators were becoming nervous. There was shouting down below on the tracks. Sparks and explosions were heard between the heats. The players were out of control, ignoring their coaches, the refs and the rules of the game. Everyone could see the melee. As tension increased below, spectators also began to argue. Fans tussled with each other breaking into bleachers, igniting fires with their sparks, knocking particles off their opponents. Injured ElemMates lay everywhere. Fireworks became exploding bombs.

"Hold onto me. Let's stick together," Carl shouted over the din. Carl held Tavia with one arm, grabbing Heidi with the other. Tavia gripped Evie around the waist.

Heidi's combusting energy lit the way as the friends clambered over broken bleachers and wended their way out of the stadium.

The plaza outside swarmed with panicked ElemMates. Suddenly the stadium went dark, the buzz of the magnets silenced. Only the soft emergency lights shone.

"Attention, ElemMates!" came Mr. Darm's voice over the loudspeaker. "I've cut the power. The games are cancelled. Everyone is out of control. My security force will escort you out. All the injured will be taken to the hospital. I am very ashamed and sorry about this situation. A full investigation will be conducted."

Tavia led the group through the darkened streets north to their neighborhoods. Rioting ElemMates punched and attacked each other. Some egged the fighters on; others tried to intervene only to be attacked in turn. Crying and wailing added notes to the shouting. Out of control sparks flew from fighters igniting fires.

"We need to fly," said Tavia, grabbing hold of her three friends. They hugged each other close lifting into the air to soar above the danger.

Arriving safely at Carl's doorstep exhausted and shaken, they agreed they had to do something. Heidi would stay the night at Tavia's since her house was on the other side of town. They'd talk in the morning.

Evie thought it time to go home. "Until next time." She closed her eyes, focusing through the explosions and smoke on the Formula in Reverse and home.

Chapter 6
Home

With the sun on her face, the smoothness of warm rock cradling her and the sound of splashing waves below, she was glad to be home. Just a weird afternoon dream. Must have dozed off. Better get home for dinner. Sitting up shattered that peaceful moment. A high morning sun blazed. Not nestled on her familiar cliffs anymore, the rocks were blackened and crumbling as if there had been an explosion. Oh, no, that explosion had been real all right. Despite the obvious explosion the Chemistry Set sat intact next to her with a few empty test tubes strewn nearby. Inside most of the containers lay neatly in their places. Strangely it looked like the box Liz had tossed to her, plain and small. Looking toward the park she could see the flashing of a police car's light and barricades around the shoreline path.

"Hey, kid," shouted the officer jumping out of his patrol car. "Get away from there." As she moved away, he darted around the barricade toward her. "Wait. Come over here."

"Uh-oh," she thought tucking the box inside her shirt. "They know. She'd be thrown into jail for vandalism and arson and made into an object of scientific experiment like ET, that innocent alien almost studied to death. As she cautiously approached the officer she noticed her clothing was not only dry, but as clean as it was when she had put it on. Well, she'd better be cool nonetheless."

"You Evie Sparks?"

47

"Yes, sir."

"Your parents are frantic. They've been looking for you all night. What are you doing here of all places? Some crazy vandals were up to no good last night. Huge explosion and fire. Luckily the rocks stood up to it. You know anything about it?"

"No, sir, I was just walking by..." she hesitantly lied, not usually too good at it.

"You realize your parents have started a county alert. Come on, I'll take you home."

Boy, was she going to have a lot of explaining to do when she got home, she thought. Luckily no one was around in the park to see her. The patrol car went the usual way up the coastal drive out to the north of town passing rolling fields and orchards. Her grandfather had bought their 1700's ruin of a stone farmhouse in the 1960's for almost nothing and modernized it. Two stories rose on top of the original foundation with spacious living areas.

A six story stone and glass tower blended into the old stone base. It contained the library that overlooked the orchards and views of the ocean.

Her parents, Rob and Dr. May Sparks, waited outside the rose garlanded picket fence as the patrol car pulled up. They were so glad to see her that the questions didn't start until after they made her eat. Although she really wasn't hungry, the pancakes with late season raspberries from their garden topped with homemade whipped cream went down just fine.

Actually they did all the talking sitting around the round oak kitchen table.

"Is it our fault you ran away? We're so sorry we haven't been spending enough time with you. Me with my herb studies and gardening, Dad with his writing deadlines. We only found out from Liz that you were upset, that you didn't do so well on your first science quiz. She said you'd wandered off alone to the park after school. Then you didn't come home all night. You've been missing all morning...We called the school, the police, everywhere. Oh, honey, we are so, so sorry..."

"Everyone is talking about the explosion. The cops looked everywhere for injured people. We prayed they wouldn't find your body over there. Luckily no one was hurt. Seems at that time no one was even walking nearby. A few dead seagulls and some dead fish washed ashore," said her dad.

On and on it went with lots of hugging and kissing to distract her from her pancakes. They were OK parents. Not their fault they had such passionate interest in their work. She envied their dedication. Mom, a horticulturist, taught and did research in Cambridge, and then came home to her garden. Dad use to teach but now managed to sit in his study full time churning out huge novels and magazine short stories. In the past Evie didn't share their interests. "I can't see scrambling around in the dirt chasing after a little seed nor sitting all day in a chair tapping out stories. Now I'm starting to get it." She mused while her parents talked at her. "..Hmm, I guess Liz didn't mention our tiff over the toys we found in the dumpster...guess we'd get in trouble for shoplifting. She probably feels bad about the bum deal she gave me, taking the good stuff and leaving me with the chemistry set. That sure did hurt considering she knew how bad I'd been feeling...But hey, her loss. Look what I got."

Out loud she interrupted her parents' chatter, "Mom, Dad, hold on a minute. Don't you want to hear what happened to me?"

"Yes, we sure do. Something strange is definitely going on. While you were missing, your computer went on by itself. We heard this loud, high tone, or maybe music. We rushed into your room to see this strange though very polite being on the screen. He spoke to us saying it was nice to meet us and how he was so happy to have Evie in their midst. He introduced himself as Dr. Plutonium. I tell you we both froze in shock. I figured it was a weird spam," her dad said, his voice quivering.

"Well, I don't know what to believe. But my child was gone for over a day and that huge explosion in the park…and now look at this." Her mom pulled out the morning paper where the headline screamed about the closing of the Ozone Hole. But I do know we are definitely going to take you to the hospital to make sure you're ok. You didn't even tell us if someone attacked you or hurt you…" said her mom tensely.

"Please, let me tell you. I had the most amazing adventure! You wouldn't believe it. I know you think I'm off my rocker, that I was drugged or something. But not true."

She changed the beginning of the story to protect the innocent saying she had found a chemistry set in the park on the shore promenade. She explained who Dr. Plutonium was. When she described the Ozone hole crisis, her mom began to cry and her dad gripped her hand. "Everyone is going to get really bad sunburn poisoning. Many people will get skin cancer and die. But it is even more horrible for them. You guys should have seen how the rays smash them up. It was horrible."

Ignoring Evie's comment about the beings she had met, the scientist mother couldn't help interjecting, "Oh, yes, I've been reading about this. All the aerosols from our sprays and refrigerators we release into the air disrupt the atmosphere."

Evie described everything in great detail: the crystal plants, floating beings with orbiting sparks. Her face lit up about the thrill of flying and her pride at making cloth just by thinking. They did smile when she said she was determined to do more to clean up the Earth. "Radiation can be helpful in small doses, but it is destructive when it is out of control," she said gravely.

When she was finished her parents sat in silence for a bit. With a worried frown her Mom spoke up. "That's quite a story, Darling. After you get checked out and rested you will tell us what really happened. Who hurt you? Maybe you didn't realize they slipped you drugs. Those strange beings we saw on your computer screen must be some terrible hacking trick. Who would concoct such an elaborate scheme to get a kid to plant bombs? What happened to that Chemistry set? I'm surprised you forgot one should never pick up any unattended packages, especially one just left in the park. There's probably something terribly wrong with it. That's why it was thrown away. In any case you are certainly old enough to know you don't just fool around with chemicals, even ordinary ones. You could have been very badly hurt mixing chemicals you know nothing about, nor ignoring the directions."

Now her mom was getting angry at her irresponsibility with the set. "You were probably knocked unconscious. Everyone is saying the destruction at the park is extensive. We didn't connect you to it at the time. No one found the Set. Do you have it? In any case, Rob, we must get her to the hospital."

Her father sat back, thinking, that twinkle in his eye. "It's a good one, Evie, a real good one. Maybe you want to write it down." Everything in life was always a story or material for a story to Dad. He put together words the way Dr. Plutonium put together molecules. His boundary between what others considered real and what is imaginary was thin and porous. He always said, if he had lived in ancient times he would have been a Story

Teller, a narrator of folk tales, myths and legends. He made sure his children knew them all. Bedtime stories for Evie and her older brother were often his own made up fantasies.

Then he got serious. "You know fairytales and myths are really lessons. Most are universal. Many tell about the journey from ignorance to enlightenment. The heroes and heroines struggle in darkness, wander aimlessly and lost, struggle against terrible trials and tests until they overcome adversity and gain their reward. Some begin when the hapless traveler stumbles by mistake upon the magic object that takes her into strange imaginary lands to confront amazing creatures. With effort the traveller transforms, gains powers and saves victims to finally win the treasure or the crown.

Perhaps this is the beginning of your Quest. You found your magic object, entered your strange land with supernatural beings and saved them from a terrible attack. Who knows where your quest, your path will take you. Keep your eyes open. I do hope however that this journey will not do you or anyone any grave harm. I also hope at the end of your quest you attain your reward. In any case, if the bump on your head knocked this story into your head, it's a winner."

Her Mom rolled her eyes and began to clear the dishes. "Rob, you aren't taking this seriously. There's a lot of destruction out there. That computer hacking is frightening and Evie is spouting delusions. Evie, please go change and we'll go to the hospital."

"Two good ideas, I'll write down the story and get changed," she said using her new found conciliation skills, relieved at an excuse to go to her room. "The story should be great for my English class assignment."

She slipped from the kitchen into her cluttered lair. Her

sanctuary was still filled with her international doll collection and figurines that she viewed more as sculptures than playthings. She stashed the Chemistry Set in her closet, turned on the computer and began to change her clothes. As the computer warmed up, her mother appeared behind her.

"Are you almost ready? I really am taking you to the hospital."

Dad came in and plopped onto the bed next to her desk. So annoying when she wanted to be alone. "I hate when people hang around me when I'm trying to write," her Dad laughed, hovering behind her as the computer loaded.

The screen start up made a musical hum different from the usual one. An unusual new animated screen with swirling clouds and supernovas appeared. Her parents eyes riveted to the screen, their smiles gone, their faces white. "Oh, Evie, that's what we saw before when you were gone". Evie hadn't put that there. She stared in wonder as the now familiar letters and formulas appeared in animation. As her parents leaned over her shoulder peering into the monitor, flashing, glowing red letters filled the screen with the words: "THIS IS TOP SECRET. BE CAREFUL WHOM YOU TELL. SWEAR THEM TO SECRECY. THE WORLD IS AT STAKE! A high-pitched tone screamed from the computer. Her parents gripped the back of her chair and whispered, "So what is all this? Is this a joke? Ok, we promise. We swear," her parents said in shaking voices.

"So, you see? Now do you believe me that this is a message from them. The whole story I told you is real."

Her dad whispered in awe. "So, they needed you for help? They think you can do something. They say you have super powers?"

"Daddy, I really helped. I flew. But more important, the Elem-

Mates, the people there, listened to me. I helped everyone work together. I didn't really do anything more than that. Not sure I'm actually a super hero. I'm no superman who stops floods and earthquakes with brute strength."

Her still skeptical mother put in, "Evie, I'm not sure what to believe. It could still be a terrible joke."

"While I'm always ready to erase the fine line between fact and fantasy, what will happen if you break that line? I'm worried about your mental health. But we did see an image of some strange lit up person on your computer screen that's for sure. We were both pretty shocked." Her father's voice was serious.

The family spent the rest of the day at the hospital where Evie had a thorough check up and a battery of tests. Evie braved the terrible blood taking needles and relaxed in the pleasure of her parents' undivided attention. The conclusion was she was in good health. Going over her test results and chart the doctor noticed she had grown 2 inches since her 13th year check-up. She did have high levels of minerals in her blood, some not in vitamin tablets. Her oxygen count was very high as well as her blood pressure. Was she taking anything she shouldn't be? Her whole system looked like it was on stimulants. He recommended rest for the rest of the day, drinking lots of fluids and full meals. An appointment was to be next month. Take no vitamin supplements, he instructed. If the extra minerals remained in her body, they could be toxic and they would need to flush them out.

Chapter 7
Blast Site Treasure

Evie felt great Monday morning after her adventures, hospital visit and a good night's sleep. Her stomach was free of that nauseous "I have Science Class today" feeling. The days got better and better. She opened her locker to find the computer game CD and a note: "Sorry I was so selfish. Enjoy. Are you all right? I hope so. I've got your back in Science class. Love, Liz". What a good friend, it's going to be hard keeping secrets from her.

Science class was first period. Liz had saved her a seat next to her and squeezed her hand as the class settled down. "Did everyone read the Science Section of the newspaper? Did anyone read any interesting articles since we last met?" No matter what unit they studied in their general science textbook, Ms. Melillo always tried to relate science topics to the real world and current events. Evie always liked this part of the class, although she never read any outside articles. She listened to her classmates read about new inventions and discoveries making the dry textbook stuff come alive.

Liz stood up. "I read about that explosion in the park the other day. No one seems to know what happened. Supposedly it was a very powerful explosion, but it only hit a very small area. "

Everyone began talking excitedly. Ms. Melillo raised her hand for quiet. "As a matter of fact I'm very interested in the subject myself. Since I am a geophysicist, the officers approached me for my advice. The blast was very powerful, stronger than an atomic bomb, yet it only affected a twenty-foot area. The granite itself actually melted. You'll see me quoted in the article. They are investigating terrorist information. The materials are too advanced for the average citizen to obtain. The authorities have allowed me to take some samples for testing. Does anyone want to work with me on this?"

Evie's hand shot up. "Hmm, maybe Ms. Melillo can be a help," she thought.

"Evie! Great!" Surprise and pleasure showed on Ms. Melillo's face. "Anyone else?"

No one else raised their hands. Instead they all turned giggling and smirking toward Evie. For once Evie just grinned back.

"Ok, class. Has anyone else a current topic to discuss?" she asked bringing the class back to attention. Paul, the new kid, stood up waving his news clipping. He easily got everyone's interest. Cute, with dark, wavy auburn hair, he seemed to have already made friends and become crush material for the girls. "It's right on the front page. He displayed the article's huge headline reading "Ozone Hole Closed".

The class understood the enormity of this event. They had been studying the atmosphere and how spray aerosols and toxic chemicals broke a hole in the earth's protective ozone shield letting radioactive rays to penetrate to the surface. No matter how uninterested in science they were, the students knew the opened hole meant higher chances of cancer, an end to hours in the summer sun. As relieved comments circulated the room, Paul quoted scientists perplexed by the sudden change in the atmosphere.

Ms. Melillo admitted she knew little more about the event. While the students all engaged for once in discussing this scientific phenomenon, the teacher noticed Evie quietly doodling then leaning over to whisper to Liz. "Class, why don't we use today's class time for research? Everyone is dismissed to go to the library." She instructed.

As everyone else filed from the room, Evie and Liz approached Ms. Melillo. "Come on, Ms. Melillo, let's go do some field research. Can Liz come too?" said Evie, her face serious though Ms. Melillo detected a twinkle in Evie's gray blue eyes. Evie's high cheek bones, almond shaped eyes and heart shaped face ending in a delicate pointed chin gave Evie an impish look that at times made Ms. Melillo, rational scientist that she was, think Evie had something magical about her.

"Can Liz speak for herself?" asked Ms. Melillo pleased with Evie's new eagerness.

Liz did average work in class, usually showing little excitement for science. "I was the only one who brought in the article about the blast." Liz pointed out softly.

"Yes, that's true. Of course I would love both of you to come. We'll meet here after school." She smiled warmly at her two new budding researchers.

"What a day!" shouted Evie over the wind tangling her wavy dirty blond hair, Liz's straight dark strands and Ms. Melillo's brown ponytail as the teacher drove her red Taurus convertible along the coastal road to the town park.

Ms. Melillo showed the two guards her ID card. One guard smiled at Evie in recognition. "Hi. Good to see you again and looking so well. Guess you like this spot, huh?" Ms. Melillo cast her a questioning look.

"Sure," Evie said turning away from the guard avoiding looking at Ms. Melillo. "This is my favorite spot. I always love watching the waves crashing on the bluffs."

"Come girls. Look over here." Ms. Melillo knelt on the charred rocks.

"Wow! Cool! Look at the oxidation and extreme crystallization of the." Then noticing Ms. Melillo's surprised stare Evie finished lamely with … "of …those pretty colored rocks."

"It seems you studied a bit on your day off, Evie. Is there something you want to talk about, about your day off?" asked Ms. Melillo quietly.

Evie studied the ground intensely for something to say.

"Hey, wow! These rocks look like jewels!" Liz's squeal broke the tense silence. "Can we take these, as samples of course?" She attempted a scientific tone as she caressed sparkling blue, red, green and purple stones sliding them into the sample bags the teacher had given them.

"These crystals certainly look like semi-precious gems," said Ms. Melillo squinting through her jeweler's magnifying loupe at a blue crystal as big as her thumb. "I haven't seen these minerals in this area before, and I've done a lot of research. Perhaps the blast pushed them up from deeper in the earth's crust. The cliffs are mostly limestone and marble, which is why the town is called Marblehead."

Her face was flushed with excitement. She picked up and examined other loose and charred rocks and scooped up water pooled in the broken crevices. Her fingers trembled as she carefully placed samples into different containers. "I'll run some tests on them at my lab. Maybe consult with my colleagues at the University." Consumed with scientific fervor Ms. Melillo could think only of her research. "Come girls. Please put the sample bags and tools in this container in my trunk. Where can I drop you off?"

Back in Evie's bedroom Liz poured crystals from her pockets onto Evie's bed. Evie sat in silence while Liz exclaimed over her treasure letting them run through her fingers. "Wow, Evie. Wonder if these are worth anything. They are so pretty even if they aren't valuable. We can make jewelry out of them. Or even mosaics. You could make some cool art with these, Evie…" until she noticed Evie just staring off into space. "Hey what's up with you? You still mad at me?"

"No, not at all. I'm thinking I'm so glad you came and did the after school research with me. It makes me happy you want to make something out of these rocks together. But I need to know, are you still my best, most trustworthy friend?" Evie whispered. "Can I trust you to swear with your life to the gravest ultimate secrecy?"

"Of course", Liz murmured worried by Evie's serious look. "C'mon, what is this secret? Tell me." Liz said smiling expecting Evie to relate the latest gossip.

"OK, This is no joke. If you're in with me, you're in with me for life. Your life will never be the same. But I can't keep this to myself any longer," Evie said gazing intently into Liz's eyes.

"Yes," Liz whispered.

"I caused that explosion on the cliff, me and that chemistry set we found behind the toy store. When I ran off from you, I went to the bluff by the promenade and just started fooling around with it. It was or shall I say, is, actually a beautiful set." She went to her closet and pulled it from under some boxes. At Evie's touch it transformed to its full size. Liz gasped at the inlaid gold and gems.

"Oh, my, this is really a treasure. I swear it was a little plastic case when I tossed it to you. Is this really the same case?" Liz's eyes widened as she examined it closer opened the lid and gently picked up the vials. This is also very, very weird. It definitely changed size. Even I realize, this is finely hand crafted. I bet these are real semi-precious stones. This could be thousands of years old and extremely valuable. So you said you opened them and mixed them. Then they must be real chemicals."

"I know. But you know I love fooling around with paints, or things like paint. So that's what I did, forgetting it was a chemistry set. I mixed them in one of the rock crevices into a cool multi-colored swirl. But then it started doing a reaction, bubbling and smoking with colored flames. I heard tones, and vibrations and designs floated into the air. I swear I saw letters and symbols like skywriting and heard voices. Then a big explosion…" Evie told Liz her whole adventure ending with…" When I came to, I grabbed the box before the cop saw me. And I can go back anytime by repeating the formula supposedly of the reaction I created."

Liz looked at her with disbelief. "You must have knocked your head and imagined it all," she managed to say. After a silence, "Whatever it is, this chemistry set definitely sent you on some adventure, real or imagined. What are you going to do with it? It must belong to someone. I bet someone planted it to see what the person would do with it. It's probably a moral test to see if you'll try to return it. You are obviously being tested.

"Maybe you're right. Even the ElemMates kind of said they didn't know where it came from. They were happy I appeared. They see it as an chance for me to connect them with our world. In any case I felt good saving their lives from the rays. It was fun playing the diplomat helping solve their differences. This Chemistry Set could be more than physically valuable. It could be a kick in the pants to help me grow, create and help others. One thing for sure is I mixed something up that got quite a result. I'll look for the person who left it, find out about it and why they left it. For now I'll keep it safely in my closet."

They sat quietly for a bit. Liz absentmindedly played with the pile of gems.

"Do you believe anything I've told you?"

"I'm thinking. This is a lot to take in, Evie. But if you really mean what you say about wanting to help, then I'm with you on that," Liz said taking her hand.

"But you don't believe me do you? I mean about Atom City and the ElemMates? I'll prove it," she answered vehemently. "Come with me next time."

Always up for an adventure Liz agreed, "Ok, let me know, yeah, whenever, sure."

"Come," said Evie pulling Liz by the hand to the computer, gems tumbling to the floor. She silently recited the Formula to herself.

Chapter 8
Watering the Sahara

Instantly hot blue sky surrounded them. Evie stood upright
and steady on her feet still clasping Liz's trembling, limp hand
tightly. Liz crouched by her feet, leaning on her legs. They were
surrounded by hot, rippling golden sand as far as they could see.

Evie had expected to arrive in Atom City. But before she
could panic, she heard familiar voices. Soon she could see
Octavia's windblown form and Heidi's red mop approaching,
their electrons flashing around them like halos. She noticed an
unfamiliar ElemMate with them.

"Hi, Evie. So glad you came so quickly. But who have you
brought?" exclaimed Heidi noticing Liz. They reached out to Liz
who tentatively stretched out her hand giving a meek smile.

"This is my best friend, Liz. I tell her everything. When I told
her about my adventures with you, I don't think she believed me.
Still, she said she'd join me. She's always up for new adventures.
Right, Liz? You believe me now? But I thought we'd be visiting
Atom City. Where are we? "

Tavia said "You are in the Sahara Desert. This is Silvia Silicon. She and her family need our help."

Silvia and her family had polished, transparent glass bodies,
hair made of tiny sandy colored grains, wide, light beige eyes and
fourteen orbiting electrons.

"We are Silicon atoms, grains of Africa's desert sands. The

small amount of water that has held us in place is disappearing so our family is scattering beyond the edges of the desert. No roots, no moisture holds us down to the earth. We can fly the world on wind currents, but we really want to be securely anchored. We could if we mix with water made by Oxygens and Hydrogens and ElemMates like Nitrogen and Carbon to create fertile land and plant life. Evie, we know you are good at helping us all work together in new ways. We hear that your Evium properties are protective and binding. So we thank you for coming and bringing your friend. Perhaps she, too, has powers to help."

At this moment a moist coolness heralded masses of Oxygen and Hydrogen families coming to help. Evie smiled. Liz regained her usual composure, returned the smile and stood up. Nonetheless her eyes were still wide with shock and wonder.

"See, Liz, it's all true, the ElemMates are real. Like them we are now compacted down to one atom size. You may find you have special powers like me. I can fly. I weave powerful cloth from my hair. Everyone is opened to your ideas, so speak up. Your athletic abilities, more concentrated here, will help."

"I tell you, Evie, I couldn't ask for a more exciting adventure. Thanks for bringing me here."

"Oh, this is nothing. Wait 'til you see Atom City. Perhaps after we help here we can go relax in their city. Liz, it's made of gems like the ones you poured out on my bed."

Masses of ElemMates gathered in to welcome Evie and Liz and help the Silicons. Liz noted distinct character traits and clothing among the arrivals. She couldn't take her eyes off their beating hearts made up of clusters of small spheres visible through their translucent bodies. When Tavia embraced Liz, she felt refreshed, calm and energized as if she had taken a breath of fresh air.

"I remember Evie's first visit. I think I was able to comfort her a bit then," said Tavia. Liz's shyness dissolved. She hugged Tavia back.

The crowd quietly gathered around the Silicons. "What we wish of all of you is to help guide nature to give us water. We need real, plentiful, sustainable water." The Silicons shielded their faces, holding each other as the wind whipped and buffeted their bronze facets.

Tavia and Heidi reached their hands toward the Silicons, their electrons crackling as they embraced.

"Water, water, there must be water deep down. Infrared photos from airplanes reveal tons of it slipping away. We need to find it and channel it back," Evie mused aloud. Her concentrated brain cells remembering information she never realized she knew or understood. "First step, then, is to find those reservoirs. Oxygens, what if you bond with the Hydrogens to become water? Since water molecules attract others, you might be able to find a trail or make a new one."

"Heidi, why don't you go ahead with Evie? I'll stay here to keep an eye on Liz," Tavia said although Liz seemed ready to plunge into the action. Truth was, Tavia felt a bit put out by Evie's taking charge without discussion. She realized Evie was new in Atom City and getting used to her new-found powers. Nonetheless Tavia was usually the take-charge one, getting cooperation with her subtle, conciliatory manner. Perhaps, Tavia thought to herself, she had been looking forward to spending time with her new friend, and was feeling jealous when Evie announced Liz was her "best friend". Tavia had never worried before about the best friend thing. She already had so many friends.

Heidi was ready. She grabbed two of her Hydrogen cousins

and shoved them toward Tavia. "You three make a great three-some, a fine trailblazing first water molecule." Heidi scanned the Oxygen family gathering around. She took hold of Tavia's brother's hand. "Mind if I join you for a second one?" She flashed her blazing smile at him and slid to his side. Her sister joined them linking her arms through both of theirs.

"Ok, we'd better begin." Heidi shouted. Throwing her arms over the two ElemMates' shoulders they began a circling dance. The other three ElemMates began their own group spin. Liz looked on amazed. Spinning faster and faster soon the ElemMates became a single blur. Then in a flash of light, two huge drops of water appeared where the ElemMates had been. Crystal clear, sparkling in the sunlight, Liz could just make out the six Elem-Mates' forms within the drops.

"OK, follow us. We've got the trail" came Heidi's garbled voice from inside one of the drops. The two water molecules sped forward as if pulled by a magnet.

Behind them Liz saw other newly formed water molecule drops glide swiftly to follow. Liz found she could run fast enough to keep up. They trekked for miles, hundreds of miles at super sonic speed. Liz laughed basking in her newfound powers. She found her strides could make her airborne. Using her innate agility she found she could maneuver to stay in the air. Playing as the group followed the trail south and slightly west, Liz stretched and twisted her muscles launching herself into exhilarating acrobatic swoops, dives and spins.

Suddenly Tavia's water molecule stopped, hovered over the sand and soaked abruptly in leaving only a small dark stain. The parade of water molecules followed suit, each one hovering then disappearing into the ground as if a vacuum sucked them in from underneath. Since they were all atomic or nano-size slipping down between the grains of sand was no problem. Down, down they went zigzagging and twisting around the grains of sand. Because the grains of sand were made of mostly silicon molecules, Silvia Silicon and her cousins worked together to make sure all their Silicon cousins helped keep the path between the grains wide opened.

Liz stood back watching the dry sand absorb the glistening stream. She found Evie farther back helping to keep the crowds focused on the trail. Evie turned surprised to see Liz unaccompanied. "Liz what are you doing here? I thought Tavia was staying with you?"

"Tavia wanted to get into the lead. She was the first molecule to drop underground. But I've gotten into stride. Evie, I can fly!"

"You can? I figured you'd be a good flier. I did have confidence you could take care of yourself. Still, I'm sorry we left you alone. Now, are we ready to go under? Just swim."

Both girls dove into the sand. Evie confidently managed a smooth surface dive. Liz jumped up, flipped and did a swan dive into the sand. The sunlight disappeared. Soon the only light in the pitch darkness was the sparkling glow of trillions of electrons orbiting each ElemMate. Water molecules plowed forward like the cars with many sparkling electron headlights. The pathway was lined with the Silicons and other ElemMates whose electrons created a well-lit row of streetlights.

"Wow! Look at some of these crystals. I bet these are precious or at least semi-precious gems down here. They look like the ones from the site, and Ms. Melillo said she thought they could be real gems. And look! That's gold...or fool's gold. And there, that's silver. At least they look like it. I know there are tons of minerals here." Evie exclaimed, finding it difficult to keep her eyes on the group.

Liz ogled with her. They were just girls eyeing store window displays at the mall. "Evie, you'd never have been able to appreciate all these colors and details in this light even with your wonderful artistic talents. I am so enjoying this, Evie. My senses are sharper, too, even my sense of smell. What is that?...Oh, look we've reached a deep underground reservoir."

A minute later a teeming crowd of water molecules blocked their way. Everyone cheered. The incoming crowd rushed to embrace the reservoir's surprised water molecules. Tavia pulled away from Heidi's Hydrogen cousins, approached the reservoir water molecules and bowed in greeting. Her strong voice resonated against the cavern walls quieting the multitude. Through the surface of each molecule three faces looked towards Tavia. "Greetings. We came from the desert in search of you. We hope to convince some of you to return with us to the Sahara Desert surface, to resettle there and help us to make it live again."

A reservoir molecule composed of an Oxygen and two Hydrogens stepped forward. The Oxygen ElemMate spoke in a rich gurgle. "There were periods in ancient times when we settled there. We keep trying to set up tiny settlements, but we are never really welcome. Our molecules are not embraced. We merely slide off and are sent streaming far away."

"But you have to, you must return. The Sahara's sands are spreading. The life on its borders is dying out. Please! We'll find the roots to hold you. Will you give it a chance?" pleaded Evie, her mind searching for the perfect convincing words. "What to do first," she said with conviction, "is we need to construct canals to get there and build a new reservoir to give you a permanent

67

home. This home where vegetation can root and build up rich soil will fulfil our promise."

"Between the two of us and all of you ElemMates, we'll do it!" Liz added. The girls grinned at each other and got to work planning irrigation canals.

The ElemMates gathered to watch the girls design canals that would rival the great waterworks of the world.

"I remember reading about how the ancient Andeans constructed intricate waterways in extremely arid lands," explained Evie to the crowd. She sketched out in the sand intricate canals needed to bring back the water in the sand. Liz used her math skills to calculate dimensions, locks and other logistics. It took only a few minutes to complete and memorize the plan.

"Now to get the job done. What does everyone think of this plan? Anyone know how to accomplish everything? How to dig the canals, bring in vegetation…"

The ElemMates got busy. Tavia instructed the water molecules to convince the reservoir molecules to join into a loose chain for the transport through the canals to the new site. The Nitrogens and Carbons would contribute to the Oxygens and Hydrogens to generate plant life.

"Listen everyone," Heidi said her booming voice carrying over the crowd, "First we must gently encourage the sand molecules and minerals to move aside for our canals. Then while we flow through the canals, let's loosely bond with ElemMates living next to them. We can try to convince them to join us to help bring dead land to life, that all kinds of minerals are needed to encourage healthy plant life and soil."

"We're with you," came the unanimous reply.

"How do we 'loosely connect'?" Liz asked Heidi.

"Good question. I just thought it sounded dramatic," said the hyped up red head.

Evie stepped up. "Diplomacy. By making friends. Show them the love you showed those shinny gems you played with on my bed…then use the old team captain charm to move the players into winning formation. You can touch them or even their orbiting electrons. Make eye contact and politely ask them to move over. Just as you encourage your team mates, I know you can get the water molecules to follow you." Evie said.

Evie turned to give Tavia a hug. "We'll all work to convince everyone."

At first it felt silly talking to the dirt walls and gemstones, asking them to move. But on closer look with their new high power vision and adjustment to the dark, they could see the trillions of ElemMates making up the dirt. With a bit of convincing the grains of sand and gems vibrated enough to move. Bit by bit the massive crowd moved back. Space opened up. Silvia and the girls cajoled and gently prodded directions. Soon only a smile and a nod made the tunnels grow and the miles pass. Evie referred to the visual map in her head for direction. Liz engineered the tunnel dimensions. Tavia and Heidi guided the water molecules into an even flow. Meanwhile Carl and Nyla encouraged their life supporting cousins to join in to resettle and fertilize the desert.

Once in a while a large gem resisted. "I have been here for millions of years. I do not intend to move now!" resisted a tough diamond. If Cousin Carl couldn't convince him, they'd leave him be…unless he was blocking the tunnel route. Hydrogens would provide a small explosion to convince the stubborn ElemMate to move aside.

The tunneling proceeded at a steady super fast rate. In a

few hours they had tunneled back to central Sahara. Everyone cheered when they crashed through to the surface. The girls, the Carbons, the Hydrogens and the Silicons were the first to bounce high above the desert in a geyser of fresh water.

Soon the water collected in a vast lake and continued cascading. Those arriving sent word to the far north, east and west so new channels formed and new lakes and streams appeared in valleys and crevices.

Silicons dove blissfully under the water happily sticking to each other and other ElemMates. They formed thick fertile mud that anchored them securely into the ground.

Everyone danced around in the water. "Wait", Evie said, "Not to spoil the party, but we have to ensure the water stays. We need to have plants germinate, send down retaining roots and provide organic material to the sand and water to make life-sustaining soil. So who knows how to make a plant?"

Nyla piped up. She oversaw the parks and agriculture in Atom City. "You need all of us: Oxygens, Hydrogens, Nitrogens, Carbons, Sodiums and many others. Let's gather for a big Bonding Party! Course our Bonding Party will just get it started. We'll need to make tons and tons of molecules to grow a real oasis here. It's complicated. We'd have to bond for a long time to allow plants to grow and evolve. I'll get my plant factories humming triple time back in Atom City to mass-produce the stuff. We'll transplant it back here later."

"...For now though, let the fun begin!" Carl shouted. He grabbed Heidi blushing and giggling. The ElemMates formed a tight circle and began their circling dance, spinning faster and faster gyrated and singing the same eerie tune from the blast site. Electron sparks grew into pulsing flashes.

At first only a bright green sprout of grass emerged from the mud. It grew quickly right before their eyes. From a tiny shoot it sprouted stems and leaves, then buds. The buds burst opened into a multitude of brilliant flowers. The blossoms shot out hundreds of seeds, each landing in the mud and sprouting more new plants. The action repeated itself over and over again, quickly planting fields of a wide variety of flowers, trees and shrubs as far as the eye could see.

While Evie and Liz watched the desert bloom with rapt attention, their friends reappeared. "Phew! That was a job. There are plenty of roots now to make a start." Carl said, his dark skin ruddy with exertion. Heidi emerged pale pink, her freckles standing out more than usual. Tavia floated quietly out to embrace the others. In silence the group watched the plants spread and grow toward the horizon

The late afternoon sun reminded them it was time to go. "Great meeting you, Liz," said Carl. "Next time, Evie, bring Liz to Atom City."

Liz was full of questions. "Where is Atom City? How do you get there? When can I see it?"

"I guess we'd better be on our way home, too. I think we've all done enough adventuring today." Evie said cutting off more of Liz's questions. After good-byes all around, she took Liz's hand and recited the Formula to herself.

Chapter 9
Budding Scientists

Liz opened her eyes on Evie's bed. "Wow, you wouldn't believe the dream I just had. How long was I out for? It was so real, so amazing! Guess your storytelling really got to me. I dreamed of the atom-sized people you spoke of. They're beautiful with those sparkling flashing lights spinning around them. I even made friends with them. We did this whole thing in the desert making an oasis."

"Liz that was no dream. I took you to where they were meeting. Yes, that sure was exciting for me too. You handled it great. I think they liked you too," said Evie sitting on the bed next to Liz.

"I still don't get it. How did we get there? You said those beings we met were a single atom of a mineral element. How does that happen? And were we their size? And how did we or let's say you get these superhuman powers?" Liz asked.

"Ah, I guess I can't answer. Guess I just let the whole thing happen. Wait 'til you see the city. It will blow your mind even more. But I love it. I don't know if it all comes from that Chemistry Set or if it's the gateway. Not sure if it was by accident, or if I was chosen. They seem glad I came, as if they needed help from somewhere. From what I can tell there are some problems going on in their city. I'm thinking some of it is being caused by human events. Seems there's too much radiation from somewhere. They talk about politics, something about the radioactive ElemMates trying to take over the city by force and violence.

In any case they think maybe the Formula is the process that concentrates all the atoms in our bodies making them hyper-function and amplifying all our body functions. And Liz, look what you did out there in the desert."

"Well, I hope my "friendship" skills will be improved, Evie. I'm so sorry I haven't been a good friend." said Liz taking Evie's hand, then pulling her to dance around the room with her....
"Oh, I was flying, moving at jet speed. It was amazing...and I love how those ElemMates dance and spin themselves into other things." Liz stopped abruptly and whispered, "Seriously, though, did we really do those things? Did we make hundreds of miles of canals and tunnels and redirect water from deep aquifers into far off lakes?"

"I think we did, with the help of the ElemMates. Do I believe the logic of the ElemMates as living being? They aren't like your usual science fiction monsters. I am so comfortable with them. I'm thrilled with their world. They live together cooperatively, working out their problems by the laws of Chemistry and nature. I'm enjoying this too much to explain it away. But I am glad you came with me and you saw it was real," said Evie.

"Evie, can I come in?" her mother called knocking gently at her bedroom door.

"My Mom and Dad know a bit. I'm not sure what they believe. Maybe don't tell your parents at this point, ok?" Evie whispered opening the door for her Mom.

Mrs. Sparks briskly entered the room and pulled opened her paisley curtains. Morning sunlight poured in. "Did you girls have a good sleep? I see you are all dressed already. Liz, your Mom called last night. I told them you two were working on a project.

Seems you forgot to tell her you were sleeping over. Perhaps give her a call after breakfast. I've made some raspberry pancakes for you. Oh, and I left out today's newspaper. Check out the headline about an amazing occurrence in the Sahara Desert. It's all over the TV news also."

She gave Evie a quick kiss and Liz a pat on the shoulder as she left the room.

"Oh, no! I had no idea all that time passed. My Parents must have been worried sick when I didn't come home yesterday afternoon. Luckily it's Saturday and I am usually here," moaned Liz scrambling to gather her stuff. Yet both girls felt surprisingly fresh for not having slept all night.

For once the pre-class conversation revolved around a news-worthy subject Monday morning: The Sahara Desert flooded and vegetation is sprouting like mad. Lakes formed with lush oasis's created almost overnight. Ms. Melillo led a captivated class with discussions about rain and air current patterns, soil composition, irrigation techniques, water resources and desert plant growth.

Paul asked questions about the weather in the desert. "Would it change with the new environment allowing for regular rainfall to sustain the new plant life or will it dry everything up as it has for centuries?"

Ms. Melillo answered each question succinctly posing more questions inviting more discussion from the class.

Liz and Evie exchanged looks with no need to read each other's mind: Smart guy and cute with wavy auburn hair. What's his story? …Hmm, they hadn't considered the weather in their Sahara project.

Ms. Melillo cut the discussion short. "Class, I hate to bring up more mundane matters, but it's time to discuss your Science Fair projects. The Fair is the first week in May. Start submitting ideas to me. We also have a final test at school's end on the whole textbook so we must stay on track with reading, assignments, papers and quizzes." Groans were heard around the room.

At the end of class Ms. Melillo asked, "Does anyone wanted to join Evie and Liz to help with research at the Blast Site down in the town park. We sure could use more hands there. They are assisting me in geological research. Paul, how about you?"

He blushed, but fixed steady large brown eyes with thick lashes on the teacher, "No thank you. I'm in the Orchestra and the Jazz Band. We have practice every afternoon."

Four other students volunteered. Ms. Melillo updated everyone on her research. "I've found some amazing information about the stones we found. Those stones are of a variety of minerals, many semiprecious and precious gems and rare metals. We're researching to see if there are any new minerals or new discoveries. I know there is limestone in the cliffs. Limestone in time becomes marble, hence the name of our town. Many minerals seep into limestone and soft marble to give it the colorful veins and patterns everyone loves. What we need to find out now is if the new found minerals were indeed always there and the explosion's pressure and heat caused them to emerge, or whether the indigenous elements recombined into these crystals. We'll have to collect some more sand samples and analyze them in the lab. I'll also send them to several colleagues at the University who specialize in rare mineral creation."

No one had been to the site since last week. Two policemen stood at the barricades that fenced off the charred, crumbling cliff area blocking the view. So when everyone gathered behind the barricades the transformed area shocked them all. The black, burnt stone had turned to rich brown soil. Tiny shoots of every shade of green sprouted thickly from the soil. Many green stems supported buds and leaves. Tiny streams of water filled what had been rock crevices to irrigate this growing garden.

"Well, everyone. Now we have so much more to study. Add Botany to the list," Ms. Melillo said hyped up with excitement. She gave everyone small shovels, clippers, tweezers, gloves and tiny plastic bags and vials to collect samples. "Be very careful with the samples. Just clip a very little sample of the plants." She pulled Evie aside. "Isn't your Mom a Botanist? Do you think she may want to come and help us identify some of these plants?"

Evie called her Mom, who arrived in minutes ready to get her hands into the dirt. "Ms. Melillo, thanks so much for letting me in on this. I have a state of the art laboratory greenhouse at my home. Would you mind if I take some samples there?"

Now besides the gems, tiny seeds, stems and buds were carefully examined.

Evie found a curious crystal. Tiny different colored stones curved into a ring shape like a wedding band. She found several of them where she knelt in the dirt. No one else could find any. Strangely when she moved to another spot, she unearthed more right under her knee. Later thinking she had found yet another one of these crystals, it turned out to be a ring shaped seed. Again it seemed they appeared where she knelt in the soil. No one else found any. She carefully used her tweezers to save the samples.

With the warm October sun on her back and the camaraderie of students and scientists working together, Evie felt content. It reminded her of the feeling she had joining with the Elem-

Mates in the Sahara.

The girls continued to help Ms. Melillo after school several days a week. They learned to dig carefully through the sand and dirt using the eye loupe to find miniscule samples, to carefully use tweezers and gloves to store samples and write detailed descriptions of the samples. The school lab became a comfortable place. Ms. Melillo taught them how to test the minerals and plant samples using higher level equipment she had borrowed from the University. Their lab skills and knowledge of Chemistry, Geology, Mineralogy and Botany surpassed many High School students who now wanted to get their hands on the exciting materials.

Paul stopped in a couple of times, observed for a few minutes and left. Evie noticed he visited more and more often and stayed longer. He would walk around the room looking at everyone's work, asking questions. She liked to think he hovered longer at her station. Otherwise Evie was fully engaged in the work. It was easy getting to know the others in the work-centered environment. Four other students came every day. Several even invited her to hang out with them. Liz only worked a couple of days a week because of her sports obligations.

As the days got cooler, Dr. Sparks, Evie's mom, nurtured an increasing number of sprouts and seeds in her home lab. Mom's greenhouse and gardens could have rivaled the great botanical gardens with their ornate glass greenhouses. Originally Evie's architect grandfather had built a curve glass structure using technology and materials advanced for the 1960s. Her Mom had added simpler glass rooms and poured cement bunker-like enclosures with skylights. The latter were used for her more confidential experiments.

Not really into plants herself, Evie was grateful her mom

showed her how to germinate the seeds.

"Look here's how you do it. You have to nick each seed with a knife first, then soak it over night." The next day Evie filled pots with fertilized moist soil, mixed in some she had brought back from the site and placed them on a shelf in direct sunlight as her mom instructed. Next she tenderly tucked a single seed into each pot. "Eighteen for good luck, for life" she murmured giving them a light sprinkling.

Her mother studied the seeds carefully, referring to her extensive plant data. "I can't figure out what plant these seeds are," she said perplexed. "I know Moonseed flower has similar ring shaped seeds. It has orchid-like blue flowers and bright red, poisonous berries. Well, we shall see won't we?"

Despite the cooler weather, the tiny plants at the site continued to grow quickly. By mid November some plants were bushes, tall ferns, saplings and blossoming flowers. Scientists came from schools and universities to observe. Papers were being written.

Because of the interest, Ms. Melillo and Dr. Sparks decided to organize a Conference in the spring for scientists to exchange research, discuss papers and hear lectures.

Evie's grades improved. She found she got her homework done quickly and efficiently after working until five o'clock in the lab.

Instead of working in her room with all its entertaining distractions she took her books to the family library, the jewel of their home. Usually her Dad had finished his writing for the day in his office next to the library. Oriental rugs, Tiffany lamps and overstuffed chairs and sofas created a cozy Victorian parlor within the stark modern six-story tower. As a last golden ray burnished the rich oak desk, she unpacked her laptop and plopped into the leather armchair. By the time the purple twilight blacked out the view through the six story windows, Dad had switched on the many lamps. Tiny spotlights highlighted paintings and artifacts on shelves and walls.

Dad collected books. He had a huge collection of folk tales from around the world in every era of human history. Lately she had been looking at books of the early scientists, called "Alchemists" who wanted to turn common metals into gold.

Dad pulled out "The Sacred Way". "Remember we were talking about your journey toward your dreams? How everyone makes their path to adulthood and onward through their life. Just about every culture has unique ways to go about it. For some the journey is a real voyage with great risks, nightmares and monsters the traveler must vanquish."

All this mystical stuff gave Evie the shivers, not sure if it was fear or excitement. "Dad, look at this illustration in "The Sacred Way". There's a winding rocky path through woods and along an ocean side cliff to a mountain top. Doesn't it look like the landscape right here? It says the Greeks would walk this special path in darkness then climb up to the light and an inspiring view. It all sounds so poetic, so mysterious to me," Evie sighed.

After some thoughtful silence her Dad said, "You know your voyage begins at birth. This past year you celebrated your Bat Mitzvah, the Jewish rite of passage to begin your adult journey. Think of all the arduous tasks you have fulfilled so far. Your Atom City adventures are part of your journey. However you travel, and whatever forks you take remember Mom and I are here for you." He kissed the top of her head and went off to help Mom get dinner.

Another day Evie flipped through a new, glossy coffee table

book showing all kinds of symbols. One was a ring, the continuous circle of life. Evie visualized the tiny crystals and the seeds both set in ring formations.

"Water", another powerful symbol, symbolizes a cleansing, a new beginning. People take special baths or are blessed with water at important stops in their lives. It struck Evie that she had indeed fallen into the ocean and was revived in the fountain of Atom City.

Evie was ready for new beginnings and the next step in her journey.

The Science and the Myths became mixed up in her head like the crazy Formula she recited. It got her mind all revved up with Science Fair Project ideas. She had already secreted a bunch of the colorful ringed crystals. It was curious that no one else had found any. Her new found nameless seeds were just beginning to sprout in their pots.

Liz unloaded glassware from the lab's sterilizer. "Well, I'll tell you. I'm in love with diamonds. As they say 'they're a girl's best friend'. They're made from carbon under great pressure, right. Maybe we can go talk to Carl Carbon."

"Not a bad idea. I've been trying to think of a project studying the creation of crystal gems and gold to tie it to jewelry making. Sort of a necklace from start to finish, a timeline starting with how the minerals become crystallized. I guess I would display the process with little samples of different minerals at different stages of crystalline growth. Not sure how exciting it would be, just a bunch of rocks on display," said Evie putting the clean test tubes, beakers and flasks into the cabinet. Not mentioning the other two germinating projects already started. "Or maybe bring everybody to Atom City for a field trip. Now that would certainly blow everyone's mind." She whispered giggling.

Liz's strong, stern reaction surprised Evie. "It would blow more than that. Could you imagine what would happen if everyone knew? First they'd think we were crazies making up a fantasy world. Yeah, we could say we were addressing the impact of Science Fiction on real Science. I've read how many of Jules Verne's and Ray Bradbury's science fiction ideas are now reality. But to be taken seriously? Forget it. Our lives will be in tatters, a media circus when scientists, doctors and reporters descend on us? Then everyone else would either react like "the aliens are here" paranoia or attempt to exploit or make personal use of Atom City. Governments and criminals would of course hound our families and us and take control of it. Remember ET," said Liz aghast just thinking about the repercussions of Evie's lightly given suggestion.

"Yes, I guess the idea that everyone could use their new found powers and intelligence to become socially and morally evolved people who would live in peace and cooperation is truly Science Fiction for our species. Sadly, that idea of peace, love and brotherhood is the real fantasy that could never become reality. I must be careful to keep The Formula a secret. I'm so bad with that. How will I keep it from you? But I guess I really must take your point to heart," said Evie solemnly.

"In any case, we've worked hard and deserve a bit of fantasy excitement, right?" Evie whispered, her eyes twinkling. "So let's go to Atom City for some remedial Science Fair help."

This time they stopped at Liz's to ask if she could stay over and picked up her things. It was Friday so there was plenty of time. At Evie's they downed a hearty snack, told her mother they were working on their Science Fair Project and may visit Atom

City. Her Mom laughed but worry lines creased her forehead. "Be careful, enjoy."

"Seriously, Mom, please don't come in." Evie warned as she closed her bedroom door.

Eagarly Liz grasped Evie's hands as the smaller girl thought The Formula. Liz would finally visit Atom City.

Chapter 10
Political Parties and Poison

Tavia hovered head down high up in the air over the city. She desperately needed to center herself. All the frenzy in the last few days was making her as tense as the gangs of rioting Radioactives. Doing great earthly deeds exhilarating as they were frazzled her. Evie's and now Liz's arrival was exciting, their help in the crises immeasurable. But it had shaken up her life. She couldn't think; she couldn't write; she couldn't relax. She needed to center herself back to her usual serene composure. Yoga helped. Tavia took a deep breath of her oxygen in and let a deep breath out. The cool air soothed her agitated electrons. Refreshed, she felt like herself again.

And her offer to help Gilda Gold campaign for Mayor now that Mayor Plutarch was giving up politics to concentrate on his medicine, added still another responsibility. Tavia wondered who else would run. She wondered if sweet, softhearted Gilda was really the right one to take over as Mayor of this no longer peaceful city.

She floated down to Gilda's Gold Palace, its lacy spires standing out from the silver-colored gleam of the Silver's, Platinum's and Palladium's long slender palace spires. Tavia never tired of her city's architecture.

Arriving at the Gold's courtyard Tavia was surprised by the

large crowd milling around. "What's going on?" she asked a Platinum ElemMate.

"Gilda's making her announcement. She's trying to gauge everyone's opinion."

Tavia dashed up the back staircase to Gilda's private rooms. As usual, Gilda glowed in the warm light that attracted everyone to her. Now her electrons vibrated excitedly.

"Oh, Tavia, I was hoping you'd show up before I gave my speech. Where on earth have you been? How can I give a speech without your speech writing help? Could you help go over it with me? Oh, I am so nervous. Am I even doing the right thing in running for Mayor?"

"Of course you are. You are the most clear-sighted citizen, benevolent and untarnished. Let me see the speech." Tavia spent the next hour editing and punching up the writing. It felt so good playing with words to get just the right emotional effect with the greatest drama.

Gilda practiced it a few times. "This is perfect, Tavia. Perhaps you should be running for office."

"I'm more of a behind the scenes leader. How about this, if you win, I'd be happy to be part of your administration. Count me in as Press Secretary," said Tavia toying with the idea none-theless. "Get real" she thought to herself, "haven't I been a fixer in this town lately? Doesn't everyone call me when there's trouble? Perhaps I'll see how things go and suggest myself as a running mate. Actually, I enjoyed taking charge of the Ozone Hole with Evie."

Suddenly Sonia Sodium burst into the room crying her salty tears. "Beryl Beryllium is running against you, Gilda. She's my neighbor and is forcing me to campaign for her and her Radioactives Party. She's got the Lithiums and most of the whole west side of town committed to her. The South Side is already in her corner. But I don't want to be with her. She uses lies, violence and magic to convince everyone she can solve all the problems. Oh, she scares me so much. I think she even uses poison potions."

Gilda and Tavia wiped her eyes and patted her shoulders. Tavia said sternly, "We'll just have to gather our own team. We can count on Heidi and Cal Calcium from your side of town. I had heard rumors about this Radioactives Party. She's gathered a strong power base with the wild, anarchist Radioactive Elem-Mates. Not sure of Plutarch's stand on this. Although he is a Radioactive ElemMate he is a Moderate believing in self-controlling radioactive activity. He is wise, compassionate and rational. Perhaps he'll support our Atom City Party which believes in peaceful cooperation."

"I hope he does. Everyone loves him. We must do whatever it takes to make things better in this City. Beryl is taking advantage of the recent turmoil and ray attacks," said Gilda.

"Beryl plays dirty and has so many secret tricks," sniffled Sonia. She had us over to her castle for a fund raiser. Gave us a tour of her dungeons where she makes her potions. She had all these weird bottles in ornate old carved chests."

"Weird carved chests and pretty bottles? Isn't that what Evie said she found in the chemistry set? Do you think Beryl planted it? I wondered what brought this whole Evie business here. Evie has no clue to how she got here or why. I wonder if Beryl has some plot to use Evie to get her way. Things have certainly been stirred up since Evie came."

"But, Tavia, Evie has done only good since she came. Perhaps Evie has integrity and inner strength and can't be manipulated," said Gilda thoughtfully. "Perhaps we can explain what's going on here and she'll support us. She seems to want to fix things very much."

"The Problem is, she is a just a kid. Her friend Liz, obviously a courageous, competent leader seems to respect and care for Evie. Both are totally overwhelmed with our city. In any case we definitely need to give them a heads up.

Remember, Gilda. You've got a strong following yourself. Everyone knows you get things done. You support lots of city groups: business, community, industry, arts and science. You've backed ways for the Radioactives to use their power constructively," said Tavia, heading for the door.

Liz was awestruck by Atom City. They arrived in front of Carl's apartment just as he emerged heading to Gilda's palace.

"Well, well, look who's here. No world crisis today, huh. Just thought you'd drop in to pass the time?" While his wide grin showed he was obviously glad to see them, he seemed to be rushing out. I'm due at Gilda Gold's Palace. It's all this political stuff. Mayor Plutarch is stepping down. Gilda wants to run, but she's got no experience. And she's such a softie. Not sure she's made of the right stuff. I do hope Tavia is helping with her speech. Come, let's go."

Liz thought Carl's dark chiseled face and jet-black hair very handsome. Sort of like the Ancient Greek athletes she'd seen in paintings. His bright smile made her feel warm and comfortable. "So sorry we didn't let you know. Also, we came looking for some advice on some Science Projects we have to do." Liz apologized.

"Ok, after Gilda's, we can meet everyone to hash out some ideas. This is your first time here, Liz, right?" Carl waved his arms in an arc to take in the city spread around them. "Sure beats the Sahara. Have you looked around, seen the City yet?"

"Oh, it's incredible. We just flew in. Great aerial views! Everything sparkles." Liz said now focusing only on Carl, deciding he is one of Atom City's marvels. There had been so much going on in the Sahara, she had barely noticed him. He pointed to his apartment tower flanked by crystalline flowers and green-jeweled trees. Her jaw dropped at the fantastic architecture of neighboring apartment complexes, brilliantly sparkling gardens and spraying fountains.

Evie was glad Liz was handling her first visit to Atom City. She was glad she could just take the time to enjoy the city at leisure. They walked passed a garden brimming with multi-colored flowers shimmering in the sunlight. "Look at these gorgeous flowers! Have they just been watered 'cause they look like jewels," Liz exclaimed.

Evie explained, "The flowers are well watered, but in truth many are actually jewels. They grow crystals here."

"Yes, you remembered, Evie. Each ElemMates family donates some seed crystals from their neighborhoods to put in the community gardens. Then our gardeners cut and polish the metals and minerals as well as care for our organic flowers," Carl explained.

Now Liz was tuning in to the sights of the city. She knelt down to examine the flowers stroking their petals. "They don't feel like stone, they are soft like real flowers."

Evie joined her. "They are so delicate, so finely shaped. As if some craftsperson spent a lifetime carving different gems into colored blossoms a millionth of an inch thick, then set them on stems."

"Well, we do have fine craftspeople with lots of time on their hands," Carl laughed. "Come let's head over to Gilda's. Later we can give you a quick tour of the city and relax at a café downtown."

Heidi and Nyla joined up with them and together they headed southwest toward the Gold palace.

They turned onto Phosphorus Place, passing Arsenic to the corner of Tin and Lead Streets toward center city. A right turn on Gold Avenue put them into a neighborhood new to both girls. The girls took it all in, their heads swiveling from left to right to up to down. In each neighborhood, each ElemMate family inhabited a whole city block, constructing their buildings of their own minerals. Looking north they could see Cobalt's celestial blue arches. "That's our Town Hall. You'll find the courts and the cops, the fire department, the school board and the Mayor's office," pointed out Nyla.

"Look," shouted Evie, "beyond it in the distance. It's the Eiffel Tower!"

"Oh, that's the Iron Family's lacy "Eiffel Tower" looking building. Yes, their claim to fame, they say," explained Heidi. Flanking the Town Hall to its right a cylindrical structure made of silver gray discs displayed a huge sculpture of a nickel at the top. "That's the Nickel Mint and their money trees. They make the city's coins and paper money."

"See those trees? While most trees are crystals, many are organic and grow like regular trees. Each tree is a one-celled plant condensed down like you are." Heidi pointed out.

In the distance the blue-green Statue of Liberty crowned by huge shiny copper pennies could be glimpsed.

The corner of Gold and Silver Streets, their destination,

dazzled. Glittering Gold, Silver, Mercury, Platinum and Palladium towers almost blinded them. Gilda Gold's gold palace gates faced kitty-corner to three other grand palace Gates: Platinum, Palladium and Silver's Gates.

"I think it's almost time for Gilda's speech. I'm sure she wants to meet you two before she gives it. She's hoping for your human support," Carl said.

"Yes," crowed Heidi. "I'm ready to party. No matter the occasion she knows how to entertain."

They entered through ornate gates into the grand lobby. There was Tavia arranging signs, buttons and campaign literature on tables by the door.

Evie rushed over to her with a hug. "Hi Tavia. This is so exciting."

Surprised and relieved to see Evie and Liz, Tavia really needed their support.

"Listen, guys. I, that is, we hope you two will want to get involved in Gilda's Mayoral Campaign? We need everyone. The Silvers are on board. Brace yourselves, you are going to see the real workings of Atom City politics today," Tavia said excitedly guiding the group through the ornate grand hall.

Music filled the air. Hundreds of ElemMates dressed in fancy costumes floated and twirled in a graceful dance, their starry electrons mingling in rhythm. Sweet and spicy scents made the girls hungry. Did ElemMates need food as they did? As they walked through the huge ballroom carved with fantastic golden sculptures, the dance music suddenly stopped and a trumpet blared. The crowd grew silent and stepped back to let the visitors greet the Gold ElemMate up on the dais. Sunshine seemed to glow around her.

"Hello, so good to meet you. I am Gilda Gold," said the would-be candidate in a brocade gold gown. She wore a crown with waving gold streamers ringed by triangular gold shapes over her curly gold hair. She shook hands with Evie and Liz and directed the group to soft golden couches inlaid with rose quartz and blue lapis lazuli.

"Now bring on the food" Gilda called to servers. Golden platters arrived with delectable golden treats for the girls. Overstuffed gold satin chairs were drawn up to the solid gold table. Waiters served them a bit of everything: yellow cheeses, golden chicken garnished with crystallized ginger, saffron rice, banana pudding for dessert with lemon soda to drink. It was somewhat embarrassing to be the only ones eating, but they managed to eat just about everything.

"So, I hear you have come for a relaxing visit. Though Carl says you are also on a fact-finding trip for your Science Projects. Perhaps we can help you with some ideas," said Gilda, making conversation during the meal.

Evie explained, "It's the annual school wide Science Fair. Kids chose a scientific concept and try to demonstrate it using models and displays. Lots of schools around the world participate. In the spring all students set up an exhibit of their experiment, and judges choose the winner. Winners then compete in State and National and International competitions for scholarships and grants to do more experiments. I'm thinking I'd love to do something with my experiences in Atom City."

"Me, too. Though I haven't been as involved as Evie. I also want to create a project using what I've learned. Both of us have been working with our Science teacher studying the geology of the blast site, you know, where Evie did her experiment. We are learning lots of scientific methods and lab skills. We were thinking we could find something really exciting to demonstrate. Of course it must be real science." Liz added.

"I actually think I have gotten an idea since I've been here today. I'd like to grow those crystal flowers. Maybe I could go to each ElemMate neighborhood for crystal seed donations, then grow them on a big chart like the classic Periodic Table of Elements….Maybe I could let them grow into a great sculpture to bring in my artistic bent," proclaimed Evie all excited by the idea.

"Not to put down your idea, but, Evie, mineral crystals take thousands, if not millions of years to form. Of course you could do sugar or salt crystals, but that's not new," put in Liz.

The group pondered in silence watching the ElemMate guests dancing around the ballroom in a graceful waltz.

"Hey, time's no problem," volunteered Heidi. "We could help a little, sort of work with the factory here and speed things up. How fast do they need to grow?"

"Hmm, I know humans have grown some gem crystals in the lab, though pretty small ones. Industrial diamonds are commonplace. Are you allowed to use outside facilities and resources? Some, like salts, as you said are pretty easy. You need to begin with a seed crystal. Perhaps with our Atom City technology, it could work." said Carl.

"At this point we have four months, until March. I will definitely try to find an industrial diamond place. Perhaps doing all the elements is too much," said Evie.

"And what about you, Liz?" asked Carl.

"I'm pretty interested in diamonds," she answered, blushing a bit. "I don't know. There's the huge pressure needed to change carbon into diamonds, I know. And yes, I could check out industrial diamonds. Then there are those "Bucky Balls". Carbon molecules formed into what looks like soccer balls...and since I'm the Captain of the Soccer Team, it could be really cool. I hear that the Bucky Balls are made into strands and woven into very strong, light materials."

"You have certainly been thinking about this a lot." Carl smiled. "Let's all do some thinking."

"Not to change the subject everyone, but Gilda and I want to fill Evie and Liz in on what's going on here. Atom City, as Evie saw on her last visit, is no Paradise. You saw what we went through with the rioting," said Tavia seriously. She described the worsening political situation. Sonia repeated her experiences with Beryl Beryllium.

The girls were intrigued about the possible origin of Evie's weird Chemistry set.

Heidi jumped in. "OK, ok, enough serious thinking. We have guests on vacation. Here we're at Gilda's Mayoral Announcement Party. Let's show them how to have fun." She pulled Evie toward the dance floor, twirling her around.

As Evie dodged dancers, tables and servers with food, a tray of quivering purple and green dessert caught her eye. She leaned close to the sweet smelling confection recalling the green sugar crystal her friends had created for her. Just as she spooned a bit toward her mouth, the Chlorine soldier from the Ozone Hole battle rushed over and smacked it out of her hand. Loud laughter echoed throughout the great hall. The crowd grew silent.

"Beryl, you come out and show yourself," thundered Gilda. "Is this your idea of contesting my campaign by trying to poison my guest?"

A tall female ElemMate emerged laughing from the crowd.

Beryl Beryllium's pale silvery skin, strong featured face and broad shoulders set off her elegant deep green satin gown studded with emeralds. Her smooth green hair highlighted in silver coiled around her head. Turning toward Evie she said, "I'm so glad to meet you. I have been looking forward to getting to know you. I do hope you are ok, Evie. It really wouldn't have hurt you, too much. It might also have helped you see things in a new light. Indeed, I've been looking forward to meeting you."

She faced Gilda and the crowd of guests like a practiced orator. "I know everyone else here knows me, Beryl Beryllium. I thought it would be a dramatic way to stir things up a bit to announce my candidacy for Mayor. Thanks for letting me preempt Gilda's announcement on her own turf. I take this opportunity to be the one to officially welcome Evie and her friend to Atom City. You can thank me or not."

Gilda stood up and came forward to the edge of the dais. Her voice resonated through the great hall. "Yes, I am indeed announcing my candidacy for Mayor of Atom City. We need someone with honesty and good will to combat your underhanded politicking. While we honor Evie who helped the world as well as our own city, you attempt to hurt her. What's your logic? She saved you and your family, yet you attempt a deadly trick against her? My platform is centered on fostering living together cooperatively and working to do the same for the whole world. What is your platform? Fostering antagonism and violence? Supporting rioting in the streets and hooliganism? Please leave right now, you are not welcome in our palace."

Beryl laughed again and with head held high strode proudly toward the exit, waving to the crowd, "I have strength and support throughout this city. I have more depth and breadth of knowledge, more wisdom than Goldie Locks here. And how do you think Evie came to be here in the first place?" Nearing the exit she turned, raised her arm and proclaimed in a loud resonant voice to the crowd, "I am leading the Radioactives Party of Atom City. We include all citizens who believe in self-fulfillment. My platform is Freedom to use your powers as you want and the Right of the individual over the group. All are welcome Radioactives and Non-Radioactives." Then she flounced out of the ballroom.

The ensuing silence gave Gilda a chance to respond. Her voice carried clearly through the crowd. "All of you know I am a steady, solid constant, my qualities have been displayed for eternity. If we are united in the face of change, we can thrive. You all know I believe in diplomacy, consensus and working together to accomplish what is good for the whole City as well as individual rights. I hope you continue to endorse our long standing Atom City Party." Then smiling, Gilda spread her arms to the crowd. "But that's enough politics. We are here to dance and enjoy ourselves." She beckoned the orchestra to recommence their music.

Meanwhile Evie stood silently next to her Chlorine rescuer, spilled dessert oozing at their feet. His fresh from the pool scent overcame the sickeningly sweet smell of the poison confection. "So sorry about that," he said. "Beryl and her magician friends like to concoct poisonous tricks. It did look delightful. In fact Beryl's treats do taste sweet. But one taste of that may have killed you."

"Whew," Evie breathed in relief leaning over to whisper to Liz. "My Dad would love this fairy tale: Golden Princess and dashing soldier in a magical kingdom save Girl from witch's poison. That's what I get for being such a pig, grabbing food and not watching what I eat." Evie recalled Beryl's passing comment that the dessert was NOT poison. Was she lying?

After some interesting conversation about gold jewelry and sculpture, Heidi's nervous energy made her impatient. "Come on gang, let's get this tour moving."

"Wait, I'd like one dance with Evie before you go," said her Chlorine soldier. The sprightly orchestral music filled the hall. He took Evie's hand and spun her onto the shining marble dance floor. Carl grasped Liz's waist twirling her into dance. Gilda danced with a Fluorine, and the others easily found friends for partners. What a sight! Electrons flashed and vibrated around each of the thousands of richly costumed whirling, dancing ElemMate guests.

When the music paused, Gilda announced to the crowd, "It's a golden afternoon, everyone! I'm taking this party down to the Primordial River Promenade. Refreshments on me at the Beach Front Café! Boat rides on the Primordial River for all!"

Gilda glided gracefully through the crowd toward the large exit gate. The crowd followed joyfully down the avenue passed Dar Stadium Arena through grassy Proton Park to the Promenade, a wooden deck shaded by palm trees. Cafes with umbrella-shaded tables lined the walkway. Everyone trouped past banners and streamers decorating wrought iron railings and lampposts. Some settled into cafes. Others descended from the promenade to the sandy beach. The rest walked out to the boat piers.

Chapter 11
Evium, A New ElemMate

Heidi led the group of friends along the pier to the gaily painted pleasure boats. Liz looked forward to rowing. Evie loved any kind of boat ride. Just about to step into a waiting boat, Evie glanced down at the water and recoiled, scrambling back onto the dock.

"Yuck! This water is disgusting. It stinks like rotten eggs. Look! I see all kinds of rotten looking stuff floating in it, and it's steaming. It's bubbling! Oh, my, it's even glowing. This water must be so toxic, so polluted we'd lose our hands if we put them in," she gasped holding her nose. "I don't think I'm into boating in this water."

"It's fine, fine," laughed Carl. "Don't worry it won't hurt you. True there is a lot going on in our river. It is indeed steaming and glowing. But it has always been that way. It is the Primordial River, the water, the steaming pool, from which life formed. The 'stuff' are not pollutants. They could be particles forming new atoms, molecules and new life forms. Some mutate, evolve, thrive and develop. Others won't survive. Everything in Earth's history is there: ancient forms and forms just being created as you watch. You only need to reach in to scoop it out."

Intrigued Evie said, "You mean I could fish out a prehistoric dinosaur cell or the cell of a creature no one has seen yet? Wow." Evie climbed into the boat. The others followed. The girls stared into the water while Carl rowed. They all took turns. Liz rowed next, moving like a shot through the calm water.

While Tavia rowed, Carl pointed out the sights along the river. "Come on girls, look around." The river divided the city into a north and south with most of the city on the north side. They could see the bustling downtown, the civic and government, shopping and office buildings as well as factories. The south side seemed quieter. Spacious classic and modern mansions, museums, the City University and Prometheus Amusement Park occupied bigger plots of green landscaped hills.

"It is beautiful. I hope we get to visit the south side soon. Meanwhile I see there are nets under the benches. Can we fish?" Evie suggested.

"Sure, if you really want to. We usually don't fish though. The nets are mostly here for lifesaving. We usually like to leave what's growing in there alone, but ok," said Heidi handing her a fine mesh net.

"Me, too, me, too", said Liz plucked a net from under her bench.

Together the girls gleefully tossed the net. It fanned open in the air, splashed into the water and slowly sank. Soon the fine mesh filled with all kinds of exotic fish, creatures, plants and shells as well as unidentifiable objects. They pulled the shimmering, oozing writhing mass closer to the boat. Liz stood to heave the net in when she lost her balance and tumbled into the water.

"The net! The net!" yelled Carl. Evie found another empty net stored in the boat's prow, shook it out and threw it to Carl. He and Tavia quickly took each corner and flung it out into the water. Evie impulsively jumped in after Liz. In a second Liz's smiling face surfaced. Evie bobbed up seconds later.

"Ooh, yeah, it's like a bathtub complete with bubble bath and salts," Liz exclaimed happily floating on her back, her arms pillowing her head.

Evie paddled around plucking interesting looking objects from the water, tossing them into the net that had hooked to the side of the boat intact. Swimming out away from the boat, diving under the surface, Evie snatched more and more treasures. Bobbing up for air, she flipped onto her back to float next to Liz, her treasures balanced on her stomach otter style.

"Ow", shouted Evie. "I'm being pinched. Get me out of here!"

"Ew, something's sticking to me, I'm getting out," Liz sputtered heading back to the boat.

Heidi and Carl pulled the dripping girls back into the boat. The giggling girls were covered in river flotsam. The objects Evie collected still stuck to her stomach.

"Look at yourselves. You've attracted everything from the water!" Heidi scolded. "Those free-floating electrons think you are an atom's nucleus. Minerals think you are a seed crystal to attach to. We don't even know what some of the substances are in there. Actually we don't really know if they are toxic to humans. Who knows what all that mix will create reacting to each other and your bodies. We should get them right up to the Wise Center right away. Luckily it is right up from the shore road."

"But Carl said it wasn't dangerous," Evie argued.

"Yes, but he isn't human. The ElemMates that can dissolve in water stay away. We should just check you guys out to be sure," said Heidi, trying to pick off the debris from the girls' clothing.

Worried Oxygen ElemMate bystanders gathered close around the girls to give them extra fresh air. Others lifted them up, floating them toward Radon City Hospital like princesses leading a procession. "We're fine, aren't we Liz?" Evie protested. "Don't forget the stuff from the net, I want to check it out, maybe take it home" Evie shouted back to their friends tying up the boat at the dock, feeling energized from her dip. It took only a few minutes to the entrance where Dr. Plutarch Plutonium met them with a staff of emergency workers. They took the girls to a room with a full body scanner. This scanner, unlike the ones at home, checked every electron, proton and neutron in their bodies. Once all the foreign particles were removed, Liz's atomic make up was back to its normal perfect shape. She showed no radiation or toxic exposure or signs of any viral or bacterial invasion. In fact both girls' super condensed state gave them super strong immune systems.

But everything did not check out so perfectly with Evie. The machine beeped and flashed warnings. The readings were unclear about foreign body invasions, radiation and toxic poisoning. The foreign electrons so easily removed from Liz refused to budge from Evie's body. Instead they began to orbit around her in concentric rings with each ring angled at a different level and slant.

"Evie, how do you feel?" asked the doctor looking into her eyes and throat and checking all the monitors to which she was connected.

"I feel great, really energized. Better than I've ever felt before. Not so sure if these orbiting electrons are going to get me dizzy. How long will this last, Doctor?"

"I'm not sure. This is a new phenomenon. Those electrons seem to be forming a pretty precise and steady orbit around her. Dr. Plutonium quickly counted the electrons and rings. "My goodness, you are turning into an atom, a huge atom!"

Liz tugged on the doctor's jacket frantically. "You've got to save my friend. Please, please help her. Why am I ok and she is turning into a strange creature."

"So far she is fine. All her vitals and organs are getting stronger and stronger. Her brain function is gaining complexity and strength. "

"Are you kidding?" Evie exclaimed incredulously. "You are saying I am becoming an element, a new kind of element? Me? How can that be? It doesn't make any sense. If I am an element, what are my properties?"

"I don't know" the doctor pondered. "Let's scan you again."

After the technicians checked and readied the scanner, another slow, scan was taken. The data checked out as before.

Plutarch said, "You are now a very large atom, larger than the largest ElemMates in Atom City, even larger than any synthetic elements made by humans. Your properties are completely unique. You have already discovered some of your powers. Like us you can float and fly. You can stretch your hair and extremities into amazingly cloth you can shapes with your mind. You are impervious to the strongest radiation. You have control of the special Equation that allows you and someone you hold to transform from Human to the size of an atom. You are already enjoying your increased brain capabilities. Now you may have even more properties."

The doctor continued examining her and the monitors. "Look! These crystals you had resting on your stomach match your electron configuration and weight! Amazing! That means they have taken on your properties and become one with you. You attracted rudimentary unformed elements and made them your own. "

Evie thrilled by her new state turned and stretched her arms and legs, "Wow, I am so much more flexible. Now I can reach my leg around my neck."

"Oh, help her, Doctor!" Liz shrieked, "She's glowing like a neon rainbow. And those crystals are growing right before our eyes. It must be the radiation or toxic stuff from the water. Please stop it."

"Don't worry, Liz" said the doctor checking the readings again on the scanner. "Now the readings definitively show absolutely no radiation going in or out of her. The scanner shows she is perfectly fine, better than fine. And being a highly radioactive ElemMate myself, and a scholar on the subject, I know the symptoms. Don't worry, she is fine." Plutarch responded, calming Liz's fears.

Liz relaxed a bit and took in the beauty of the crystals growing around Evie's body, the multi-colored glow emanating from her like an aura and the electrons sparkling around her. Now the crystals had grown to the size of silver dollars.

Evie stood up an admired herself in the lab's mirror. "Gorgeous, but it is a bit cumbersome. I could probably handle it if they stay this size." But they didn't. Everyone tried to pry them off to no avail. Plutarch tried a laser zap. Not even a sliver chipped off. Carl's diamonds, the hardest element, didn't even leave a scratch. Weirdly, hard as they were, they stretched and grew the more they were pulled.

"You know," said Carl who'd been quiet all this time, "maybe do what I do when my diamond crystals get a bit much for me? Why I just pluck them off myself. No one else can give me a trim. Guess everyone takes care of their own crystals. Go ahead, Evie, try it yourself."

Sure enough Evie could pluck them off easily herself. Everyone watched relieved as she easily removed the bigger ones and pinched others back to smaller sizes. At a certain point she could not remove any more. Her now full multi-colored crystal gown spread flashing prisms of light as she joyfully twirled. Her orbiting electrons made her hair golden waves and her skin pink gold.

Tavia counted 180 electrons. "Wow, you sure it's 180?" Everyone recounted to the same number. "That's gotta be lucky." Evie said her high-powered brain whirring. "Eighteen is the Hebrew number, "Chai", which means "Life". I'm "life times ten". I'm also the number of degrees that make up a semi-circle."

Evie felt good in the flowing gown. Despite all the crystals the fabric was soft and smooth. She fingered the material thinking how it would look when she stretched the fibers and wove them into the moldable cloth. Peering closely at one of the bigger crystals on her sleeve, she gave a start of recognition. These crystals formed into a ring shape. Indeed these were the same crystals she found at the Blast site! Now she realized they had come from her own body.

All business now she headed toward the bin holding the tangled net and all its treasures. "Ok, enough primping over me. Let's see what we brought in from the river."

Everyone gathered around the bulging, dripping net. Plutarch carefully scanned for radioactivity and toxins. Miraculously everything proved safe. Everyone gleefully explored the contents.

"Oh, look, Liz, I found a Bucky Ball." Said Carl pulling out the 16-sided piece of carbon. "If you like these, I can get you more from my cousin, Bucky."

"Oh, wow, great. Thanks. But isn't everyone forgetting something. My friend Evie here just became a new element, a huge beautiful, tough, stretchable one of whom I am very proud. Shouldn't we celebrate? Shouldn't we name it, er, her?" suggested

Liz. "If I may, I've got an idea. What do you think of Evium?"

"No, no I couldn't have my name in it," Evie said modestly. "How about something about color like Rainbowium or Prismium?"

Tavia, the wordsmith said, "Those names are descriptive, Evie, but you not only discovered the new element, you became it. As you get used to yourself as an element, an ElemMate, you'll learn even more and more about your properties. Now you find you can produce, adjust and re-size these multi-colored crystals. Who knows what else you'll discover about yourself. In any case what does everyone else think of the name? I like Evium, myself."

"Yes, yes, Evium!" they unanimously cheered.

"OK, ok. Thanks, everyone. So, hey, Doc, what do you want to do with the rest of this stuff? Should you research it in your lab or put it in the city museum? Can we bring some of it home and find scientists to help us study it? Can we take some samples? Wonder if I'll look like this when I get home? That wouldn't be good." Evie was a bit apprehensive as she pulled off one or two of her crystals and sealed it into a container.

"We'd love to study the contents in our lab and display it in the museum here, if you don't mind," said Dr. Plutonium. "How about if you go enjoy the city for a bit while we collect all the information. We can meet at the museum later. Help put up the display. Then we'll pack up some samples and gather crystals from ElemMates for your projects, and perhaps some little gifts."

Heidi, impatient to be on their way exclaimed, "Time to continue our tour of Atom City!" The friends strolled out from the Medical Center and walked along the river road. ElemMates sat in cafes, walked along the beach and rowed on the river, the girls' dunk in the river forgotten.

The group strolled west through the beautiful gardens of Proton Park.

Darm Stadium impressed Liz, captain of the soccer team. "Oh, this is an incredible stadium. Kind of like one I saw in England on the Sports Channel. Can we go in? What sports do you play here?"

Heidi explained the City's game, Particle Collider. "We'll have to take you some time. Each team races around their own track in opposite directions. At a high speed, the dividers between the two tracks are lifted and players smash into each other. Their parts, their particles scatter. Detectors count the particles from each team. The team with the most scattered parts wins A bit like your football, I guess."

"Sound a bit rougher than our football. Even more rough than rugby. So all the players whose parts scatter die?" asked Liz, upset by the brutality of the game.

"No, ElemMates don't die, not in this way anyway. After the action, the players go to the ReConnection Room, where electromagnetic machines reconnect them, for the most part that is. There are permanent mishaps of course," said Heidi with a fan's fervor. No one mentioned the riots that happened at the last game.

They continued straight west for the Atom City Mall. Carl suggested Dubnium café nearby. "Don't worry, Mr. Dubnium disciplined his sons and has restored the Café after their fight there." But Tavia had become very sensitive about the high tensions among the ElemMates. Still, it wouldn't be fair to not support Mr. Dubnium's business. The café on the plaza just outside the mall overlooked a more industrial part of the river. They sat among other tables full of chattering ElemMates watching large ships unloading goods for the business and factories nearby. Carl ordered ice cream sodas stirred with rock candy swizzle sticks. The Dubnium boys served them politely without smiling.

They relaxed in delicate wrought iron chairs entertained by the parade of shoppers. Sipping sweet, refreshing Atom City water, Tavia opened up to Evie.

"Evie, I know you are younger than me. But somehow I feel a connection with you. We both love to fly and float and relax and enjoy just being. Yet we both like taking the plunge, so to speak. I loved fixing these big crises with you. I think we make a good team."

Evie was touched. "Oh, Tavia, that makes me feel so good. I feel our connection, too. Maybe because we both have an eight in our atomic number. Seriously, I hope we can do more adventures together."

"The adventures are great. But I'm more concerned at this point by the troubles in Atom City. The Radioactives want to take over. They want anarchy or a totalitarian city where physical power trumps fair laws. We need a strong person to run against Beryl. I'm not sure Gilda can do it," said Tavia leaning close to whisper out of the others' earshot.

"That's big stuff, sure, I'm finding I have some leadership potential, but I haven't done any politics. Tavia, you seem to have more verve than Gilda. Maybe you should run. Let Gilda do the parties and fund raising. From what I saw someone has to stand up to Beryl. But is she really a power hungry witch? She does seem awfully sharp. She actually made friendly overtures to me. I'd actually like to see what she's up to in her lab. I'd love to pick her brain. Of course at this point I wouldn't trust her. Still, maybe Beryl can be won over instead of defeated. Anyway just my ignorant observations," Evie whispered back.

Evie glanced across the table at Liz, Carl and Heidi. It seemed to her Liz and Carl leaned very close to each other. Carl's arm stretched around the back of Liz's chair, his fingers touching her hair.

The Western Bridge spanned the river from the Mall's plaza. Views of the river were spectacular. Turning to look back, one could see north all the way to Terra Mountain in the distance. They headed south to the less congested South City.

The bridge ended at a plaza with signs directing visitors to the Promethium Amusement Park and the museum.

A bit early for their museum meeting, they scampered to the Amusement Park. No one could resist a ride on the roller coaster. Every amusement crackled with non-stop fireworks. Evie wasn't so sure she was into the stomach churning rides, but Heidi and Liz grabbed her arms and secured her between them. They all screamed with joy, until an errant firecracker shorted out the ride. Luckily they were near the end of the ride.

Breathless after the rides, they headed toward their appointment. A magnificent glistening dome supported the Museum's white limestone facade. Figures recounting the City's history were carved into the huge stone blocks. Colored crystals and minerals emblazoned the roof. ElemMate visitors, scholars and workers scurried everywhere with notebooks, easels and magnifying glasses.

Dr. Plutonium arrived as they did. The group entered a door marked "Authorized Personnel Only" when Octavia flashed her press card to the guard. A few ElemMates sat at dark oak tables copying ancient manuscripts with gold quill pens. Octavia spoke quietly to one of them who pointed to a small door set in a carved stone archway. Another guard ushered them through it into a gleaming, brightly lit room full of modern steel cabinets.

The conservator, a bright-faced Europium ElemMate appeared with a bin holding the contents of the net that had ensnared them in the Primordial River. "Actually we really don't have the display ready for the public, but the Primordial River Net Findings have been catalogued, photographed, tested and recorded. Years of research will still be needed. Our designers are working on how to exhibit it all. Lucky you, you can still see it all close up before it's put into the cases. Your dredged up treasures will be part of all our displays of ancient and new discoveries."

The group peered closely at the strange, sparkling objects stuck in bronze glowing ooze.

"This ooze looks really cool. What is it? Can we take some?" asked Liz reaching out to it bare handed.

"Hey, Liz, remember all the protocol we learned from Ms. Melillo. If you don't know what it is, don't touch it. We should get some gloves," said Evie.

The elderly ElemMate Conservator handed her gloves and a scoop. Evie spooned a shiny blue globe from the rubbery substance into a container he gave her. Bubbles skittered over its surface. "What are those?" Everyone peered over her shoulder.

The Conservator informed them, "It is pure oxygen. This solid, hard, transparent globe is an ancient form not found today. We have been excited about our studies of it." Octavia leaned close fascinated to see an ancient ancestor.

Evie picked up the scanner waving it over the mass. The scanner clicked and beeped displaying common elements until it flashed an, 'unknown substance' in its window. The mineral had no crystalline structure. It was made up of tiny spiracle cones like orange and cherry soft ice cream swirls. "This is perfect for Ms. Melillo since she took us for ice cream, and since it seems unidentified, it should keep her busy."

"That's it then. I'll have it gift wrapped, please." Liz joked.

Evie peered into the bin and chose several objects. One sparkled like gold with many pointy projectiles. This looks like a star. Is it safe? Can I have that? Another was a plant-like green corkscrew with soft feathery tendrils. Her final choice looked like a fossil of a snake biting its own tail. All checked out as safe.

Then, as promised, staff members fanned out around the city to collect seed crystal samples. To their surprise a crowd of Atom City citizens stood waiting outside the museum exit. Each offered a container with their family seed crystal. It was explained that the compressed samples would uncompress in the same way Evie and Liz expanded back to normal size at home.

"Would it offend you if we didn't take the toxic or radioactive seeds," Evie asked. "I think it may cause trouble back home."

Even Beryl came by offering her family emerald. "So sorry for my behavior, before. I do get so caught up in politics. Please don't eat this sample. And perhaps on your next visit you will visit my Palace. I have a fully equipped lab in my castle basement. I'd love to pick your brain, verbally of course. And I really have no secrets. More than willing to share my studies with you." She said sweetly, tightly gripping Evie's hand.

Gilda came with a pot of gold for her. Bucky Carbon, Carl's cousin, gave Liz a few more of his prime Bucky Ball samples.

She addressed the whole crowd. "Liz and I thank you all so much for your gifts for our project. With your help these crystals will grow large and fast to show humans all your symmetry and beauty. We hope our projects will be worthy." No one thought to ask about stopping their growth.

"We can't really gift you seed crystals at room temperature. Here's a bit of hydrogen and oxygen gas." Tavia and Heidi handed her the gas samples in tiny delicate crystal vials.

Carl gave Liz an extra diamond crystal: "For your project or just to keep," he said winking.

"Well, I guess it's time to head home, Liz," Evie sighed. "Thanks all of you for pulling us out of the river. But for my part, I really enjoyed the swim." Evie took Liz's hand, hoped she'd look normal when she arrived home and thought The Formula backwards.

Chapter 12
Project Crystal

"Wow! Unbelievable! That was some fairy tale! It beats the Grimm brothers even without the Beryl character," exclaimed Evie flopping back on her bed, gray blue eyes in the clouds. "And Liz, I am a fairy tale princess, though I could never dare show up at school looking like a psychedelic rainbow," noting with relief her normal still scrawny teenage body.

"Well, I thought you looked great, but I'm glad you were able to take those crystals off. That could have been pretty horrifying if they'd grown any bigger and didn't come off. I'm glad those things didn't stick to me. Anyway, the whole thing was an incredible adventure. Thanks so much for taking me. And you know what I think? It was no fairy tale. It was real," said Liz with conviction sitting up at the edge of Evie's bed. "I definitely 'suspended my disbelief'. I can accept both, that the ElemMates are small particles of elements, and fully living, breathing, thinking beings."

"Are you referring to a dark, handsome guy with a dazzling smile?" teased Evie.

Liz threw a pillow at her. "Come on. We have work to do. What time is it anyway?" she said laughing. She glanced at Evie's bedside clock. "Oh, look it's only 9:00 p.m. It seemed like we were gone for longer. You hungry? I'm famished."

"How could I be after that feast? Course we got lots of exercise, flying, and swimming." Evie laughed leading the way to the kitchen. The girls managed to polish off everything on the heaping dinner plates Evie's mom had left wrapped in the refrigerator.

Evie's dad dallied in the kitchen with a piece of cake and coffee. He was taking a break from his writing and welcomed talking with the girls. In the relaxed glow of the kitchen lamp, the girls told him all their adventures. Her father couldn't get enough of what he called "The Evie Tales".

"So looks like you really took lots of steps on your journey, both in actual steps, in your physical development and in politics. Atom City sounds so beautiful, almost blinding. Interesting they like to copy our architects' designs," he said between sips.

"Well, that's why they want to connect with Humans. Their properties are set by nature, the laws of chemistry, not rational thought or artistic passion," she answered.

"I've been reading that so much of Human creativity is indeed based on the brain's chemical-electrical reactions," said Dad. "Now what about your body chemistry? Not to embarrass or pry into your physical changes, but I wouldn't tell Mom you have ringed crystals growing from your body. She'd have you in intensive care in a sec. Can I see them?"

Evie pulled up her sleeve to reveal her usual pale olive tinged skin with its fine light blond hairs. "They are only there when I say the Formula or enter Atom City," she explained.

"Looks ok to me. I don't see any rings. Still, remember the doctor wanted you to check in in a few weeks."

"Dad, they were the same crystals I found at the Blast Site. I

111

might study them for part of my Science Fair Project. Perhaps I can claim a new element."

"Cool. Right now it should all be confidential. From Mom's recounting of politics in the Science world, there's lots of intrigue. Be careful."

"Yes, Dad, you also promised to keep this confidential. I know if people take it seriously, it could literally be earth shattering information," said Evie.

"Of course, Evie. Who do you think I am? As your dad my foremost concern is for your safety," he replied offended.

"Dad, I know you care and I also know you are a true storyteller. It will be so difficult for you to resist, not only putting it on paper, but embellishing it even more, if that's possible." Evie reached over to hug him.

"Truly they are your stories, yours and Liz's. Keep them well. Use them well." He replied squeezing her hand. Now, besides your new element, how will you translate these adventures into a real science project? Let me know if I can help."

"Umm. Guess we have some thinking and research to do." Standing up she patted her Dad's head, put their dishes in the dishwasher and followed Liz back to her room.

Liz pulled a chair up to Evie's large desk and opened her notebook. Then the cold reality hit them. The containers, where were the containers? Evie had never attempted to bring anything back from her adventures. Could the containers still be in Atom City? They frantically searched their clothes, the bed and the whole the room.

"Wait a minute. Don't move," commanded Liz. "Maybe the containers are here in their original size which of course means atomic size. Now, if we are very lucky the containers may still be in our hands. Maybe they slipped into the cracks in our hands and are stuck there. 'Course if they've slipped out, we're sunk."

"Good thinking, Liz. We'd better cover our hands before we do anything." She rummaged in her art cabinet for a box of latex gloves she used when she painted in oils. "Now what? We can always go back, but everyone was so nice donating, and so many different elements were collected, I couldn't ask again."

"No we couldn't do that. Not only did the whole city go to a lot of trouble to get us the seed crystals, but remember what we did to gather some of the stuff from those nets. I'm not sure we should go back for another dip. Though truthfully, I really enjoyed that water. It was the perfect temperature and those minerals were like a fancy mineral spa bath," said Liz, her dark brows knit together over long lashed dark eyes. Her chin resting on propped up elbows on Evie's desk.

"You enjoyed the swim, too? You seemed immune to any reactions. But you are so right. We have to do as much as we can ourselves on these projects. Not sure how much help we're allowed. Maybe if I can try to visualize the scene without saying The Formula, it would be enough."

Evie closed her eyes and tried to picture the ElemMates crowd outside the Atom City Medical Center bearing their tiny gifts. In her mind she visualized the activity, seeing ElemMates placing the packages in their hands.

"That's it! I realize we have the containers safe in the lines of our hands. But now what? I certainly don't want to wear these gloves until the Science Fair. Having invisible crystals is no experiment; more like a hoax, the Emperor's New Clothes. No one is going to believe us. We have to make something happen with them," complained Liz.

"You're forgetting something, Liz. The seed crystals are growing rapidly. Hopefully in a few days we can see them with a microscope. They decided to wait until Monday.

The girls got to school early Monday and quickly set up the school microscope. Pulling off the gloves they examined their hands. Nothing showed. It took awhile to scrape tiny samples from every crevice in their hands. Well practiced in making slides after all the time working there, they dabbed their skin material onto fifty sterile glass slides, covered them carefully and observed each on the lab's most powerful microscope. The effort paid off. They saw some faint irregularities.

"Take a look, Liz. Do you see the disturbances, even tiny black specks?" Evie called out peering at the fortieth slide. Should we tell Ms. Melillo now?"

We can say we also made some slides from our hands that perhaps had some contact with materials there. That would be the truth, really. She'll think we are very thorough scientists…. which we are" said Liz giving a little punch to Evie's shoulder.

When Ms. Melillo walked into the lab they explained. "We scraped our skin when we came home from the Blast Site and from when we were working on the samples in the school lab and made some slides of potential microscopic residues. We took some of the school's slides. Hope you aren't mad at us," confessed Evie in a low voice.

"Mad? That's great," their teacher said. "I am so proud of you guys for taking the initiative. I actually was lent a high power microscope that can actually see individual atoms. Is that why you girls are wearing gloves? Are you thinking there are still samples on your skin? Worth a try, I guess."

It was so exciting to see one of the most advanced microscopes. After school, Ms. Melillo showed them how to use it using some of her slides.

The sights through the Electron Scanning Tunneling Microscope astounded them. "Look, I see something" Evie exclaimed. "I see tiny shining things. Oh, my, I see them! Are they really atoms? Are we actually seeing real atoms?"

"They sure are, girls," Ms. Melillo said. She looked closely at their slide four. "Such good slides, we can even discern some of your skin's atoms mixed with the crystal minerals. Great work girls." They took turns seeing the crystal seeds containing a few atoms. "Okay girls you're on your own. I have work to do in the classroom. Call me if you need me."

As soon as Ms. Melillo left Liz put slide six under the "And look! There's my Bucky Ball," exclaimed Liz peering in at the 15th slide. "And there's my diamond next to it."

The girls pranced around with excitement At 5:00 exhausted and relieved yet pumped with the possibilities, they packed up their slides.

"You girls are growing into real scientists. Feel free to use our school lab whenever you want. I'll make a copy of my key," said Ms. Melillo coming in to lock up the lab.

During the week the girls checked the slides during their usual after school lab time. It felt good to use their new key instead of hunting for the custodian or waiting for Ms. Melillo.

On Thursday Evie put a slide on the regular school microscope platform on a whim. Surprised she called Liz to peer through the lens. "Oh, look, Liz. I can now see them on this microscope. Can you believe how fast they grew? We don't even need the ETS microscope. If they are growing so fast, I wonder how long the containers they came in will hold them."

Liz looked a bit worried. I guess we'd better think seriously about where we are going to set up this crystal structure. It may be pretty big by the time of The Science Fair. And it had better be a strong and secure base. You have to admit we have bitten off a big project here. Obviously the adults are interested too."

"You're not kidding. I've heard the chemical companies send spies to steal student's ideas. ...I know, we can use my brother's workroom in our basement. You remember he was always down there fiddling with his mechanical inventions? Guess it got him into Carnegie Mellon for Engineering. It's got a lock on the door. He used to lock it to keep me out, but Mom made him leave the key in the kitchen drawer when he left."

"Won't he get mad? I recall he always yelled at us when we went down there to play in the rec room."

"Nah. He cleared it out when he went away. Took all the important stuff up to his room. Actually, it's time I made it my own. He's not even coming home this summer. I could use it for my art studio and our lab. It even has a sink."

They rushed back to Evie's house. No one was home. Her mom was still at the local greenhouse nursery where she worked with the farmers on crop improvement projects and rented a little research space there. Dad's office was empty, probably at his favorite hang out, the town Library. The girls took some cookies and milk down to the finished basement.

The workroom door stood ajar revealing a large room filled by the sturdy Ping-Pong table topped by the plywood board worktable. They cleared it of broken computer, toaster and TV guts spread around among piles of old toys and magazines. Knowing the value of this so-called junk the girls carefully fit it onto the rusty metal shelves built along the walls already filled with dusty gadgets, and kitchen and hardware items. Afternoon sunlight streamed through a high casement window. They swept the floor and opened the basement's outside door to let in some fresh air.

The 9 by 6 foot table got a good scrubbing. Liz found a large piece of Plexiglas leaning in the corner, which they laid over the worktable and also scrubbed clean.

Finally Evie switched on the overhead spotlight. The girls opened their packs carefully extracting the slides.

"Well that's it for me. I'm bushed and I have the final soccer tournament of the season tomorrow. We sure did a lot, got our ideas and materials planed out. Are you up for working Sunday?" Liz asked getting her things and one last cookie. "Wish me luck in the tournament. Then that's it for soccer until spring."

At dinner Evie's parents asked about their projects. Her Mom had such good things to say about working with Ms. Melillo and was grateful for her interest in Evie.

She said she and Ms. Melillo were working hard on a Blast Site Conference. It took a lot of time: the logistics of permits, invitations, booking speakers, accommodating foreign visitors. They were thankful many scientists and volunteers were helping out. Maybe Evie, Liz and their friends would want to help.

After dinner and good nights to her parents, Evie got to work. She took a long bubble bath and brushed her hair. Next she put on her iPod to listen to her favorite downloaded celestial 'New Age' music. Then she turned on her pink light bulb in the stained glass lamp.

"Evium Evium Evium," she chanted silently. Suddenly electrons ignited right before her eyes, the colors swirled around her and the crystals in every color sprouted from her skin. This time she calmly let the crystals grow. She felt she was floating. The crystals made a rocky shell around her as they grew larger and more profuse. Still she let them grow until they sheltered her in a blue, green, red, orange, yellow, pink and purple crystal rock.

Finally she pushed them away from herself thinking herself back to normal. The swirling colors and orbiting electrons disappeared. Evie marveled at the crystal rings strewn at her feet. She carefully scooped them up. One sparkling multi-colored ring, almost six inches in diameter, weighed almost nothing. In her desk drawer was the plastic envelope containing the ring-shaped crystals she'd gathered from the Blast Site. She added the ones she'd just created then quietly she slipped to the basement to add them to the other crystals on the table.

Sunday Liz showed up ready to work. She related the events of the tournament. Their school had lost. She'd made some bad plays and felt bad Evie hadn't attended. But when Evie showed her the ring, her soccer woes were forgotten.

"I've decided I'm going to make a huge picture of the Periodic Table of Elements Chart with a big square for each element and place each element crystal in the square." She spent the afternoon carefully drawing the classic chart using several different reference designs and colored in headings, information about each element and the areas describing the different types of element groups. Then she placed the big Evium crystal in a square for yet undiscovered elements in an area to the right of the chart.

Liz sat with her laptop researching the formation, location and uses of Bucky Balls and Diamonds in industry and products. She couldn't help being sidetracked by the wonderful images of famous diamonds and diamond jewelry and figured, why not do a two-pronged project. She would do a research report and display photos, and then display models of the different forms of Carbon such as diamonds, graphite and the 16-sided Bucky Balls. She laid out her crystal slides on a separate board then carefully placed it on one of the empty shelves.

They both would incorporate their work with Ms. Melillo's research at the Blast Site. Ms. Melillo expected the students to hand in a first draft of the project before the Winter break, which was in three weeks. So intent were they in their work they didn't even check the crystals until late in the afternoon. They were upset when they saw the slides all in disarray with the slide covers cracked or fallen off. At first they thought someone or thing had knocked them over. What they saw under the bright spotlight over the table was a shock.

"Look at this, Evie. I can see the crystals with my naked eye! The crystals grew and cracked the slide covers and the slides." Incredulous the girls examined each slide. There they saw many crystals crowding each other for space on each slide. They were the size of tiny black specks.

"Oh, boy, these are growing awfully fast. In a few days they'll each need their own slide. What am I saying…they'll be big enough to pick up. Oh, I hope we haven't created a monster. Guess it's good I used this 6 by 9-foot board and chart. Maybe I should reinforce the board and get wheels on it to transport it. Luckily this is a walk out basement right from this room. Liz you are also going to have to build some bigger display case, although you are only using two forms of one element. Let's see if Dad will take us to the hardware store." Evie said talking a mile a minute.

While shopping at the hardware store for supplies to make supports and displays, the girls described the crystals' behavior to Mr. Sparks. At first he was a bit frightened by the whole thing. "I'm used to fiction and the security of knowing it isn't real. This is serious." When they showed him the crystals, though, his eyes shone with excitement. "I guess we better keep these events under wraps for now and see how it develops."

"What we told Ms. Melillo was we took dust and skin samples from our hands and gloves after we worked on the minerals found at the Blast Site. She was pleased with our scientific thoroughness and accepted the explanation. But she doesn't know that not only are the crystals growing, but they are growing fast. And my crystal ring would really confound her.

The only other explanation for it, Dad, has got to be magic. That's really getting into your department, huh?" Her Dad stared at the crystal ring and the slides strewn on the table deep in thought or, Evie knew, deep in his imagination.

"Dad, I have the feeling this project is going to be a major test for me, definitely lots of possible stumbling blocks on my journey."

"Well, girl, you may fall, but you have lots of supporters to help you keep on track."

Ms. Melillo allowed the girls to borrow a school microscope to use at home. By the next week they could pick up each crystal now the size of a grain of sand with tweezers. Evie decided to try to identify each element seed. "Darn it, we should have had each ElemMate label their seed gift." She said with frustration.

Liz thought she could see the tell tale shape of the Bucky Ball, but wasn't sure. "At this rate of growth, perhaps with research we will be able to see more next week," Liz said trying to be positive.

By the next week, a week before the concept work was due, the crystals had grown to 1/8th of an inch. And lo and behold, under the microscope Liz could make out tiny letters and numbers etched on each sample. "They thought of everything", exclaimed Liz, "They labeled each sample. We're saved!"

"Oh, look, and here are the four gifts all wrapped and labeled." Evie put them aside and later hid them in the back of her bedroom closet.

Liz located her two samples and placed them in the wooden case she had built. Her plan was to let the diamond and Bucky Ball grow, create objects or models made from the mineral, then report on the industrial fabrication of the real items. She was excited about forming the Bucky Balls into filaments that would be woven into materials to make a cool carbon fiber hockey stick. Of course she would also use the diamonds to make some jewelry and demonstrate with photos and charts how industrial diamonds are used in cutting and grinding machines.

Evie began placing each sample in its proper place on the board with the chart on it. "These are actually growing so fast. Crystals usually take thousands of years to grow. I hope they don't keep growing like some horrible nightmare and take over the world. What if they continue to grow during the Science Fair? That sure would be trouble to explain. In any case, Liz, did you find more than one diamond as I need one for the Carbon spot on the chart."

"I must confess Carl gave me several. I'll put one on your chart. I have an idea for you. If you can get the crystals to fill the square then force them to grow upward, you could create a set of columns."

"Yes, I like that. Maybe when they get tall enough I'll be able to guide them into architectural structures to make the whole thing one fantastic castle. If it kept growing, it would become a large, ornate Crystal Palace. Who knows, if it gets big enough, it could become the size of a real palace…though I think that's kind of off the scientific radar, too much magic not enough science."

"I think it could be the coolest science project. You'd be showing how crystals grow in an artistic way, a great, beautiful, dramatic demonstration of crystal growth of different elements. Not magic, just mineral elements growing normally, well, uh, sort of normally," Liz finished sheepishly.

"Yes," Evie answered sarcastically, "Normality is the key word here, and you know it. We are going to be in the spotlight, more in the news than that Blast Site.

"How about this: Everyone is going to make models of the scientific concept they are exhibiting. Students always make stuff out of plaster, plastic, clay to represent the real thing. We can say we sculpted everything to look like the real thing. If the crystals grow large, all the better. We'll say we sculpted enlarged versions for better clarity in the demonstration. Perfect for you since everyone knows you are a great artist. Ironic and a shame to say the real thing is fake," said Liz.

"So let's get started writing down our proposals, outlines and notes to hand in next week. I'll say: I will study crystal growth of elements using research, models and demonstrations. For the Bucky Balls, um, let's see. To discuss different allotypes or forms of the element carbon: Coal, Graphite, Diamond, Bucky Balls and to demonstrate their structure and creation." She dictated out loud as she scribbled in to her notebook.

"Sounds good. And for Evium, I'll write: To describe and research developments in the creation of new elements, including man-made elements. I'll discuss discovery, properties, structure and properties and talk about manufacturing and possible uses," Evie wrote.

The weeks before the holiday break were busy. Final tests were coming and papers and projects were due in all the classes. Evie dedicated much care to the Science charts, plans and sketches for the Science Fair Project, making them works of art.

Evie thought she had everything under control. The crystals were growing an inch every week. The Science Fair materials handed in on time. She was confident about her finals and papers in all her subjects except Math and Science.

"I can't believe you are still nervous about Science. That first test was in another lifetime. You are not Evie Sparks, one time science flunky. You are Evie Sparks, super hero, Chemistry genius, discoverer and creator of Evium, a blossoming artist and most important my best friend," said Liz trying to bolster Evie's confidence and secretly glad all her strengths had not gone to her head.

"Old habits die hard, right? I'll blow it from nervousness." Evie just couldn't shake off the feelings of dread. Just looking at the Science Textbook made her nauseous. She tried to study, but the words seemed to disappear. So silly, she knew she now understood everything in the book. As the days passed she found it more and more difficult to concentrate on schoolwork.

She began to take more and longer breaks in all the subjects to go to the basement to check out the crystals. By Finals Week the crystals were over six inches high. Each crystal almost filled its square on the chart. Strangely she found she could easily manipulate the crystals as if they were clay. She poked, pinched and pushed them creating lacy holes and bends. Like a gardener training a vine she caused some crystals to elongate, some to merge together, and others to twist making windows, doors, domes and arches. Not concerned with convention, she formed irregular organic shapes and narrow towers. The crystals were soft enough to respond to knife cuts. She chiseled the crystals into fantastic figures. Gold and silver dribbled, gilded and laced everywhere like metallic sauce over every flavor of ices. An Evium ring grew into a grand circular entrance way.

The day of the Science test arrived. Evie felt sure in one area: she had turned every page in the textbook and notebook. What that translated to on the test was another story. Ms. Melillo handed out the tests. When Evie focused on the first question the words blurred and her hands sweated. Blinking a few times she tried again, but the whole page was a grey blur.

"Evie girl," she said to herself, "Cut out this nonsense. Relax." She closed her eyes and tried again. Still a blur.

Evie concentrated her thoughts. "Come on, you have power, flying high over Atom City, blocking neutrinos with your body, stopping CFCs from wrecking havoc, building canals, reciting complex equations. Yes, equations. I'm Evium, Evium, Evium." Opening her eyes, she picked up the pencil and finished a minute before the bell.

Chapter 13
The Science Fair

After the break the girls buckled down on getting their Science Fair Projects done by March 14th when students would set up their exhibits the day before the exhibit in the school's gym. They had to be careful that all the data was accurate and well researched using legitimate channels. It certainly would not do to quote Dr. Plutonium or Octavia Oxygen or experiences in Atom City as research sources. The Internet, the Library and phone interviews with some local scientists they'd contacted supplied information, graphs and images. This lent legitimacy to their probably illegal, unscientific, unexplainable project.

The girls had to wait until evening to bring the display to school when her father could help lift the huge platform holding the crystal structures. He would also help Liz transport her smaller project and set it up. Growing up with his architect father, Mr. Sparks was comfortable with lifts, pulleys and building supporting frames. This was his first glimpse of the finished project. While he harbored doubts about the reality of Evie's stories, this solid confection hit him with reality. It would be a challenge to get it to the fair.

"Whoa, Evie. What the heck! Did you sculpt this? With the stuff we bought a few weeks ago? You are some artist!" he exclaimed hoping it was no more than an incredible work of art.

Indeed the structure now rose almost five feet off the table within mere inches of the basement ceiling.

Liz was also astounded by how much the structure had grown in the week she had been away working on the text, photos, report and data to put on the tri-fold display for her own project. At that time her own diamond crystals had grown to 8 Inches. Her Bucky Balls had become big enough to form into long strands. She had used Evie's tools to weave her growing Bucky Ball filaments into fibers, then into mesh. Making a model for every stage, she had plenty of fiber to mold a hockey stick blade. This afternoon her mother had driven her over to Evie's with her not so small exhibit. Mr. Sparks helped unload her one square foot board wrapped tightly in black plastic bags as well as all her tri-fold panels describing her experiment, and secured them in his van. Under the dark wrap Liz knew her crystals had grown immensely. She had a glittering array of gigantic diamond crystals and oversized Bucky Ball carbon models.

"Evie, you've turned your science experiment into an incredible doll house. This is huge. Is it still growing? We hadn't really thought through the growth thing. I was kind of disturbed by my 2 crystals growing to a foot tall, but hopefully they pass as models I made myself," said Liz examining Evie's work.

Dad's eyes widened in shock. "You mean you didn't sculpt this. These are actual mineral growing from those crystals?"

"Well, Dad, sort of. You'll be proud to know I manipulated them like Mom does her Bonsai trees. I was able to pull the crystals into different shapes and sizes, bending them, curving them, splitting them, and flattening them to create this castle. ..." Cut short by the look in his eyes she stammered, "Dad, you can't say anything to anyone. You remember you promised before you'd keep this quiet."

"You're not kidding. Do you realize the implications of this? We're going to attract everyone from treasure hunters to the government to every scientific corporation."

"Dad, let's not worry about the other stuff now. Just focus on getting this packed up and safely to the Fair."

"Just focus on the physical, here. Try not to think about what Evie and Liz have done. Give me a story I know is fiction. This broken line between fiction and reality is freaking me out. Focus on the screwdriver," Rob muttered to himself.

Evie's dad screwed in the wheels underneath the wooden board. Then with a jerry-rigged contraption of pulleys, bungee cords and brute strength the three of them hoisted Evie's castle structure to the floor. A soft, navy, flannel blanket covered the crystal castle. The bungees held the blanket in place. Using a ramp attached to Dad's van, the huge dark mound was pulled inside and secured. Evie had her data, illustrations and research mounted on foam board and on a display tri-fold. She carefully packed them next to Liz's. By the time they got to the school gym only a few stragglers were left. No one paid attention to the covered form next to their display table nor to Liz's black plastic wrapped one on the table. The girls laid out their charts, diagrams and reports. The school had supplied easels and platforms for their tri-fold displays.

The next morning the gym bustled like the busiest of trade show conventions. Crowds of parents and visitors from their town and the region surrounded tables with maps and descriptions. There were representatives from Universities, corporations, Educational organizations as well as journalists and town officials. Students were putting on last touches and fussing with their displays. The girls quietly removed the covers from their models.

There lay the largest carbon Bucky Ball ever seen nestled next to the world's largest diamond. Evie adjusted the huge multicolored ring at the top of her glittering palace.

A few students wandered over to their table commenting: "Cool, what are these?" and "Oh, wow, look at this castle. What is it made of?"

Matter-of-factly Evie answered, "These are diamonds. This is a Bucky Ball. That's Evium, a newly discovered element. The castle is made from all kinds of minerals that we found at that Blast Site in the park."

"Oh, really?" they said awed and impressed. "Is the diamond real? Are all the stones that look like jewels, are they real?"

After a silent pause Liz quickly replied, "No, of course not. These are just models. Models, they're models." She repeated loudly.

The two girls hadn't rehearsed what they were going to say. "Hey, I thought we were going to say we found the stuff at the Blast Site. Ms. Melillo and the scientists backed us on that." Evie spoke into Liz's ear to be heard over the room's din. "We really must agree on this or we're in big trouble."

"Evie, did you bring some of the samples we really did find at the Blast Site? We can show those in front, then say we built the models larger to reveal the details. I think everyone including the adults will accept that. I really did have to weave the carbon fibers and make the hockey stick. You really did form and manipulate the crystals to make the palace. You have your data and images of the stuff we found at the site, right?" Liz said confidently.

"OK, then, that's it," Evie said as Ms. Melillo approached smiling. Luckily Evie had brought the pebbles and slides from their work with Ms. Melillo. She quickly laid them out.

"Hello, girls, beautiful models. You both really worked hard. I knew Evie you'd go wild merging your science and artistic passions., their teacher said beginning to study their data.

More and more people flowed by, a gasping, exclaiming, admiring crowd formed at the Crystal Palace.

Evie responded nervously to everyone's questions. "Heh, heh, guess I went a little wild with the chisel, huh?"

People moved in closer to examine the sculpture. Each of the numerous twisted crystal towers seemed made of a different glittering gem carved into fantastic faces, characters and shapes and encrusted in frothing gold and silver.

"See, everyone, it's all here in the report" Evie said regaining her composure. "We studied the mineral elements. They are all here on the Periodic Table of Elements. Many elements can form into crystals depending on different conditions of time temperature and pressure. Not all the elements are represented. That's why there are only eighty samples instead of one hundred and eighteen. Many of those are gas or highly toxic and radioactive, or survive only seconds. I took some liberties showing most of them all together for demonstration purposes…Then I let my artistic impulses took over."

Everyone smiled congratulating both of them, everyone except Ms. Melillo. She was examining everything very carefully. "I have some questions for you girls," she said frowning. "I think we need to talk privately, later, don't you think," she said walking off.

"She knows," Liz mouthed silently to Evie.

Everyone smiled congratulating both of them.

Sure enough Ms. Melillo returned at lunchtime when the crowd thinned. She had a portable microscope with her. Quickly she examined the diamond, the Bucky Ball and the samples on the table including the Evium. She studied the palace through her powerful jeweler's loupe. "OK, girls, I know I gave you a few samples but not this many, and indeed we did find tiny mineral fragments. You did a great job with the research and data. I'm glad you were able to show the photos of the individual atoms from the samples you saw in the Electron Scanning Microscope. But these crystal models are not made of sugar or salt nor are they glass, plastic or clay are they? These are real crystals. They are the real minerals which I see you have accurately placed in their proper position on the Periodic Table of Elements Chart."

"Yes, Ms. Melillo." They both said meekly, fear on their faces.

"Well, why didn't you share this with me? Those crystals are amazing. How did you do this? And what, I beg you, is this ring? I want answers, or I'll have you disqualified and reported for I don't even know how many infractions." Then she turned and strode away.

The girls were very upset. They had not thought of Ms. Melillo's feelings after all she had done to help and support them. "She thinks she turned us on to the whole thing, bringing us to the site, working with us in the lab, lending us the microscopes. We did pocket more samples at the Blast Site than we should have. We really should tell her more. But what?" asked Evie.

"I don't know. We or I should definitely apologize. After all I was the one who pocketed the jewels on the ground. How about if I offer to give the rest back," said Liz.

The girls meekly knocked on the teachers' lounge doorway. Stone-faced Ms. Melillo beckoned them in. "We're so sorry. Here you trusted us, and I let you down. We thought if I told you I'd taken the samples, you would be angry at us and not let us work with you. I was a kid in a candy store, I admit. I didn't know what they were, just that they were pretty. Later when you tested them, I was too embarrassed to give them back." Liz apologized.

"Listen, really. We appreciate all the support you've given to us. It all just happened! We really don't know how everything grew so fast. One reason we didn't tell you is we thought we would be disqualified if you were part of it. Ha! Guess we were wrong." Evie's shrill voice shook with frustration.

Liz was crying.

"I am the supervising adult. I do confess some of my anger is envy. I'm sure you noticed how excited I've been. This was my big chance to discover something. Instead I passed the torch to my students. I should be proud of you. There is so much more research to be done, that's for sure," said Ms Melillo placated.

The gym was even more packed when they returned. The other school classes and teachers were required to come. Groups from other schools and of course parents were expected. But there were many more adults than was usual for this event. Usually a few University scouts, local journalists and nearby corporations who funded the exhibit attended, but it seemed the whole town, the whole region was pouring in through the double gym doors with the crowd flowing right to their display. Camera flashes amplified the gems glint and sparkle. Which were the judges?

Meanwhile the crowd around their display continued to grow. Cameras flashed in their faces as well as on the jewels and castle.

The girls tried to enjoy the attention and the rest of the fair. They answered questions from the excited, interested crowd.

Later Evie was able to slip away to call her mother out in the relatively quiet hallway.

"Oh, honey, are you OK? How's it going over there? I was just about to come over to tell you some great news. Turns out your Grandfather owned the land where the Blast Site happened. He had donated it to the town for the park, but the title had never been legally transferred to the town. That land is still ours."

Evie felt weak. "Please, come now, Mommy. I need you now, Mommy. Ms. Melillo suspects the gems are real and wants an explanation," she whined. Her mom said she would come right away. Comforted, Evie meandered slowly back to the gym. For the first time that day she could take in other students' projects.

Wonderfully sculpted explosions hanging high overhead caught her eye. Auburn haired Paul stood under them explaining the life cycle of a star. That was the least of it. His awe-inspiring Photo Astronomic images of the universe in action rivaled images from the Hubble telescope. Real works of Art.

He was explaining to a group of students and, Evie assumed, judges, how he built the huge telescope on display, took amazing shots of the universe and discovered a new star. With help from family and neighbors he had set up the rotating dome observatory from a kit in his back yard allowed him to connect remotely with professional, international research observatories. With access to thousands of astronomical pictures, he compiled them into one image.

Evie studied his display. This guy is really something, Evie thought. And I'm sure he doesn't have strange atom-sized friends to help him. She got up her courage to ask a few questions. "Have you named your star yet?" She blurted realizing with all his technique and science, naming the star was the least of it.

"No. I haven't had the time with all the tweaking of the images and building the hanging models. My project kept mushrooming. First when I got the kit, I planned to just build the telescope. I put so many hours in, observing the sky myself, gathering the data, connecting with the big observatories. Soon I was connecting with professional and amateur astronomers all over the world."

"And of course you still have your music. Any time for that?" asked Evie.

"Sure. I always make time for it. It calms me down and helps me release tension," said Paul abruptly averting his deep brown eyes from Evie's.

Both were silent. "You could give the star a musical name." Evie mumbled awkwardly. "Well, anyway, bye, hope you win."

"You, too," he said under his breath, not looking up. Evie noticed his intense blush before she turned away to hide her own burning cheeks.

In a fog, she made her way back to her display. The short respite was the last quiet of the day. Crowds continued milling around their exhibit. Everyone wanted to know where they had gotten the crystals and how Evie had made the palace. It felt good now to have Mom there. She saw Liz's strained face relax a bit when her own mother arrived. The girls put off the thorniest questions by referring to their tri-fold display and written report.

The Mayor was ecstatic about the display. He wanted to display it in the Town Hall after the Science Fair ended as a commemoration of the Blast Site Event and the geologic history of the town.

By late afternoon, Evie realized to her horror, the structure had grown a few inches higher since the morning. Luckily the crystals had thickened further, but had not spread wider over the supporting base. When a few people who had been there all day commented on the growth, she laughed, said it was wishful thinking and joked about magical fast growing crystals. Yet her unease increased. Liz shot her worried looks, noticing her own crystals had continued to grow. Her whole hockey stick seemed swollen.

Evie needed to think. She needed to talk to Plutarch. That evening Evie, exhausted went right to bed after a light supper.

"Plutarch, Plutarch, I need to talk to you?" She thought to him. "Our crystals are growing like crazy. People are noticing. Our teacher thinks the crystals are real. The Palace really is magic. I feel like the apprentice in the "Sorcerer's Apprentice", out of control of my own beginner's knowledge. Everyone knows crystals don't grow so fast, nor in that form. Some don't even form crystals. They're demanding explanations. I'm so scared business people and criminals will force me to make more to sell. Or maybe kill us for the secret. I feel like the girl in Rumpelstilskin who is imprisoned and forced to spin straw into gold," cried Evie, her tears wetting the pillow.

A voice replied, "Except, Evie, you have the power of Rumpelstilskin. You do have the power to spin evium fibers into lifesaving fabric. You, Evie, my artistic friend, can also spin gold into straw. Dear artist, use illusion. Turn those minerals into more mundane materials. Use your strong Evium brainpower to figure it out. Relax and concentrate."

Evie believed she'd sent her thoughts to Plutarch; she also realized the conversation could have been all in her head. It didn't matter. It was the thoughts that counted. She chuckled at that feeling more confident. She indeed had the power to weave evium. She could turn that gold into straw.

"Evium, Evium, Evium," Evie chanted, to focus her mind and turn herself into her powerful element form. Relaxed now, she concentrated her thoughts on the structure wrapped in the school gym. It was up to her to remedy her own mess. She had to turn the real into real art made from real art materials. Evie lay thinking, her electrons zipping around her wildly energized. How to replace real crystals into fakes.

Happily her powerful mental skills translated each crystal's atomic structure into common plastics, paint, clay and foil. Some chemically more complicated than the real thing, they were easily obtained in any art supply store.

Then she repeated the process on Liz's diamonds.

The next day the crowd at their exhibit was even larger than the day before. Word of mouth had attracted a larger public. The structure had continued to grow. It now stretched a foot over the base on each side and was over six feet tall. Evie hoped it had stopped growing for now. Liz's jewels, now fake also, were world record size, her hockey stick perfect for a giant hockey player.

She told Liz what she had done. Now they could enjoy the attention. The issue today was, the Mayor, the head of the local art museum and the head of the city Natural History Museum all wanted the sculpture. Evie suggested it resided four months at each site and perhaps finally in the town park.

At lunchtime the judges ordered everyone out of the exhibit hall.

Ms. Melillo took this time to hand out the tests they had taken. Liz got and "A". Evie had an "A-" because she had answered a question describing the element Hydrogen as "a loud mouth with red hair" and Oxygen as "a dependable friend".

Then she pulled Evie and Liz aside. "You girls really freaked me out yesterday. I went back this morning to examine your structure. I don't know what I was thinking…or thought I was seeing. You did such a realistic job on it I was truly fooled thinking it was real. I am amazed by your skilled use of mundane art supplies to create such a masterpiece."

An hour later an assembly was called. Even with all the hoopla about the Crystal Palace, Evie was shocked when she heard her name and Liz's. Liz had to yank her from her seat. "To tell you the truth," the Judge said, "it was a difficult decision, so we have awarded First Prize to the girls who worked on the crystals and possibly discovered a new element and to the boy who built the Observatory and discovered a new star. An' International Science Competition scout invited the three of them to enter their competition next winter.

Evie gushed her thanks. "Thank you! Thank you." She said pumping the judge's hand. "I've never won anything before!" Liz grinned next to her. Paul stumbled blushing, head down onto the stage behind them. Then with rare stage presence Evie took the microphone for an impromptu speech: "Just want to thank Ms. Melillo for all her extra help, all the scientists we interviewed, my parents, my partner and friend, Liz, and of course all the elements that made it possible."

Stepping down from the stage, Evie thought the Crystal Palace had grown just a little bit bigger. Perhaps it would be best outside, she thought.

The next day was the final day of the Science Fair. The exhibits were to be dismantled at the end of the day. Evie's blue award ribbons looked nice until she spilled soda on them. People continued to crowd their space eager for information. At 2:30 a truck arrived to take The Crystal Palace to the Town Hall. The girls packed up Liz's project, the charts and reports and piled into Mom's car.

When they pulled into the driveway they couldn't believe the scene there.

Reporters from everywhere waited nosily on the front lawn. The girls tried to answer honestly, being very careful of their secret. Basically repeating their award speech they gave most of the credit to Ms. Melillo who had gotten them so interested in geology, had included them in studying the Blast Site, and had taught them professional laboratory skills. Most important they said their teacher had infected them with the excitement of scientific exploration. And of course they gave credit for their parents' support.

"Evie, what are your plans now?" asked a reporter.

"Oh, too many ideas. First I have to finish my homework and get through the rest of the school year. Then I plan to relax." Everyone laughed. "Ms. Melillo has invited me and Liz to continue doing research with her. Some of the judges and representatives of national competitions approached us, so perhaps we'll enter a National Science Competition next year." She said nervously, but getting the hang of public speaking.

"But Evie, you may have just discovered an amazing new mineral. You have created a museum quality sculpture. Excuse me but you must have some dreams you would like to share." insisted another reporter among the clamoring news people.

Evie stopped to think. The reporters politely silent. "I think…" she began slowly, "I'd like to start a science organization for kids. It would be like an open science club, but real fun, like a party, where kids could contribute and talk about all kinds of science…. and how art can be part of science…and how we can all contribute new ideas to help the world, to help fix the awful stuff going on." Evie continued excitedly. "It would be all the sciences plus the arts. Teachers, scientists and even big companies would help us out. Maybe grown ups would even donate money so we could really do experiments and make new things. Kids could work with the grown-ups to raise money for our projects!"

"You sound as if you have been doing a lot of thinking," piped up another reporter. "What about your art? We hear that it's your passion."

"As I said, art would be part of it. That includes all the arts, including music, dance and literature. The subjects have been intertwined all through history. New scientific ideas inspire art; art puts new ideas together to inspire science," Evie finished surprising herself by her orating skills.

"And you Liz, what are your plans and dreams?" a reporter asked the tall girl.

"Umm, well, Evie kinda said it all." She said as the crowd laughed good-naturedly. "I have the same basic plans as Evie for the summer, thinking about the science fair competitions next year, doing research and lab work. Evie did forget to mention we are still kids. And school is not over. Now I'm going to buckle down to finish the year. Once school's out I plan to have fun, hit the beach and do lots of swimming. Course I'm also captain of the soccer team which begins practice in August." Turning toward Evie she continued. "But, hey! I'm with Evie. That organization idea is great. Could really be cool fun. Count me in all the way on that!" She leaned over to Evie and whispered, "And I'm with you for every adventure that comes our way."

More questions bombarded the girls until Mr. Sparks whisked the girls into the house saying, "Thank you very much for coming. No more questions, now."

Chapter 14
Gathering in the Garden

By the next week the Science Fair excitement died down. Evie and the other lab assistants met at the Blast Site and in the school lab. Up in the northeast, spring usually didn't arrive until the end of April, but the plants at the site that had sprouted in November had miraculously flourished and grown all through the winter. Still wearing their winter jackets in the early spring afternoons, the group studied plants more than the stones. "Maybe we should call this place The Garden not The Blast Site anymore," Evie suggested. They promoted the idea by painting some signs and nailing them up around the borders.

Her favorite cliffs were transformed. The Blast Site, land now acknowledged to belong to the Sparks family was officially renamed Sparks Garden. The family and town created a fund for its upkeep and preservation.

Meanwhile her "crystal palace" sculpture had stealthily grown despite its inanimate materials. Evie borrowed the lab spectroscopy analyzer to find the craft materials had reverted back to the real minerals and growing with no way to stop it. Soon it broke the base of its pedestal in the Town Hall. Everyone agreed the sculpture belonged in Sparks Park. It was placed on the bluffs of the original Blast Site.

One day coming in late, Mom sat glumly at the kitchen table in the dim evening light.

"Oh, Mom, you ok? You mad at me? So sorry I didn't check

in. What did you do today?"

Her distracted mother said, "Guess I'm overwhelmed with organizing this Conference on top of my work. Besides all the publicity for Sparks Park, I'm trying to do a million things. The big day is only a month and a half away. Just a little stressed, that's all. Anyway, I'm going to get some work done here. Do you have homework to do? Would you mind getting dinner going?" Dismissing Evie and her needs, her mother rose heavily from her chair and out to her greenhouse.

Evie brewed Mom a cup of tea and brought it out to her with some crackers and cheese. She admired her mother's self discipline and organizing skills. She watched her mother type away on her computer, her black hair neatly tied in a ponytail.

Evie sucked up the last of her lemon ice cream soda careful to save the marshmallow and whipped cream for the spoon. Ms. Melillo always treated them to a snack before they got to work in the lab.

Today she seemed especially excited. "We've received hundreds of responses to the Conference. The hotels are filling with reservations. Scientists with research on the oasis that sprung up in the Sahara Desert will present papers. The Oasis in the Sahara will host our sister Conference, which will connect to ours via satellite. Remember we read news articles about it in class, how all of a sudden ancient waterways and ancient aquifers gushed to the surface? Diverse plant species sprouted and grew miraculously fast. Everyone wants to figure out how this event occurred. I hear many people are heading there calling it a new Eden. Oh, I'm so excited!" she said grinning.

"Yes, I've seen some videos of it. Have you noticed many of

the plants are similar to the ones we've found growing in Sparks Garden? Have you noticed there are tropical plants in our garden, and northern vegetation in the one in Africa?" Evie said.

Liz said, "I've seen those videos. They shot footage from helicopters. Shockingly green in the middle of the white Sahara, a true paradise with plants of every shape and color. They showed the tent city all set for its International Science Conference for the Greening of the Sahara."

Ms. Melillo said, "We're also going to set up tents for our temporary city right here. I'm also stressed with all the work. But I'm loving all of it."

Evie and Liz helped as much as they could.

The whole town got involved. Already on the tourist maps as an well-preserved Colonial New England town full of old stone houses and quaint gardens, builders and restorers spruced up the buildings, replaced cobblestones in the streets, and crafted old-fashioned signs. There would be side festivals featuring Colonial American foods and entertainment. Owners of historic homes were transforming them into temporary Inns to accommodate the overflow visitors. Visitors were already arriving a week before the date. Foreign languages filled the town's old winding streets.

Besides entertainment offerings at the town cinema and theater, free street performances kept the early arriving scientists and their families occupied. After school the students hung out in town instead of going to their after school activities. Liz laughed hysterically at Punch and Judy Puppet shows. Evie and her new lab friends joked around on the antique carousel. Her dad had a Storytelling Booth.

A warm, sunny New England Spring brought on Spring Fever. All the native flowers blossomed at once. First came purple crocus, red, pink and orange tulips, bursts of yellow forsythia and clouds of pink cherry blossoms. A few days later Evie's favorite flowers, the lilacs, unfurled in lavenders and deep purples. Roses began to vine around picket fences. Strolling her spruced up town Evie noticed features the builders in Atom City emulated: The old white church tower, the majestic stone columns at the Town Hall and the fine stained glass in the church windows.

Evie joined her mother on a rare walk together up the seaside promenade that stretched from the park through wild flower fields to the back of their property and continued up to a bluff a few miles further north. In the Sparks Garden they discovered more unknown plant species. Her mom pointed out a flowering plant with orange, blue and yellow centers.

"Look, Evie, this is the plant I've been germinating from the seeds you found. Seems they're growing everywhere. Strangely I just read they've found ones like this at the Sahara Garden. This is probably a related species. Both have long curved red tendrils surrounding the bright orange, blue and purple. I agree with the studies it may be confused with orchids, morning glories and Moonseed Flowers.

Like those flowers I read these can also be toxic. Their scent heightens the senses and stimulates the nerves. Teas brewed from the leaves of this flower have caused visions. Several botanists reported seeing a strange, beautiful microscopic world within our world. They found just a pinch of its green pollen from the powdered stamen is an aphrodisiac, a love potion, when dabbed on the skin of both lovers. It reduced and erased tumors. A tiny grain of the dried seeds, crushed, powdered and mixed with oil kills pain; too much will cause paralysis.

Some uses are untested and could be dangerous. Blossoms,

leaves and stems made into pills can heal serious mutations, and even bring some out of a coma. The waxy tendrils can horribly transform the body or cause death.

I've been working so hard to find the genetic and chemical composition. Come see."

Her mother took her to her lab to show her all studies. Evie took it all in.

Evie begged her parents to book one of the tents offered at the Conference so they could rest up without coming home through crowds and traffic. The Tent City had been set up just south of the growing garden. Designed to make guests feel like they were in a desert oasis, tents were furnished with gauzy mosquito net draped cots made up with African fabrics and large lounging pillows. A wood floor platform, electric heaters, lamps, a screened window with flaps that zipped closed and bathrooms were modern amenities. Hospitality staff left Middle Eastern snacks of fresh dates, hummus, pita bread and olives.

Evie's parents said she and Liz could sleep there if they liked. The first evening Evie flopped onto a cot. Looking out through the net and the opened tent flap Evie gazed at a hazy full moon until its hypnotic spell put her to sleep. They could really pretend to be at a desert oasis, back in the Sahara Garden they had made.

The Conference was a small city bustling with thousands of guests. A large reception tent welcomed everyone. For security even the organizers and their families needed to sign in and obtain badges. Next morning the Welcoming Committee guided guests to the dining tent and showed them around the tent city. A welcoming orientation speech gathered the hundreds of visitors in the main dining tent. Literature and schedules about small talks and displays at various scientists' tents were handed out.

The girls chuckled that it was a Science Fair for grown-ups. Vendors had purchased booths to sell plants and all kinds of science equipment. Science oriented entertainment tents interspersed the serious science booths. The vendor and entertainment tents and booths were arranged in a wide avenue through the center of the park which ended at the cliffs overlooking the ocean with Evie's now 20 foot tall sculpture perched on the edge.

The orientation tour culminated in a Dedication Ceremony there honoring the Sparks Family for creating the park. The Committee for the Conference thanked the town and the international science organizations that helped bring this event to fruition with hopes to make the Sparks Garden Science Conference a first of many. The Committee honored Evie for her sculpture. The crowd ooed and ahhed at the towering metals and gems twisted into spires and arches glittering in the sunlight on its new brushed steel pedestal.

At noon the second day her mother met with colleagues. Evie warned, "Mom, be careful sharing too much information with someone you don't know. Don't you want to get credit for a new scientific discovery?"

Her mother responded indignantly, "I believe it's collaboration in science that moves knowledge forward. Keeping secrets does not help advance science, only lines the pockets of greedy individuals who in the end get left behind when inevitable errors are found."

Paul suddenly emerged from one of the tents.

"Paul?" gasped Liz forgetting everyone in town was at the fair. Evie was too shy to look at him.

Paul smiled though his blush. "Oh, hi, Liz, hi Evie."

"So," began Liz to Paul. "What do you think of all of this?"

"U-uh," stammered Paul also surprised to see them. "I think they organized it pretty well. I hear Ms. Melillo is going to present the work we, uh, you guys worked on."

"You know, Paul, you did spend time hanging out in the lab. It could have been your name along with ours on the research," said Evie.

"Well, you guys are still working on it, right? Maybe I can join in. Orchestra is ending. I'll just have my Jazz Group. I play clarinet. Are you going to be working on it this summer?"

"Yes. Oh, yeah, sorry, I forgot. You are big into music. So, uh, how's the orchestra and jazz going? Do you perform on your own ever?" said Liz keeping up the chat.

"How's the star gazing going?" Evie attempted conversation.

"Oh, fine," he mumbled. A heavy silence fell among the kids.

Evie tuned into her mother's voice nearby. "The more I research, the more I am amazed by tribal healers' medical and chemical knowledge. They claim certain herbs and minerals can really transform them into different beings, into animal or mythical creatures and travel to other worlds."

"Ah, you mean the use of herbs to reach different states of consciousness. Yes, every culture from the beginning of time devises ways to see visions that can lead to insight. There is such a fine line between reality and imagination. It definitely warrants study," another scientist replied.

Evie worried about where this discussion was leading and if it was betraying her secret. She hadn't thought about her mother's view of her adventures. Evie shot her mom a hard look.

Evie's dad announced he was going to the tent to write.

Paul slipped away, mumbling about practicing.

As part of the Ms. Mellilo's research group, the girls had spent time in different areas of the Sparks Garden, but never had the chance to explore it for fun.

"Come on, Liz, we've got some research to do, too. Don't you think? Oh, I hope my mother doesn't tell her colleagues too much. That stuff about how visions can seem very real really got to me. Heck, this Garden sure seems real to me. I can't believe this whole thing is our doing. There are so many consequences we didn't think about. Nothing is simple, huh? What have we unleashed? It's like we made a Garden of Eden and everyone is eating from the Tree of Knowledge," said a worried Evie pulling Liz deeper into the dense garden.

This was no formal garden. Every day the garden expanded taking up more parkland. Thick new exotic tree trunks matched height with the town's ancient oaks and maples. Huge ferns and deep hued blossoms tripped them at every step. Vine tendrils grabbed at calves and ankles, growing right before their eyes. Giant palms heavy with ripe coconuts bowed low enough to pluck. Liz cracked one open on the tree's trunk. They drank the juice and picked at the crunchy fruit.

"So, are you really worrying about all those heavy thoughts?" asked Liz after a long silence as they sat eating and slurping on a cushion of thick moss, "I'll admit it's all important, but I know you. I think you were really concentrating on the auburn haired guy."

"Aw, lay off."

"Well, would you look over there at that pool of water and the waterfall! Sure looks inviting. I propose we jump right in to clear our minds." Liz took off her shoes and plunged in, sundress and all. Evie followed. The water was perfectly refreshing. They swam, splashed each other and let the waterfall shower them in surprisingly warm water. Evie wondered if the source was from Marblehead or the Primordial River.

Later the girls met up with her mother and father at their tent. Evie opened up to her mom about her concerns about keeping her research secret.

"Evie, first of all I'm very impressed you're interested in my work and memorized so much of it. Now you must trust my integrity and professionalism. You are always welcome to work with me on the testing if you want," said her mother, a bit put out at Evie's doubting.

"Yes, I'd love to. Mom, together we can discover more secrets of this plant. But we must be discrete." Evie repeated, honored to be included.

Changing the subject Mom said, "Oh, by the way, Dad found this lying here when he got back to the tent after lunch. Looks like our flower is thriving in Sparks Park."

Someone had threaded a the very flower they were discussing through the handle of her backpack. It sent its intoxicating scent straight to her heart. Behind her closed eyes she had a sudden vision of the musician's fine hand brushed with emerald pollen strumming the petals, gently pulling them back to let ring shaped prisms drop into his hand.

Chapter 15
The Sacred Way

Evie's mother lovingly studied her daughter enjoying her flower. Under the scrutiny she noticed her daughter did not look right. "Honey", she worried interrupting Evie's reverie. "Are you ill? You've been burning the candle at both ends. You are due for a follow-up checkup with the doctor. Perhaps everyone doing research on the original Blast Site should be checked. We don't know what particles are getting into our systems. Low-level radiation is definitely present. From what you've told us it could be you've absorbed more than anyone. If you really have incorporated that new crystal into your body, you could be in grave danger. Who knows what you picked up in that Primordial River and even from unknown vegetation you say you saw in Atom City. Whatever I believe about Atom City, I do believe all the substances are probably at this Site. And now that everything has grown and multiplied in the garden, the intensity would have multiplied a hundred fold."

"I'm just a bit tired, Mom. I know in Atom City there's more uncontrolled radioactivity than usual they tell me. The thing is, the usually well-behaved, regulated radioactive ElemMates have decided to take over Atom City and rule it by force. I was bombarded with radiation, but I fended it off. I admit I did okay. I'm finding I've got a lot of strengths," Evie said.

"What? You were bombarded with radioactivity? You might have radiation sickness or worse. How could you take such risks?

Oh, why must you do these things? You're only a kid, Evie." Her mother clasped her in her arms. May was not sure how much she believed of the Atom City stories, but her daughter had definitely been exposed to unknown materials. "Honey, I don't want you to save the world if it's going to destroy you. I want you to grow up healthy and strong. Then you can take on the world. These adventures are getting too dangerous."

"Not to worry about that, Mom. I tested negative for radiation contamination at the Atom City Hospital. Their tests are pretty precise. But I admit all of this adventure, all of my size changes, all my new abilities are weighing me down," said Evie morosely.

Evie's mother agreed with that. "Your body has definitely been going through many stressful changes. For goodness sake, remember you grew three inches at your last doctor visit. Just looking at your pants cuffs, you have grown more since then. Fast growth can wreck havoc with your metabolism." The Scientist Mother justified Evie's fantasies and illness with logical health information. "Besides school and the stress of the Science Fair project, you are doing college level research from this garden. You are taking on a lot for an almost fourteen-year-old girl. Speaking of almost fourteen let's talk about how you want to celebrate your birthday after this conference ends, ok?"

Evie sighed and took a deep breath.

Her dad sat beside her and stroked her hair. "My little girl, I'm also worried about you carrying too big a load. Your fantasy world is too real; your real world is too serious. The road you are travelling is getting a bit rocky. You need to step back, my love, relax. Take your sketch pad as you used to when you were upset. Remember how you brought your pencils and paper everywhere? Afterwards you always felt refreshed. Why not go draw in the garden now?"

"Funny you should tell me that, Dad. This all started because I was upset about my Science Test, and mad at Liz. I was trying to make myself feel better by mixing up the colored chemical samples in that chemistry set." She laughed a little knowing she had brought the pad and colored pencils with her. "Still, Dad, the Fantasy World is indeed real. Just ask Liz. But you know that. You saw what happened. I know you want to justify the inexplicable into fiction, a fairy tale." Evie got up, pulled her pad and pencils from her backpack and headed toward the tent flap. "Thanks for the suggestion. I'm off to the Garden."

Seeing her Mother's worried look, Evie walked back to hug her. "Oh, by the way, the Conference ends tomorrow. There's to be a final lecture slash reception tonight at 8:00. Come back in time to freshen up, Okay?" said May,

"I won't be long, Mom."

Evie headed out into the brilliant New England May sunlight. It didn't matter where she went. She practiced emptying her mind and tuning in to her body's senses. The spongy earth felt soft underfoot. Inhaling a spicy, sweet scent of some familiar tree brought back happy childhood memories. Good to know this strange garden contained ordinary plants. Settling down in the grass, she leaned back against a chestnut tree and pulled out her pad and unused pencils.

Although people were camped nearby, this garden was no city park. Indeed no one had yet mapped the whole area. There were no paths. This was uncharted wilderness. Yet Evie felt safe and at peace.

It had been awhile since she had sat alone to do art. She had felt the urge to draw so many times during these adventures and travels, but there had been no tranquil moments. Now energetic lines flowed from her hand. She focused on a gnarled branch while her hand outlined an exact copy without glancing at the paper.

Pencil lines harmonized with a musical note in her head. She thought, "Ah, I hear my mantra. I'm now at peace." Until she realized the music perfectly pitched with her spirit actually came from outside her mind. A deep, rich male voice climbed the scale. High soprano notes rustled dark leaves into lime. She was enveloped in music. The voices were so huge they might not be human. These days Evie was open to all kinds of reality. Maybe this paradise had its own angels. Maybe this garden was Eden.

A loud mechanical click stopped the music, and then restarted louder. "Dummy," she thought to herself, "It's a recording coming from a nearby tent or guest in the garden. Oh, well, it doesn't make it any less beautiful." She closed her eyes to listen.

Presently she heard leaves crunch near her. She was so engrossed in the music she did not open her eyes until she felt a warm presence next to her. She was not shocked, surprised nor embarrassed by Paul sitting next to her. She felt peaceful, content not to move a muscle. They sat in silence listening to the music. When his hand touched hers, warmth crept up her arm and wrapped around her body.

Whenthe music ended Evie looked into his eyes, not moving her hand. "What is it?"

"Aida by Verdi. It's a tragic love story about an Ethiopian princess, her Egyptian soldier lover and lots of secrets," he said softly.

He was so close to her she dared not breathe. She was falling into the pools of his deep brown eyes.

"I felt like I was in Paradise listening to the music. Or is this

151

The Garden of Eden." Evie whispered.

"I like this place. The whole garden is exotic and beautiful. This tree is a sanctuary. Its smell intoxicates me," he whispered back.

"Really? Me, too. I've been at loose ends lately, frazzled. Sketching here helps. And the music, well, sure is strong medicine," she said perhaps saying more than she should.

"Well, don't let me stop you from your sketching. I've been coming here to listen to my music the last two days. Guess I'm disturbing the peace; should have used the earphones. I also like the way my clarinet sounds out here," he said reaching with his far hand for the instrument, not moving the one touching hers, not taking his eyes from hers. Moments passed.

The insistent instrument finally dragged his hand and eyes away. He leaned back on the rough tree, wet the reed and again filled her with music. Its mournful notes somehow made her feel a deep communion with nature. She gazed at Paul, head thrown back, wavy auburn hair in his eyes conjuring Pan, the ancient Greek god of fruit and nature with his magic flute. Inspired she grabbed her pencil and drew him.

The sun's changing shadows broke the spell. "I guess I'd better be getting back. There's the final reception at 8:00," said Evie standing to go.

Paul stood, clarinet in one hand. "You know your way back?" When she nodded he reached out and took her hand. "Ok, I'll see you at the reception."

"Umm, uh, by the way," said Evie softly wishing to keep holding his hand. "Did you...I mean do you know those weird multi-colored flowers?"

"Weird and beautiful aren't they. Yeah, that was me. Hope

you don't mind. I saw them growing in the garden. Thought you'd like one." His grin was wide with no trace of shyness.

"Yes, yes, I love it. Thanks." She said squeezing his fingers as their hands slid apart. "See you."

Evie entered the tent to a bustle of party prep. Dad was polishing his shoes. Liz and Mom were agonizing over dresses. "There you are. I was beginning to worry about you. I see the walk did you good," said her mother pulling her dress over her head, then handing Evie her blue green silk. Her mother had gone back to their house to pick up their dress clothes. "Come. Here's your dress. Hurry. We're already late."

"Thanks, Mom. I like this choice."

Dad called from behind the curtain divider, "How did the sketching go?'"

"You were right, Dad. It sure felt good to hold a pencil again. I found a grassy glen surrounded by some old gnarled chestnut trees," she said eyes shining happily.

"With all the exotic vegetation around, you get all excited about an ordinary chestnut tree?" her dad asked quizzically coming in to tie his tie in the mirror in the tiny bathroom.

"Well, its ordinariness made me feel at home. The tree was an interesting shape all gnarled and twisted. Seemed to be extremely old," she answered.

"Great. Can I have a look at the sketch?"

"Uh, not now. I thought we were late." Evie said quickly shoving the pad into the bottom of her backpack.

"That's a strange reaction," her dad said, a little hurt.

Evie didn't hear him. Her mind was on other things. Aida and clarinet music filled her. She tried to concentrate on her appearance. For once it really mattered what she looked like. She liked how she now filled out the silk. Where the neck usually gapped loosely, now she actually filled it out. Her mother had brought over some extra accessories: an amethyst necklace with matching earrings. Mom also lent her some make up, helped her apply it, then pinned the flower near her left shoulder.

Hundreds of scientists and scholars thronged the main tent. Musicians played in the background. The first to approach Evie and her family was Ms. Melillo.

"Hello, Sparks family, I can't believe this is the last night already, and I haven't had a chance to see any of you. Oh, isn't it all so exciting? People are doing such fascinating studies." Ms. Melillo gushed. "Girls, what have you been up to? I saw that boy from our class, you know, Paul Malik."

The two women discussed exciting research and how they could continue to collaborate. As the girls turned to wander off on their own Ms. Melillo said, "Girls, I do hope you two will help me out in the lab this summer. I have so much to do now. Your help would be invaluable." Then lowering her voice she whispered, "I've obtained samples of soil from the Saharan Garden Oasis. It matches our samples of this Garden Site's soil. I want to analyze everything in detail. Could be exciting. You'll be paid of course."

"Wow! Thanks, Ms. Melillo. I'd love to work with you this summer, although I also have my Soccer and Basketball training. Your discoveries sound amazing!" Liz exclaimed feigning astonishment.

"I'm all yours. Nothing else going on for me this summer. Just so I have some time to hit the beach once in a while. And I guess I should work on my art," Evie said eagerly knowing her summer loomed empty. "Mom, we're going to walk around."

"Fine. Be back for the final lecture," said Mom.

The girls strolled among the food tables, sampling food piled high with exotic, international foods. Platters artistically displayed pomegranates, melons and dates. Stews simmered in spices. Liz dug into the arrangements, filled her plate and wolfed it down. Evie picked at a few things while her eyes flitted everywhere scanning every face.

Finally she saw the one she sought wiping pomegranate juice off his chin. He sat sprawled on a folding chair, his long legs resting on another chair sinking his teeth into the fruit. Evie took a deep breath and approached him. Liz plucked some grapes and followed. Just then a voice over the loudspeaker called everyone to be seated for the closing speeches. Liz dashed for good seats. Evie was torn, but followed her. As she sat down, Paul came over to sit next to her.

There were speeches and accolades from the organizers of the Conference. They thanked the international scientific community for participating to share ideas and research about the sudden mysterious appearance of this incredible garden and the new oasis in the Sahara.

Although the speeches were exciting, and Liz leaned forward on the edge of her seat in rapt attention, Evie's full attention was on Paul's hand in hers. With eyes on the speaker, the voices were merely a comforting drone. That is until Evie caught the words... "destruction of this garden...". The speaker was discussing the danger that would befall the gardens. "Who will protect these fragile ecosystems and ensure they flourish.? So many wait to exploit these riches. The Sahara garden sits in the midst of a very poor country that could benefit from its resources. The garden here faces American suburban development. You, Scientists admit you research for more than the benefit of humanity, but for your own advancement. To get to the nitty gritty of it, we need to create guidelines and rules to control and oversee both these gardens. So as scientists it falls to us to organize the Sparks Garden Science Conference into an ongoing foundation. And we must get the local and country's governments to protect it for everyone. Otherwise these gardens may go as quickly as they came. Thank you."

The sobered audience clapped and murmured in agreement. Those thoughts concerned everyone.

His hand still warm in hers, Evie caught Liz's eye which plainly said, "Hey, what's up with you two?"

Not letting go of the hand on her left she leaned toward Liz, smiled, eyes bright whispered, "Let's not worry about it now, ok?"

The music started up again. People were clearing away the folding chairs to open a dance floor. "Want to watch the musicians?" Evie asked her two friends. The three stood tapping and moving to the rhythmic jazz. Paul slid his arm around her waist.

"Do you want to take a walk in the garden?" Paul whispered.

Evie told Liz she would meet up with her in a bit. Liz raised her eyebrows and smiled.

As they left the tent, swallowed by the night, the music changed abruptly to a waltz. The two non-dancers improvised their own steps, spinning and twirling together under the stars. Embraced by her Prince, Evie was the Princess in her own fairy tale. None of her adventures or honors compared to this one. She floated in Paradise. She didn't notice her Prince may have had other dreams. Her closed eyes missed his gaze to the stars.

"Oh, how I want to go there," he whispered.

His voice pulled her back from her own reveries. "Where?" she asked. She saw his face, a ghostly blue in the moonlight, tilted toward the heavens.

"Out there, to the stars," he said quietly.

"You could be an astronaut," she suggested.

"I don't know. I certainly don't want to sit in a spaceship for years. What a thrill it was just to see that new star forming through the telescope. It was so amazing. I wanted to get closer. Wish they'd figure out a faster way to travel through space. I've got so many ideas for the technology. There's so much real research about it. Everyone wants to get out there," he said with yearning.

"The stars, the stars," mused Evie. "I've always loved them from the ground, or at least in an earthbound way," she corrected herself. "I've learned that the stars are the incubators of all the material in the universe including earth. Everything in the stars is right under our feet. But I love the grandness of space. I'd also like an adventure out there."

"Oh, but you're fantasizing. I'm serious," he returned indignantly.

"And how do you know that, Mr.?" she said smiling. "I'm as serious as you."

He relaxed and smiled. "OK, what's your plan, then?"

"Well, first I'd get the space traveler to wipe the pomegranate juice off his chin…" she laughed chucking him under the chin.

He laughed and hugged her.

Suddenly a woman's sharp voice interrupted. "Paul, Evie, where are you?"

"It's my mom," Evie whispered urgently, stepping back from his embrace as her mother appeared in a flashlight beam. "Oh, hello, Mom," anger and disappointment in her voice at the interruption.

"I'm sorry to interrupt you two. It's very late. Everyone has been worried about you two, looking all over for you. You should tell people where you are going. Paul, Your dad needs you to come right away," her mom said firmly.

She pulled Evie away from him, out of earshot. "Evie, there's a woman at the conference who says she must talk to you. She says she's a Gemologist and lives in town. Something urgent about Atom City. She's waiting up the path. Don't stay too long. Then please go directly back to the tent. Dad and I are going back to the house. Liz went home with her parents. Evie, you must come now." Her mother walked away courteously to give the boy and girl a moment alone.

"Okay, Mom, I'm coming." She called brusquely, yet excited by this new event.

Paul pulled her to him, his face in her hair. "Then we'll meet again in the stars," he whispered.

Evie wanted to stay forever. She mustered a laugh, hugged him tighter and gazed into his dark eyes. "How about meeting after this conference in our own little earthly town?"

"That'll be a lot easier," he laughed.

She left him standing in the moonlight, staring at the stars. Her mother's light shone faintly up ahead through the trees. Evie scrambled agilely over roots and bushes toward her.

There in the shadow stood Beryl. "Hello, Evie. Remember me, Beryl. Dr. Sparks, may I speak with your daughter in private?" Her mother kissed her and walked away leaving the two alone in the dark. "Evie I came to show you the path to Atom City. Thought you may want to know how close it is if you want to walk."

Evie couldn't believe she was seeing Beryl at human size here in Marblehead. "Wow, this is amazing." Knowing not to trust her, Evie was intrigued and curious to find a path to Atom City. "Why now? Why is this urgent? You've appeared in front of everyone."

"Ah, no real urgency. I wanted to check out the Conference. I learned so much. Thought while I was here we could visit, take a walk. You look lovely by the why, but you may want to take off those high heels." The silver haired woman turned and strode down a darkened path.

So holding her heels, awkward in her tight dress, Evie ran barefooted to catch up.

The path was rough and overgrown. Evie had to climb over branches. This part of the garden seemed extremely old and overgrown. Vines grew so fast they twined around their ankles as they passed. Leaves were walls to be ripped through. The mix of odors from so many blossoms suffocated her. They fought their way through stabbing thorns. The Garden seemed to have expanded in size since just this afternoon.

While Beryl strode easily, Evie had to guide herself blindly, using her hands against rocky walls. She stumbled and slipped on the rocky path.

"Ow!" cried Evie as sharp pain shot through her knee and foot. "I slipped, scraped my knee and my foot is caught in a crevice."

Evie felt sticky liquid on her knee and sharp pain in her foot. "Oh, dear I don't even have a tissue with me."

Beryl approached. "Do not move." She said feeling her knee and foot with her hands. Slowly she eased Evie's foot from the crevice.

"Oh, no, I can't move my leg. I can't straighten it out." Evie moaned in pain.

"Give me the flower. Yes, it does have your Evium in it, you know," said Beryl calmly. Beryl made a paste of the tiny seeds crushed with a few blossoms, and smeared it on her knee and foot.

In a minute the pain was gone. Evie stood on her foot, put all her weight on it and walked as if no bone had broken. "Unbelievable!" Evie said with relief. "Then, it's true. The flower really has incredible powers."

"Of course. And you're right, it's chock full of evium as you suspected."

Evie said "Why don't we just fly ElemMate style, or I say the Formula."

"But you are not an ElemMate now, just a girl. In any case, if you don't walk, you won't learn the way," Beryl said.

Despite her struggles in this wilderness, her thoughts focused joyfully on Paul. No melancholia on this trail. Her euphoria helped her practically skip up the rocky vine choked path. Ah, she thought as she clambered over rocks and into deeper crevices. A thunderclap brought a sudden downpour. They slipped and slid over rocks and slimy creepers. Sharp drops soaked them to the skin.

Finally they reach a precipice. Clouds parted to let a full moon flood the plain below. They stopped to enjoy their accomplishment and the majestic view. This is indeed a special processional, a Sacred Way.

"What is that view? Marblehead? It doesn't look familiar." Evie asked. Then she thought she saw glittering diamonds shaped spires and glistening blue bubble towers. "It's Atom City!"

"You got it. Beautiful isn't it," said Beryl. "We're at the top of
Terra Mountain.

The precipice extended into a wide grassy plateau with a gigantic Banyan tree at its center. At the tree's base bubbled a spring
whose water streamed in a waterfall over the edge of the cliff.

"Here we are at the source of the Primordial River," Beryl
announced.

They entered the great tree's hollowed out trunk where the
numerous trunks arched together to a lofty height. Moonbeams
shot through a round window high up in the arch. Thousands
of fireflies lit the space. They sat on the soft, moss covered floor.
A profusion of the special flowers sprouted from the moss and
climbed up the walls. In the center a flat circular rock carved with
strange letters, symbols and figures filled the floor.

"So, Evie, what do you say. Since the flowers are made of
evium, why not take credit and name it, say, Eviea. You see, I am
on your side," said Beryl.

Beryl poured water from the spring into a pot along with petals, leaves, stems, a tiny crumb of the tendril and one seed. "I am
making a very potent brew for us with only a tiny portion of seed
and tendril." After boiling the tea and letting it steep, she bade
Evie to pour the liquid into a cup and spread the plant solids over
the rock. The stone began to glow.

As they sipped the sweet fragrant mixture, the circular stone
glowed. "Hey, are those carvings moving or am I seeing things?"
Evie blurted.

The images jostled each other until some literally popped
out of the rock becoming figures drawn in light. Musical tones
hummed faster as the figures floated faster in the air.

"Is this a hologram? Oh, I recognize this. It's the figures that appeared in the blast I caused back home. Look, I see my special Formula, and I can hear its special music!" exclaimed Evie.

"Shh, dear child, you are correct. But here there will be no blast." Beryl said calmly. The Beryllium ElemMate took Evie's hand in a spinning dance. Watching the luminescent letters circle above the stone, they twirled faster and faster to the pulsing sounds. The dance, Evie realized, was the ElemMates' Bonding Dance.

Tiny sparks of light flashed and danced over the stone until it burst into low flames. When the flames died down the rock had become transparent glass.

"Come, look inside," said Beryl pulling her over to look inside. Evie dizzy from the tea and dancing, peered into the transparent window as though touring in a glass-bottomed boat. Far below Evie saw Atom City. Zooming upward toward them were four very familiar figures.

Tavia, Gilda, Carl and Heidi burst up from the glass and hovered above it. Suddenly Evie felt very tired. The soft moss floor was so comfortable. Before she could welcome her friends, she fell asleep.

Morning sunlight streaming through the tent flap woke her. She was tucked into the cot still wearing her dress. No one else was there. Evie lay awake trying to digest the day before. Was that all a dream, a vision from the tea? The last thing she remembered was seeing her ElemMate friends hovering above her. Her thought drifted to the idyllic afternoon and evening with Paul. In any case Beryl had revealed a path, a window and maybe a portal to Atom City right here in Marblehead.

The next morning bustled with packing. People quietly departed with lots to digest. Everyone had bitten the apple of Eden. Most were profoundly changed and excited about the possibilities to come. By midmorning helicopters and limos arrived to shuttle guests to airports and trains and back to cities around the world. The participants had been given special permission to bring sample specimens across borders.

Both in subdued moods, she and her mother gathered more bunches of Eviea flowers. Though her mom had many back at her greenhouse, she wanted to study the newest flower growth. She placed them in airtight containers.

To Evie's disappointment, Paul had left without a good-bye. By mid afternoon there were no messages on her cell phone. Well, there were the usual three from Liz. As they were about to leave the tent Evie spotted a note taped to the tent frame: "Evie, I'll see you soon. Love, Paul."

Chapter 16
Bliss in the Garden

Students' three day Conference vacation ended on Friday. Everyone had lots of schoolwork to catch up on. But Evie couldn't concentrate on work. Paul's note sent her bouncing emotions haywire. Evie analyzed every badly scribbled mark on the note a hundred times over. By the next day, Saturday morning, she was already worried: no call, no contact, no e-mail, no text, no taped on notes. Then she realized she hadn't given him her cell number or her e-mail. He didn't know where she lived. She was sure he knew her last name? Did he say he would call? When would he call?"

Ever patient Liz texted her back every time. "I don't know. Sorry. I just don't know. But you just saw him yesterday."

By Wednesday after school she was so antsy, she took the long walk to the park from her house. Fast paced walking pumped up her spirits. The walk from her house passed woods, blossoming apple trees, lilacs and tons of wild roses. She circled the garden along the northern promenade that bordered the water.

Now empty of crowds and tents the garden was a primeval wilderness. Northern pines and tropical palms towered with giant redwood trees, oaks and maples. Bamboo glades soared 50-feet high. Flowers blossomed as big as beach umbrellas. Watching the waves crash on the rocks calmed her. A few sailboats danced in the late spring breeze. She breathed the salt air and felt like herself again.

The familiar cliffs had changed. She crouched down for a closer look at the huge sapphires and rubies protruding from deep in the granite. Intertwined like delicate lace she saw heavy gold veins, silvery capillaries and minute rainbow colored crystal rings. With her finger Evie caressed the natural masterpiece. She traced a thick yellow vein along to the edge of the cliff then turned to climb down to follow it further. "Soon everyone is going to see this and want to blast out the wealth. It will be a bit of a shame to mine this stuff," she mused enjoying the physical effort of climbing on the rocks. She always loved rock climbing especially on a hot day when the ocean spray cooled her and formed warm secret pools for wading. The blast had made the slope gentler than before. Her feet easily found footholds as she traced the vein toward the waves crashing on the rocks below.

A crunch on the sandy rocks made her look up. Startled to see Paul she lost her balance and reeled backwards against the rocks. "Whoa! What are you doing here sneaking up on me? You practically scared me out of my wits!" she exclaimed flashing him a big smile.

"What I'm doing here? It's a public park. I like this spot. I've been coming here almost every day since I discovered it," he said.

"Well, I'm so glad you're here," she said sweetly, so happy to see him.

"Actually I was sitting over there." Paul pointed to a flat area just below the top." I saw you crazily dangling by one hand, balancing on one foot, dragging your fingers over the rocks. I wanted to make sure you were ok. Sorry to intrude."

"So…you say you come here all the time? The cliff up there

has always been my favorite spot. I always make myself feel better when I'm down." She confessed.

"Oh, you're feeling down?" Paul said concerned.

"To tell you the truth, yes. I've been wondering where you've been." Evie managed to blurt out. "I had such a nice time with you the last day of the conference. Didn't you? I thought you did, also. Remember you gave me the flower, and left me that good-by note? I waited and waited when we got home. I didn't even see you in school. Did you skip class for 3 more days?"

"Yes, I did. To tell you the truth I'm feeling a bit overwhelmed. We all missed a week of school. I've been hitting the books trying to get other projects done. I went in for special help with Ms. Melillo after school. I may be just getting caught up. I thought I'd see you in school. So sorry I didn't call. We forgot to exchange phone numbers. I kept thinking I'd call your parents' phone. Then I chickened out. I figured you were busy, especially with your lab work," he said defensively. "So what were you doing spider crawling down the rocks, may I ask?" said Paul changing the subject.

"I was admiring the rock formations," said Evie simply.

"Oh, right. You are into geology. Well, come on show me. Get me excited about stones and minerals," he said leaning closer to her near the rocky wall. He placed his hand over her fingers tracing a gold colored vein and traced with her. Suddenly he squeezed her hand, "Oh, wow, is that gold?" he exclaimed.

"It could be fool's gold or any number of metals, you know. We would have to test it," she said quietly. Her heart beating fast had nothing to do with gold. She looked up into his eyes to see his reaction.

She smiled into his smiling eyes. The look lasted until

a huge wave pummeled them together. Laughing they sank soaked into each other's arms. She smelled the salt on his skin. He leaned close and tasted the salt on his lips. Her first kiss sent jolts through her body. As he tightened his grip around her, she reached up to touch his cheek and his soft auburn hair glistening with water. Evie returned his embrace feeling his strong muscles beneath his wet tee shirt. She pressed her lips on his resolving never to take them away. Another huge wave cascaded over them knocking them into one of the warm tidal pools. The tide was rising rapidly. They quickly scrambled back up the slippery rocks to the top of the cliff and rubbed each other warm.

"I'll put your phone number in my cell right now, unless it's ruined from the water." Paul typed Evie's number in his miraculously dry phone. She hadn't brought her phone, but she knew she could remember it. Because of all the work he asked if she minded if he could see her on Friday.

When she returned home wet and beaming, the blinker on her parents' phone meant a message. "Hello Mr. Sparks. This is Paul Malik. I met you at the Conference. I don't have Evie's cell number. Hope it's ok to call this number."

Paul was in class on Thursday. She joined him in the library to help him with his work, and quickly finished hers. "Can I walk you home?" he asked.

"I live outside of town by the shore. It's almost three miles. I usually get a ride."

"Come on it's a beautiful almost summer afternoon. It doesn't get dark until almost eight. As a matter of fact, I live along the same road, a bit farther down, about five miles. Want to stop and get an ice cream or milk shake for the walk?"

They stopped at the café closest to school where everyone

hung out. Drinks in hand they spotted an empty table outside. She couldn't believe she was actually sitting in this cool hangout with an actual guy, a most handsome guy. She sipped her creamy mint ice cream soda watching him through her lowered eyelashes. He stirred his chocolate milkshake once, cast the dripping straw on the table, and guzzled it down. While Evie finished her soda, Paul gently rested his hand on her thigh. It felt like liquid gold radiating from his touch. Trying to stay calm she covered his hand with hers, and quickly sipped the last bit.

On the walk home, he took her hand. Where the sidewalk ended at the edge of downtown, he put his arm around her waist. They walked on the shady side of the road then climbed the bank into woods. Following a tiny trail the woods opened up into a grassy glen surrounded by white blossoming pear trees and pink-blossomed willows. They ducked under the willow branches into a secluded hide-away. He wrapped his arms around her and kissed her. Evie felt the thrill of flying, only higher, the floating comfort of swimming only deeper.

Her cell phone chime brought her back to reality. "Darn, I forgot to tell my parents I was walking home…Hi, Mom…yea, I'm fine…sorry I forgot to call….I got a soda and now I'm walking home …yea, with Paul. I'll be home in a half hour."

After a drink of water at her house and a final long kiss at the end of her driveway, he headed further up toward his house. "Friday, tomorrow, ok? Want to go star gazing?"

"Yes, sounds great," Evie said reluctantly pulling away, looking up at him with stars in her eyes.

Friday after school was a scorcher. They walked to her house for snacks and a short visit with her mom and dad around the kitchen table. Paul invited her for dinner at his house and a swim at his beach before darkness enabled them to stargaze.

As they walked the shore road he told her a bit about his old home in Stanford, California. One thing he missed was his large extended family. "We have so many cousins and relatives and friends like relatives. There are always people hanging out all over the house and on the terrace. I never had to think about making friends. They were all built in."

Evie put her arm around his waist. "You are welcome to share my little family. My brother's not around much. He's out in Pittsburgh and seems to be staying out there. Our relatives are all scattered around the country."

The house at the northern point of the Marblehead peninsula was an amazing 21st century modern palace. Set right on the bluffs overlooking the ocean, it white concrete, glass, metal spires and domes. Its tower dwarfed theirs. They hung out a bit in a family room. Oriental rugs and furniture covered in colorful Middle Eastern fabrics made the soaring white walls and white marble floors cozy.

It was still hot enough to swim. She followed Paul across a mosaic-tiled terrace with incredible views of the whole bay, cove and ocean. They trudged down zigzagging steps to the family's man-made sandy beach. "Wow, this sure beats the local rocky public beach," said Evie thinking this as a second sacred walk to paradise.

There was a large white cabana on a terrace with a built in outdoor kitchen. Plenty of thick towels were stacked to supplement the ones they had brought from the house. Feeling brave Evie dropped her towel and ran into the still icy Atlantic Ocean. It felt divine.

Right behind her, he embraced her and kissed the cold away.

Then off they went, both strong swimmers doing a few laps before hopping over the crashing waves onto the beach. Evie admired his perfect teen idol body as he raced up to the cabana for towels.

After grilled burgers and fries Paul led the way up a seven-floor spiral staircase to his glassed in observatory. The small studio below the domed glass was filled with equipment, computer monitors and instrument panels. At the center a huge telescope to rival a science museum dominated the room.

"Ok, so here we are." He went on to describe everything in the room in animated detail. It went way beyond her technical ability, too much to absorb. Then silence. Only the stars in their black blanket. Her astronomer guided her eye to the lens and pinprick lights became swirling gas explosions. Monitors decoded the space data into clouds of neon colored energy with glints of young stars. "These images are as good as the Hubble telescope," he said proudly. They stood together gazing at the stars as they had in the garden a mere week ago. But now she was with her Prince in his castle under a sparkling magical canopy. In the dark Evie's evium electrons sparked.

Lots happening as the end of school closed in. Everyone had Spring Fever. School projects were in high gear. Every class had a final project or final exam preparation. Liz had reached final tournaments in her first year of Lacrosse. Spring rushed into summer.

Evie, recruited more students to help Ms. Melillo with her research, searching online, testing in the lab and excavating the Sparks Garden Site. Paul decided to officially join the group.

"Evie, when you won the Science Fair you told reporters you

wanted to organize a Science oriented club that would be fun, like a festival. Why don't we try to start it," Liz reminded her on one of her infrequent visits to the Lab.

"Good idea. Hey, everyone, why don't we go to the Garden with a picnic instead of staying in here. Anybody else want to work on starting an actual club? Anybody interested in making it really fun, wild, like those big music festivals? The core group agreed on the name Kids in Science Club. They wanted to include all the sciences. The acronym was catchy, KISC. The tag was "Get your Kicks in KISC", or one girl suggested, "Kiss KISC". Evie created a cool logo everyone liked. Ms. Melillo, busy as she was, took on the required Teacher Advisor role. She helped them with the red tape formalities: Permission slips, letters to the school administration, the Principal. Paul volunteered to write out the promotional materials. Everyone began posting on their Social Media accounts. They created a website and linked to social media, science, technology and lots of fun arts sites to announce it. They reached out for more volunteers. Club membership climbed. Ideas for activities, outings and entertainment were thrown around.

They thought of creating a Kids In Science Club Festival Event. The adult Sparks Garden Science Conference Committee helped them out by giving them their lists of venders and entertainers. Some were a bit too stuffy, but there were some exciting names to contact. Seemed many of the Science Bands were eager to play, even at discounted and volunteer fees.

Oh, they almost forgot until Ms. Melillo pointed it out, a festival like the one they are planning could cost over $50,000 dollars. An enterprising club member suggested they post everything on one of those crowd-sourcing sites. Perfect. Funds began rolling in. The town government waived permit fees and would fund security. Donations came in from town merchants excited about the money they could earn as they had from the spring Sparks Garden Science Conference.

The date was set for early September, Labor Day Weekend right before school began again.

Evie was on cloud nine these last free weeks before Study Week, Finals Week and school's end. Bliss in the Garden, she told Liz. When she was out of Liz's sight, they texted and phoned about Paul, the Club and the Festival. Weekends became parties at the excavation site and local venues. Every moment in between she spent with Paul. They had their after school and club routine: Stop at Evie's house for a snack, walk to his for a swim, then homework until Mom or Dad picked her up. There was little thought of Atom City.

She was so busy she almost forgot her birthday was coming the next week. May 28th fell on Memorial Day weekend so she'd have three days to celebrate.

And what a birthday it was.

No surprises, Paul's mom offered their house for the party. It would be fine to have the thirty people from school and the club. Mrs. Malik even extended sleep over options so parents wouldn't have to come out for pickup if the party went late. With such a big house with tons of sleeping space, it would be nice to fill the house. Evie and her mom would take care of decorations and extras.

Besides the private beach the Malik's family room opened onto an Olympic sized swimming pool in a pavilion with a re-tractable glass roof. Tables with umbrellas were arranged on the terrace. Festivities would begin with a swim then grilled burgers and hotdogs. Paul set up music outside.

Saturday after lunch Evie packed up the paper goods she and her mom had bought, her swimsuit and her blue silk dress she'd worn at the Sparks Garden Science Conference. She threw in nightclothes and a change for tomorrow unsure how she felt about sleeping over…but if people really did stay over, she'd be up for it.

Liz arrived a bit early to help set up. Thirty kids arrived at two o'clock laden with birthday gifts, and made beelines to the pool. Splashing water and mist everywhere. Screams of laughter. Water Polo, sunbathing on floats, swimming laps, diving and just lolling with all kinds of tropical fruit drinks at the pool's edge. By five her waterlogged friends slipped into guest rooms to change into dry clothes for dinner.

As Evie entered the guest room where she had left her things, Paul stopped her at the door. He kissed her and handed her a colorful shopping bag.

"Here, Evie, before you change. It's your birthday present."

"Oh, thanks, Paul, do you want to put it on the table with the other ones? Not sure when's the polite time to open them. Or maybe after everyone's gone…"

"No, uh, this is for now, to wear. I uh, got you a Birthday Dress for tonight. Hope it fits."

"OK, I'll try it on." He stood in the doorway as she pulled the delicate confection from its tissue paper. Straight out of Fairyland. A jewelry box of beads festooned the white silk tulle dress. Beads of all shapes and colors, some sewn into multi-colored rings, embroidered the wide scoop neckline, waist and hips and continued down in scattered bursts to the skirt. The short sleeves and hem were split into filmy, satin trimmed petal shaped panels. Tiny gold star sequins were sprinkled everywhere.

"Oh, wow. This is a work of art! It's beautiful!" she exclaimed fingering the thin delicate fabric. "I don't usually wear this kind of thing. A bit dressy for today, isn't it? Thank you, thank you," she exclaimed hugging him. "It looks handmade. Where did you get this?"

"I was walking in town. Saw this little place. I don't know the ladies' stores. Just thought the window looked cool. This was in the window. Course I don't really know fashion. Don't even know your size, but the woman helped me. I told her you were kind of small, not fat. She said this dress fits many sizes and body types."

Curious, she thought, how similar to her evium gown, as if a designer had copied it.

"Paul, what did the woman look like?"

"I don't know. Tall. Sophisticated, like she knew about fashion. Had a weird green highlight in her silvery hair. Nothing too special."

He left her to dress. The loose neck and sleeves secured with invisible elastic. A snug, comfortable fit, the fabric felt like cool air against her skin. She twirled in front of the mirror. The petals swirled as a ballerina's tutu. Definitely Evium Fashion. What the heck, it was her party, she thought as she flounced out to the terrace.

Lots of the girls had dressed up, too. Even Liz had a dress with some glittery threads. Burgers and fries finished with a birthday cake decorated with huge red, blue, orange, green and purple sugar orchids. Blue pool lights and colored Christmas lights lit the darkness while everyone danced.

Just about everyone stayed over. Some took a midnight swim down at the beach. Others sat quietly on the terrace or watched

TV in the family room. Evie and Paul walked along the beach and snuggled on the sand. As they kissed, she felt her evium crystals bursting under her dress's beaded ones.

Paul's mom whipped up pancakes for everyone in the morning. After a morning swim parents picked everyone up.

The next couple of weeks were crunch time for everyone. All nighters for projects and test cramming.

Finally it was over. Mid-June and freedom.

Summer was Evie's favorite season. Her life was full, bursting with work, club, beach, new friends and of course Paul.

The girls slipped into a routine. They worked for Ms. Melillo two days a week in the morning, hung out at the town beach in the afternoon. Liz had convinced teammates to help with the Club and even do research for Ms. Melillo on the days they didn't have soccer practice adding more recruits to the club. Evie entertained everyone with Atom City stories she claimed she was testing out for her Dad's new novel. Everyone clamored for more. Paul was in a Summer Jazz band. She spent time on artwork at home. But there was plenty of free time after lab work.

The KISC Festival was just about organized. Members gathered to work on it a few hours a week and socialize at the beach or at the café in town. They had auditioned tons of bands. The plan was to have music playing all day, both days. It was fun going to clubs and studios to hear groups play or listen to demos. There would be 4 bands, 2 each day on the main stage and small groups or solo performers wandering the grounds playing all kinds of music. Only rule: the music had to be about Science. Paul and his Jazz Band would play a few songs. She was excited about the popular band that had volunteered to perform.

Otherwise every spare moment was with Paul. When he wasn't with her, or on the phone, he was in her mind, in her every thought. They hiked on the shoreline cliffs, snuggled in their little glen near her house, in the Spark Park Garden, downtown and at his house. Many times he brought his clarinet, she her sketch pad. They made their own fireworks on the beach watching July Fourth fireworks.

Chapter 17
Sweaty, Sick and Sad

A real heat wave struck as July languished into August. The Sparks house only had window air conditioners though her parents didn't like to use them. They hated the closed in smell and the idea of toxic chemicals, the chlorofluorocarbons. So it was sweltering inside and out.

Saturday morning she lay on her bed, an ice pack on her forehead, and ice water in her hand, daydreaming about Paul. By eleven he hadn't called her. She rang his cell and got a message. She tried every hour for the rest of the day. Nothing. Sent him texts, e-mail. Nothing. She called his house. No answer. Goaded to action she began to look everywhere around town. Thought maybe she would run into him somewhere. Everywhere a possibility. Yet around every corner she found disappointment. She wandered to the beach, traipsed through Sparks Park and slashed through the Garden. She looked for that dress boutique where he had bought the dress, but couldn't find it. Even tried the beach. Finally on Monday evening he called.

"Hi, Paul," she cried into the phone with relief. "Where have you been? I don't know what happened to you."

"I told you weeks ago I was leaving for Astronomy Camp in California. I left Saturday morning. It was such a rush packing, then dealing with the flight and getting to this place. I couldn't call. So sorry, are you ok? In all the frenzy and fun, guess you forgot I was going."

"How long is the camp, like forever?" Evie whined.

"It's only a week, but I'm going to stay on a bit longer to visit relatives. I'll probably be home in two weeks," said Paul. "Well gotta go, they're calling us for a meeting." And hung up.

Why did she feel so bad? Why didn't he want to talk about his flight, the Camp, his activities? He didn't even ask about her and how upset she was, she lamented to herself, tears sticky on her cheeks.

She couldn't get up the next morning. Blew off the lab. She spent her free time moping at home alone in her room or tinkering listlessly downstairs in her basement lab. Glass vials she had borrowed from the lab held little evium crystals. Vials, test tubes and flasks held other samples from Sparks Garden and new mixtures and experiments made from them. Evie tried to record the experiments with scientific precision ending up drawing wild fantasy illustrations instead. She drew Atom City landscapes and doodles of Paul. Nothing came of the halfhearted experiments because she couldn't concentrate enough. Lack of energy doomed her plan to figure out The Formula. Evie felt she was the fly helplessly buzzing on her burning windowsill. She stared at the struggling fly until it died.

No one noticed Evie's attitude.

Her parents bustled frenetically at their work. Her mother deeply involved with her research paid little attention to Evie. Evie was reluctant to approach her. The Garden had so inspired her father, he wrote all day and far into the night. Every once in awhile he would confront her with some passages or ask her for suggestions. He asked her to collaborate on a science fiction novel influenced by her tales of Atom City not noticing her lack of enthusiasm. The family did try to gather for dinner, but the conversations centered on her parents' projects.

Despite her attempted work and projects, a gnawing empti-ness increased, driving her crazy. Loneliness and inertia wors-ened. Parties were too loud. She lost interest in everything. Tired of talking about work, about anything. Swimming helped a little, but the beach was closed due to jellyfish infestation and riptides. She was so agitated and nervous she couldn't focus. She couldn't sleep. Her worried thoughts whirred and buzed like annoy-ing gnats. She'd take one point of view; a minute later, take the other. Everything hurt: her head ached, stomach queasy, dizzi-ness, blurred vision, sweats, the shakes, numbness, sore muscles, sore throat and more than anything else, sore heart. Old enough to know she was sick, she was glad her mother was too busy to notice. No one insisted she follow up on the blood tests. No ques-tion she'd absorbed all kinds of substances in Atom City. Even good vitamins are toxic in excess.

She missed Paul so much. Everything else became back-ground noise to her depression. Couldn't even blame Paul for much of it. Yet she hung it all on him. She had sustained herself counting the days. Two weeks went by with no word from Paul.

When Evie blew off work for two days, Liz came by to try to drag Evie out of her house into the stifling August heat. Heavy thoughts did not go well with summer. Neither did three days a week enclosed in the lab. Kids need to enjoy summer. Even usu-ally even-tempered Liz was lethargic and out of sorts.

"Come on let's go to the beach."

Evie refused.

As they sat in silence in the hot kitchen, Evie knew she hadn't been tuning in to Liz.

Liz said filling the silence, "You know we haven't really connected much lately. I know Paul takes up a lot of your time and thoughts, as do all our projects. I guess I miss our fun together time. And now you're always down in the dumps."

"I know. I've been self centered, gabbing about my stuff all the time and mostly not in person," Evie said apologetically.

"Right. And now your thoughts aren't with me either," Liz said choking back tears.

"Sorry. I'm so down. I feel sick, sweaty and so sad. I just can't shake it off," Evie said morosely. Why don't you go down to the beach without me? There's always someone to hang with. I'm just going to stay here. I think I'll just go to bed," she mumbled.

Liz left to go to the beach alone.

As soon as she heard the screen door slam behind her friend, Evie flopped face down on the bed and cried.

She must have slept for she awoke to Liz's hand on her shoulder. "I also have this for you. It's a note from Paul. He was at the beach."

Evie sat up. "What! At the beach?" Evie's voice rose to a screech. "The one time I turn you down, and look what I blew! I don't believe it!" cried Evie. "So, how long were you there with him? What did he say? What did you say? And what's going on! I didn't even know he was back. He didn't even call me. He gave you a NOTE? Where's his cell! He couldn't call?" Evie's frantic words tumbling out rose from her heart to her throat.

"I was just sitting on my towel, and he walked by. He stood there making me very uncomfortable, so I asked if he wanted to sit down. He did. Asked where you were. I said you were home resting. He asked if you would be coming to the beach today. I said I didn't think so. He just sat there in silence. Then he reached into his beach bag for a piece of paper and wrote you this note." Liz narrated the scenario as precisely as she could.

Red in the face, Evie attacked. "A note! Who writes a note on a scrap of paper when everyone has a cell? Or a regular phone. Especially when over two weeks go by? Must be his Break Up Note." Evie shrilled. "So, what did you say? So you just took the note! That's all you did? Why didn't you ask him why he hasn't called me? Why didn't you tell him to call me? Why didn't you drag him over here?" She demanded knowing her demands were ridiculous, tears running down her face.

"Well, why don't you read the note? Anyway, for a superhero you are such a baby. I have had just about enough of your negativity. Get over yourself!" said the rarely angry Liz. Liz crumbled up the scrap in a tight ball, threw it hard at Evie and headed out Evie's bedroom door.

For once Liz missed her target, and the tiny wadded up note landed somewhere in her room. Desperate to read what Paul had written, Evie scrambled to find it. She hunted all around the room in vain: looked under the bed, behind the desk...everywhere. No one heard her sobbing buried deep under her quilt.

A few days later Evie wandered alone to the café for an ice cream. As she stood in line she suddenly saw Paul exiting, his hand resting around the tall blonde's waist guiding her through the glass doors like a gentleman and his lady. In shock and disbelief, she swung around to follow their backs. Like a bat with its night vision honed on its prey, Evie threaded her way through the tourist clogged streets. The skilled hunter stalked them all the way into town where they turned into the bookstore. "Go in? Stay out? Give up?" Her mind raced.

Her feet continued down the street. She wandered aimlessly

on to the back of the toy store. Here was the dumpster where she had found the Chemistry Set. Today there were no offerings. A walk to her special cliffs was in order. Calming down Evie stared at the waves and sailboats.

Suddenly a glance down on the rocks made her slump to the ground in despair. Paul and the blond girl sat together, backs to her in their favorite special place. Had her time with Paul all been a dream, or was this a bad fairy tale, a fantasy her frustrated mind had conjured? Her rage was enough to attack, to drive him away, down the boulders into the sea.

"I don't have to stand here doing nothing feeling sorry for myself. There's lots I can do. I've got power to get even!

I know where I'm going. To my fantasyland, my magic fairyland, Atom City. This time I'll hang out with the other side. Ah, hadn't Beryl said she had made and lured her with the Chemistry Set. Beryl, who maybe manages to live right here in Marblehead running a dress boutique as well as Atom City. I'll go to Beryl, learn her nasty chemistry and how to use it to get what I want. And I'm certainly not trudging there on the path!" She spit out angrily.

Evie stood up defiant. Her gold streaked hair flew wildly in the wind. She recited The Formula picturing Beryl and vanished into thin air.

Chapter 18
Witchery

Evie arrived disoriented. She had never been to this part of the city before. She wanted to find Beryl's castle in the North West and see what she could learn from her. Not sure if this was the North West. No one welcomed her. The streets were lined with huge twenty feet high privet hedges, which she knew hid huge, expensive estates. She peeked in through branches and ornate gates to glimpse long tree-lined driveways and immense mansions. Ominous fog and green thunderclouds replaced usually clear, sunny skies. Crystal flower petals clanked in pre-storm wind. And it was actually chilly. Shivering she hugged herself.

"Hello…hello," Evie called hearing her voice echo. "Hmm, usually I arrive where I want to. I'm a bit disoriented. Maybe because I've never been to Beryl's. I didn't give her notice. Hope she's got some time to fit me in. Looks like it's going to storm. Buck up, Evie. Thought you wanted a different kind of adventure, a more ruthless one. I'll find my way." Gazing around she could just make out the tall central city skyscrapers in the distance and headed north.

She leapt up to fly over the city for an aerial view. Suddenly the rain pelted down. The storm was intense. Stinging rain soaked her forcing her to land.

Steeling herself, Evie focused and took off again soaring through the teeming rain and pushed above the drenching storm clouds. She flew straight north over the West Bridge spanning the Primordial River, passing the deserted downtown. In the misty light the buildings looked drab. Further on salt from Sodium mounds looked grey.

Finally she saw the solid emerald Beryllium castle through the fog. She landed in a desolate space at the intersection of Lithium and Magnesium Streets. The castle was perched high on a craggy cliff, almost hidden by towering pines. A rocky path led up to the castle. Now in complete darkness and pouring rain Evie energized her evium crystals to light her way.

Evie felt strong, fully in control of her power. She hardly noticed she was totally soaked by the time she reached Beryl's gates. They swung open at her touch. The castle's rough emerald foundation supported highly polished gem walls. Thunder muffled her light knock on the door carved with knights. No response. A gold sword shaped door handle fit her hand perfectly. When she tugged the handle it came off in her hand and the massive door swung open.

A green clad Beryllium servant welcomed her. Evie cautiously entered a vast green marble foyer encircled by six storied arches. Torches lit damp stonewalls. The ceiling painting caught Evie's eye. Muscled men and graceful women in flowing gowns floated on pink clouds surrounded by elves and fairies. All the figures reached for a gigantic very real emerald suspended from the middle of the ceiling.

Straight ahead jade tiles led deeper into the castle. Evie followed the servant through numerous rooms filled with dark wood furniture encrusted with emeralds. Hanging tapestries showed tragic scenes from fairy tales: Across the room Merlin, the great wizard, alchemist and teacher waved his wand. The witch, Morgan Le Fay, stirred a cauldron in a flowering garden. Upon a closer look, her heart lurched at the image of Arthur, a handsome, ivory skinned youth with auburn hair and large brown eyes. "Yes, I wouldn't mind being Princess Guinevere," she mused out loud thinking of Paul.

"Oh, you would, would you?" came a deep female voice behind her. Evie started. She turned to face Beryl in long purple robes, holding a goblet of ruby liquid. "So you've come. Actually, I am very impressed by your accomplishments. I plan to take you under my wing to teach you so much more."

"Well, that's why I'm here," said Evie not caring that she dripped water on Beryl's floor.

She followed the straight-backed woman down a zigzagging hall tiled in checkerboard dark and light green tiles. A doorway carved with more elves and fairies opened into a cozy, thickly carpeted parlor. A huge stone fireplace with a blazing fire cut the castle's dampness. Lamps illuminated more thick tapestries illustrating a woman resembling Beryl: gathering plants in the garden, cooking and preparing them in glass flasks, ministering to sick people and animals. A large one showed Beryl and Merlin reading a large ornamented book.

A white stone swimming pool surrounded by tropical plants dominated the room's far end.

"I have so many stories and teachings for you. You know, I was Merlin's respected colleague along with Morgan Le Fay though the books don't mention me. Morgan got an undeserved bad reputation as a witch in the stories. No one even heard about me. It was a power thing you know. Back then women in power were thought to be witches.

I'll leave you alone to clean up in the pool. Then we will dine, talk and visit my lab." Beryl poured colored perfumes and oils from crystal bottles into the pool. Bubbles, sparkling lights and steam roiled the water. From another bottle she poured wine into a carved emerald goblet. "Time to think of yourself first and get what you want. Here's your drink. This wine comes from the best grapes." Beryl handed her the wine glass.

Evie weighed the fine cut crystal goblet in her hands and sipped the smooth, sweet wine. Her parents always let her sip theirs, but this was her first full glass. "I guess I'm not supposed to be drinking this," she sighed sipping eagerly.

"Oh, come on. You are in the home of a responsible adult. Enjoy your bath. We'll dine next door when you are ready." Beryl left her to her bath.

With relief Evie took off her sodden clothes, grabbed a tub pillow and sank into the warm, whipped cream thick bubbles. "Ahh, this is perfect," she sighed. Her evium crystals grew and sparkled on her skin. Sipping her wine, bubbles massaged and tickled around her, "I'm happy right here," Evie thought. The pool was large enough for swimming a few laps.

When the water cooled, and her fingertips wrinkled, Evie wrapped herself in the thick, velvet robe Beryl left.

She helped Beryl set a damask tablecloth with fanciful painted plates. It was a true medieval feast: venison roasted with currents and juniper, quail baked in a pie, spiced fruit and stewed sweet vegetables, rum cakes and mint candies. No Atom City Sweets. Real food.

"Beryl, your castle is beautiful. How come everything is made of emeralds though?"

"Actually we Berylliums are what emeralds are made of, but the green color comes from our alliance with the Chromium.

They are close family friends."

And the company was delightful. The ElemMate woman and Human girl shared their ideas and laughed at each other's wit. Beryl was impressed by how wise Evie was for her age. Evie soaked up Beryl's wisdom. Beryl told stories of ancient magic, alchemy, herbal folklore and her thoughts about the world. They talked about serious subjects like the horrendous treatment of women, especially ones that did not accept the status quo throughout history. They discussed politics.

Beryl explained her platform for the mayoral campaign, encouraging Evie to join her political party. She advocated individual freedom over compromise, team playing and collaboration.

"Oh, come, Evie. Truth is I want power. I want to control this city. I have so many ideas, but it takes a strong hand to make big changes. I've appealed to and successfully recruited the Radioactive ElemMates because they hate being restrained from using their immense energy. I want to harness their energy. Use it the way I see fit. Lately they seem to be going wild. So I have to assert a heavier hand. Most progress happens through the will of a strong individual."

"I disagree." Evie protested. "Change doesn't have to be forced on people. With information…a little diplomacy, and concrete scientific proof, individuals will do the right thing together. I believe in convincing people through all means: material goods, ideas and yes, entertainment."

"Oh, I have such plans to grow Atom City. I so want to work with you humans, to create new ElemMate materials for everyone." Beryl exclaimed excited by her ideas.

"It sounds like you could do that working with everyone: Dr. Plutonium for research and development, Gilda for her financial support, all the ElemMates who also want to develop new ways to live and work. And with the media at your back, you can convince everyone."

"Good thoughts, Evie. I'll definitely consider what you say. I did get some good ideas at your Science Conference."

"You really were there. Did Tavia and the others also appear through that window portal or was it the eviae tea? And did you bring me back to the tent?"

"Yes to everything." Abruptly Beryl stood up. "Let's go see my laboratory.

Before we go, Evie, I want to confirm your suspicions. I am indeed the one who made the Chemistry Set you found. I created several of them and planted them in locations around the world at many times in history. My aim is to recruit an apprentice. Only a certain kind of person would manipulate the Chemistry Set in the correct way to allow them to come to Atom City. Only certain individuals with the right background in the right circumstances can bring about what you have. In the three thousand years since I planted the sets only a few have partially succeeded. You were the only one in all these years to make it here. So now you know. You have obviously learned a lot. You are travelling a path and going through a lot of challenges, pain and heartbreak. I set in motion some of these rites of passage for you, which you've passed with flying colors. But your romantic trials you set for yourself."

Evie slumped back in the overstuffed chair. "You? You controlled everything? So you know The Formula? Did you control the wild garden that grew from the Blast? What about my Evium Powers? Did you devise them?" Evie paled with the realization. You set me up to win hearts in Atom City and in my own town.

Yet you deny you put Paul in my life for me to love and lose? I suspected you had something to do with the dress Paul bought me."

"Smart girl. Except for a few things. I created a general Formula, but your creativity and social abilities made it your own. Your fall into the Primordial River was all your doing. I have no control and little knowledge about what's in that river. What leached into you and caused those evium crystals to grow is all you. You know The Formula happens to be the chemical composition of evium and an ingredient in the Eviae Flower. In other words, you created that yourself. I have little to do with your properties and powers.

Actually, I'm very impressed by your abilities to create evium fiber strands that can be molded. That, my girl, is right out of the book of great Female Goddesses: women were the thread makers, the weavers, the cloth makers, the molders of pots. And like the ancient fertility goddess, you helped create the Garden in the Sahara. Speaking of The Feminine, I am taken by your close female relationships with Liz and your mother. Key to your powers is your artistic passion and your openness to risk, sensuality and beauty. Your social skills and diplomatic abilities grow stronger by the day. Finally you have proven yourself resilient and brave fighting off toxic rays and closing the ozone hole.

So, yes, I chose you well. You deserve to be my acolyte, my student in all the magic and ancient alchemist arts. I need your strong, innovative ideas. I know you have much to offer me.

While I can enter your world, I need an assistant. See, I listened to you; I don't want to rule your world, I want to connect and work within the rules of your world. A toast to Evie and all you will learn and all the power you will gain," Beryl chuckled.

Evie was thrilled with Beryl's plans for her, "I'm honored to be your acolyte, Beryl. I can really get into this. Of course you know how I'm organizing a Kids In Science Club for students, right?"

"Oh, I know. I watched from the start at how you organized everyone at the Ozone Hole and in the Sahara Desert to create the Sahara Garden. Yet you have so much to learn. Come let's go."

Evie trailed Beryl through yet another Sacred Way. In anticipation of new knowledge her evium gown sparkled and glowed. On cloud nine she trailed Beryl in a downward spiral of damp uneven steps. The wine and excitement made her dizzy winding down hundreds of stairs. By the time they reached the bottom her gown drooped, her ego trip derailed. Ah, she did have lots to learn.

The steps ended deep in the earth in a huge natural cavern. Electrical lighting was wired into ceiling stalactites. Smooth stone and steel counters and tabletops topped stalagmites. The set up of a modern laboratory mixed seamlessly with a scene from a magician's fantasy. Twisting glass tubing connected vials, flasks and beakers filled with colored liquids. Some boiled, some steamed, some thickened into slimy goo. Counters heaped with a jumble of ornate bottles contained crystals, powders and liquids. The bottles reminded Evie of the ones in her weird Chemistry Set. There were old fashion brass tools and silver magnifying glasses sitting next to modern microscopes and advanced computers. Strewn among the high tech lab instruments were all species of dried herbs and flowers. Bunches of drying plants hung from the ceiling. Intricate illustrations of plants, astrology and alchemists at work hung from the cave's walls beside photos of stars taken by the Hubble cameras.

Evie realized this was her passion, her goal, to become the alchemist who mixed magic and real science to get what she wanted for herself.

Every wall was filled with books. Tooled leather books with gilt-edged pages overflowed the shelves. She pulled a beautiful one from the shelf, devouring the illuminated drawings and writings. "Oh, Beryl, this is a wonderful lab and library. I see we have some of the same books in our library."

Finally Evie's eyes lit on her strange Chemistry Set.

"Something look familiar to you, Evie? Yes, Evie, it's an identical copy. It seemed like a stupid little toy to you at first, didn't it?" said Beryl with a laugh.

"Okay, tour's over. Now are you ready to learn? I repeat you are just beginning. See, I have been turning lead into gold over here. And over here, hope you don't mind my using your Eviae flower, I did my own experiments. I've gone a bit further. You experienced first hand the tea can cause fantasies and hallucinations. I found those tendrils may transform a person physically perhaps disfiguring a victim into a monster. Finally a bit more brings death," explained Beryl matter-of-factly.

Beryl stirred a pot here, turning up heat on another, straining liquids to leave the sediment, adjusting glass tubes to distill the pure chemicals. "I am also experimenting to find other uses for it. I worked together with many witches and healers in my time. Their teachings are at your disposal here in my library. And I must say again, I learned a great deal at the Sparks Garden Science Conference. Went to so many parties. So glad I was able to attend."

"Beryl, you have inspired me in so many ways. I'm so glad I

came. "

So Evie began her studies. It seemed they worked together for days, maybe weeks. Evie lost track of time. In between studies the two shared wonderful feasts and drank lots of wine. Delicious as it was, Evie suspected that Beryl was adding drugs to her food and drink. Sometimes her dizziness, nausea and headaches struck right after eating. Confronted, Beryl admitted they were special potions to help her learn. While they fell into a comfortable companionship, Beryl made sure not to let her get complacent. The teacher prodded her, kept her on edge, kept her frustrated and enjoyed provoking her student's anger.

"No time to waste sleeping," chided Beryl jostling her awake after three hours sleep in luxuriant silk sheets making her irritable and groggy. "I'm just toughening you up. Yes, I know you passed so many tests, but this is just the beginning of your journey."

Beryl set Evie tasks, and then often locked her in the lab alone. They had lots of disagreements and some big fights.

"What is going on here?" Evie would demand. "Are you testing my strength or intelligence? Is this a nightmare I'm supposed to escape from? Or just an evil game to jerk me around." She realized Beryl was testing her.

Evie knew Beryl was meeting with her Radioactive Party members to work on her campaign. Several times she caught glimpses of Uraniums, Sodiums, Strontiums and other Elem-Mates gathered in groups, working in offices or just bustling around.

At these times when the door was unlocked Evie would corner them to give her opinion. She tried to persuade them to work with the Atom City Party. She insisted democratic government was the fair, peaceful way to progress not an autocratic, brute dictatorship. A couple of times Beryl caught her and dragged her away.

Finally Beryl announced it was time for her to leave. "I've got to get back to this campaign full time. You have to get back to your life and your own projects." Beryl continued, "The chemicals in your brain may be weakened, some side effects from evium and influence from toxic ElemMates may be poisoning you, but I see you are still strong and resilient." Beryl knew Evie still smoldered with thoughts of revenge. She wanted Evie to keep her rage, a "fire in her belly" that would make her act without doubting herself.

"You're right. Now I am revved up to work on my own projects. You helped me see how I have the power and skills to influence situations. Thanks so much for your hospitality and teachings. Plus, I enjoyed such luxury and royal treatment. Just what I needed and wanted."

Despite such pleasant good byes, Beryl didn't want Evie to leave in a rosy glow. She rudely left Evie standing in the castle entrance way. Two guards shoved her down the long rocky steps. She hit her head on a sharp emerald crystal and blacked out until the same guards kicked her off the stairs into thorns and mud. Bruised, exhausted, humiliated, sick and full of reignited fury she remembered her real reason for coming: revenge. With one last look at the emerald castle Evie mumbled The Formula focusing on arriving in her own basement lair.

Chapter 19
Monster

Lavender twilight cast everything in her basement into grey shapes. Upstairs was quiet. Evie had no desire to check in with anyone. She had to get her task done right away. Based on Beryl's lessons and her mother's research, Evie created her own original experimental concoctions. On the shelf she found her Eviea flowers carefully dried and wrapped. She chose the biggest blossom.

Donning gloves she carefully chopped up the outside hooded tendrils and let them steep in warm water. When the liquid turned dark purple, she strained it into a purple water-tight bottle...her primary weapon to cause visions and physical transformations.

Working over a sterile plastic sheet, Evie pulled the pollen covered stamen from the center, and shook off all the green pollen then carefully funneled it into a green crystal vial with a metal stopper... love potion under a full moon, she recalled Beryl saying.

Feeling like a great sorcerer, Evie crushed a few seeds, and scraped the pieces into a thumbnail sized case with a red snap-closing lid...to stop pain or at high doses possibly killing paralysis.

Finally the petals, a piece of the stem and a bunch of leaves were plucked off. These were pulverized in a grinder. She spit three times into the mixture and molded them into tiny balls between her fingers. They hardened instantly. She stacked them in a narrow glass vial with a blue top....An undo antidote just in case...

... All four tiny containers fit into a small leather pouch on a metal chain. Evie placed it around her neck and tucked it away under her shirt. Come what may, she had options.

Her mother and father were bustling about getting dinner when she strode into the kitchen without a word, yanked open the refrigerator and grabbed some cheese, fruit and a piece of cake.

"Oh, Evie! Where were you? We were about to call the police," her dad said hugging her with relief, studying her pallid hollow cheeked face with a worried look. "Are you all right?"

"Evie, where have you been? We've been worried sick about you!" Her mother cried to Evie's back.

She turned with a glare to face both parents. "Oh, you finally noticed I wasn't around, did you? I had some research I had to do. Actually went off to Atom City for some rest and relaxation. A little get away from all the stuff going on here. Then I was downstairs in my lab. Lost track of time. I fell asleep down there. You guys were probably out anyway," she said coldly.

"You went to Atom City and didn't tell us? And you've been down stairs? Mom and I checked down there. Usually you check in when you go out. Glad you're okay," her dad said exasperated.

She had mixed feelings about being missed. Only gone three days; it seemed like weeks in Atom City.

"Evie, what's wrong? You look awful. Your cheeks are flaming red. You are perspiring." Her mother pulled her toward her and felt her head. "She's burning up, Rob. We never took her for that follow up blood test. I'm going to make an appointment for you tomorrow."

"Aw, lay off. I'm fine," she sneered. Evie twisted out of her mother's arms. "Just doing my own thing. To each his own. You get your dinner; I'll get mine." She slammed the plate on the table and pretended to eat.

Everyone sat in silence. Dad finally picked up the paper to read as he ate.

Mom attempted conversation. "You're right, Evie, I've been so involved in my research, finding so many new plant chemicals. It's break through stuff, but I ignored you," her mom said tearfully.

When Evie glanced up at her, she felt a pang of guilt at her rudeness. She missed past family dinners full of joking, story telling and laughing. She watched her dad idly separate his peas from his mashed potatoes. Her heart warmed toward him thinking, "It would be great to bring Dad to Atom City some time. In any case I got a lot out of this trip. Learned a great lesson: no more Ms. Do-Gooder, helping others instead of myself."

After picking at the food, comparing it with the recent delicacies at Beryl's, Evie stood abruptly and went to her room. Wrapped in her soft quilt she lay awake reviewing her plans. "I've given myself lots of options. No tragic heroine will I be. No mislaid plans gone awry. I've backed myself up with three options." Satisfied and eager for the next challenge, she was unaware that she was burning with fever. She slept fitfully drenched in sweat. Dreams of monsters, violence and pain swirled through her addled mind.

It was all so surprisingly easy. Much easier than any fairy tale. An automaton controlled by fever, jealousy and rage, Evie methodically fulfilled her purpose. The sight of the two of them at the coffee shop with heads together like auburn and blond lovebirds, spurred her into action.

She quietly took a pinch of the crushed seeds from the vial in one hand. In the other hand she held the purple bottle full of the tendril tea. Casually she sauntered by their table. Oblivious to her, both heads bent whispering secrets. His arm stretched out with his hand on his lemonade glass. Anger flamed higher the closer she came and the more she was ignored. A flick of Evie's wrist sent the tendril tea into his lemonade, dissolving instantly as Paul lifted the cup and gulped it down. Turning deftly, Evie dropped the seeds into what was left of his lunch. Stealing away, she glanced back to watch him stuff the hamburger and French fries into his mouth.

She felt a great surge of excitement at her accomplishment. Her head whirled. Her eyes burned. Her head ached. Evie felt her electrons shooting through her body like fireworks, jolts of electricity. Setting her on fire like the jolts of Paul's kisses. Evie shot from the sidewalk and leaped into the hot summer air, transformed into an alien with great inhuman powers. A meteor entering the earth's atmosphere, burning up before it hits the ground, she crashed to the sidewalk. Suddenly flightless, Evie ran off down the street.

Two streets away the screams from the coffee shop whet her curiosity. She followed the ambulance wails, stealing back to watch paramedics unload a stretcher in front of the café. The relief of revenge filled her. The fire in her turned to numbing ice.

She crept closer to the outdoor sidewalk filled with screaming customers. A scream came from her lips, too, at the sight of a beast rampaging around the room. Paul's white oxford shirt ripped apart as he swelled to the size of a ten foot high bull. Auburn hair flamed into red fur sprouting all over his expanding body. Fingers became cloven hooves tipped with sharp claws. Bystanders gasped as the bull-like creature lunged at tables with sharp, growing, slimy, black horns. His nose grew longer and longer into a swinging fleshy elephant trunk. His long scaly tail whipped at human obstacles in his way. Green mucus coursed from his yellow eyes and trunk. A monster worse than the Minotaur, he twisted around to look directly at Evie. She stiffened awaiting his attack before he fell unconscious to the ground.

It took ten paramedics helped by a few customers and waiters to hoist him into the ambulance. Paul was alive, but listed as critical.

Evie wandered off alone clutching the two filled containers still in the pouch around her neck. She still had the antidote blossom pellets and the love potion powder. She'd done the worst thing she could. She had her revenge. Hugging herself tightly, Evie crouched on the seaside boulders. She gazed at the crashing sea foam inches below her feet. As salty tears stung her eyes, she raged at herself and the raging waves.

"What have I done? What am I totally insane? That was no evil fairy tale prince. That was a kid, like me, who didn't want to fit into my fairy tale. And I tortured him. Ooh, no! Have I murdered Paul? Please let this whole thing be a bad awful dream. Let me wake to a mere flunked Science Test. Yeah, you wish, Evie Sparks. This is no fairy tale, and I'm no Super Hero with incredible powers, just an idiot playing with grown up poisons. Oh, I am so tired…so tired." She lamented putting her head down on her crossed arms and wept.

After a minute or two Evie lifted her head, took a deep breath

and wiped her eyes. "At least I should do the right thing. I'll go
to the police and confess. Maybe it's a dream. If not, I'd better
do something now. I better get Paul out of that nightmare fast.
I have the blossom pellet antidote. I'll go back. Don't know if it
will really work. I do hope I still have some of my evium powers
despite my abuse of them. Guess I can't fly anymore. Oh, let The
Formula still work. Of course I wouldn't blame my Atom City
friends if they deserted me now. I can't blame anyone for telling
me about the flower. They warned me to be careful. I did this all
on my own, thinking myself a witch... an angry evil witch!"

She was about to recite The Formula, then stopped herself.
"What am I going to do in Atom City, anyway? I did this evil.
I did more damage than any of those radioactive ElemMates."
She began to recite again, but couldn't remember it. "Oh, please,
please, Evie, please try," she cried to herself realizing her powers
were gone. Resigned she closed her eyes.

Liz found her unconscious down the street from the coffee
shop. Quickly she called 911 and Evie's Mom. At the hospital
tests showed she had critical levels of several radioactive minerals
in her body plus an overdose of many others. There was a substance no lab could determine. The doctors determined it sped
up all her body functions to crisis levels, causing her nervous
system and brain function to go haywire. She was hooked up to
a machine that cleanses toxins from the body. Evie's parents took
turns watching her. No one touched the necklace and pouch
around her neck.

During one of Liz's afternoon visits Evie began moaning. "I
did it. I did it. I'm the bad guy. I must fix it. Oh. What should I
do? Tavia, I'm so sorry, so sorry." Evie opened her eyes. "Liz, oh,
please. I did such a horrible thing. I've got to get to Atom City.

Help me get there." She sat up, ripped the tubes from her nose and arms and grabbed Liz's hand. "Please get me out of here!"

Liz protested. "Evie you are very sick. You've got to stay here. Let me get a nurse." Evie with a surge of energy, jerked Liz's hand away, leaped out of the bed and ran for the door. She managed to outrun the larger, healthier girl racing to the emergency exit. "Evie, wait! Don't go alone. OK, I'll go with you."

Evie turned, reached back to grab Liz's hand and pulled her after her down the emergency stairway and out of the building. Surprisingly strong despite her illness, Evie led Liz at a fast pace straight for Sparks Park. They were brought up short at the Garden entrance by barricades and warning signs declaring radioactive and toxic contamination.

"What's going on here?" Evie screamed frantically. "We've got to get through!"

"Evie, after you collapsed, many others who had been in the garden became sick with symptoms like yours: fevers, dizziness, hallucinations to name a few. The CDC found lots of toxins, heavy metals and other unknown chemicals."

"I must, must get in, get through" Evie wailed shoving a barricade aside. She pulled Liz deep into the Garden, stumbled choking through toxic fumes until they stood panting at the edge of Evie's favorite cliff. The waves smacked angrily against the rocks. The sky an ominous pre-storm green.

Grasping Liz's hand to leap to Atom City, she attempted to recite The Formula. Evie closed her eyes and creased her brow struggling to remember its components. The sound of the surf pounded in her mind. After several false tries she gave up.

"Liz, I can't remember it." After a few more tries she gave up. "We'll have to walk".

"What do you mean? I thought Atom City was only reachable by The Formula."

"If I can remember the way I went with Beryl the last night of the Science Conference. The path to Atom City follows certain coordinates of The Formula, or something. I hope to remember the path. Are you game?" Evie flashed Liz a grim smile and took her hand.

Liz didn't know if that supposed hike with Beryl was illness caused delusion or real, but stayed by her friend.

Evie followed the ridge of the cliff, stepped down into a crevice and followed it around boulders. They balanced on narrow ledges high over the crashing waves, and grabbed for handholds on slippery, wave flooded rocks. It felt like they were climbing higher and higher on unfamiliar cliffs. The path threaded through shadowy rock crevices with only a gold vein embedded in the rock to light the trail, the same veins she had traced under Paul's hand. No huge vines twisted around their ankles, but dead sharp roots and jagged stones tripped them. Thick thorns jabbed drawing blood. Winding, climbing and scuffling on loose pebbles, they finally clambered up to the precipice Evie remembered. This time the beautiful glen and pool were only dark slimy puddles. The huge tree now a charred stump.

Gazing from the top of Terra Mountain they saw Atom City in the distance. No sparkling jewel, the city was shrouded in smoke. Giant rays struck the city from above, the protective shield she had made in shreds. As if to retaliate endless rays shot up from the city like antiballistic missiles. The whole city radiated a sickly greenish and mustard yellow glow like the glow from Beryl's castle when she left. They stumbled down the mountain, heading straight for Octavia Oxygen's house.

Chapter 20
Chaos in Atom City

Meanwhile Tavia, Heidi and Carl had been working for Gilda's campaign as much as they could in their spare time. City conditions deteriorated more each day. The Party needed all the help they could get.

Heidi had the idea to host a rally for supporters at her place on the Upper Westside right in Beryl's territory. She wanted to broker some peace talks with the Radioactives and pull them back into the Atom City Party. Heidi was the ideal representative since her family and the Radioactives were in the energy business. Armed with glossy presentations created by Tavia and printed at her news office, Heidi had gone door to door to the more moderate Northern and Western Radioactives trying to get them to come to the rally and re-join the party. She enticed them with ideas to use their radioactive energy to help the city as well as their own families. Her first "returnee" commitment had been the Strontium family despite the fact that many in their family acted as Beryl's guards and soldiers.

Tavia made three stops on the way to the rally.

First stop to get Mayor Plutarch to help the campaign failed: He had no time for politics. The ER had lines of beds in the corridors with all kinds of casualties most due to gangs and street violence.

Second stop, Sodiums, their allies on the West Side. Beryl campaign posters plastered building walls. Usually friendly Sodiums shunned her. Tavia found Sonia huddled in her room, ashamed to be coerced to help Beryl whose henchmen threaten to dissolve them and their homes.

"Where is the Atom City Security? Where are aid workers? Where is the media to report this?" fumed Tavia.

"Beryl has either paid them off or barred them from entering with her own security forces. You are the first reporter to show up," Sonia confessed.

"Ok, ok, let me think. I will definitely write this story. This city is succumbing to a dictatorship." Tavia thought for a bit. A strange thought came to her...what would Evie do?... What would a true ElemMate do?... "That's it! Diplomacy is the way to go. Our Constitution decrees: 'ElemMates will bond and join to create not destroy, to connect in peace.' I'll talk to Beryl. I was going to scope out her headquarters anyway. So now stop handing out those horrible flyers. I'll head over there now."

Tavia floated carefully east through the debris filled streets to her third stop, the emerald castle. The Beryllium Family was usually very popular in town.

She couldn't understand why Beryl, would want to promote a platform of anarchy and dictatorship with the Radioactives. The castle's main ballroom had been transformed into a bustling office. ElemMates from all over the city worked at each station.

Tavia finally found Beryl in her favorite sanctuary, her basement lab.

Beryl stood up as Tavia entered. She poured a glass of wine for Tavia. "Oh, hello Octavia. Thought you'd be coming by soon. I knew you'd get bored over there with Miss Goody Gold. While she primps with her parties and baubles, we're trying to shake things up. We want action and mystery. Yea, Mayor Lame Duck Plutonium wants everyone to know the facts. There's more to life than boring facts. No one wants to hear his preachy sermons on proper ElemMate behavior to always be in control, to do "right". Everyone wants fireworks. They want fairytales and magic potions, the unexplainable, chills down the back and good old bloody street fights.

Oh, and by the by, your precious little Evie? This new Atom City Hero. Guess what? She paid me a nice long visit. We bonded, a meeting of the minds. I take the credit for bringing her here. I confess I made that pretty Chemistry Set that set things off. Now it's my turn to be at the top."

Tavia was so shocked and upset by Beryl, she fled the room without a word, raced through the castle and out into the fresh air. Running helped vent her fury. She stopped to rest in Quark Park across from Heidi's neighborhood.

A quick rest on the park bench with her eyes closed and some deep breaths, released all the tension and frustration. Tavia would not be cowed by Beryl, and would stick to her conviction to write an article and publish everything in the city paper. She wrote the article, and sent it straight to her Newspaper.

Her boss agreed to publish it. "It is time to take a stand. It's a matter of ElemMate Rights. We can't just sit and watch while a Dictatorship takes over! While corruption erodes our values!"

The meeting at Heidi's went well. Many heads of moderate Radioactive ElemMate families attended. Gilda presented some of her thoughts on re-uniting the two Parties. The Radioactives' electrons sparkled cordially in agreement, shook hands and promised their votes. Gilda bonded with some Mid-City Radioactives about developing new medical tools.

With the meeting a success, the next step of the plan was to fan out to the rest of the city taking the message from west to east and down to the big more extreme Radioactive families in the south.

Heidi and Tavia accompanied Gilda back to Gold castle to pick up more campaign materials for their canvassing trip south and east.

"I'm glad you like my plan to work door to door from West to East and South. I'm surprised I succeeded in making so many appointments since I thought animosity was so high. Thanks for joining me in this. It's too much work for one person," said Heidi.

"I appreciate all my friends' efforts for my campaign," Gilda said. "Yes, it sure would help if Plutarch came on board. Do you realize that when he isn't at the Health Center, he hides out at his estate behind his strong gates? He's become a target, a kind of traitor to his Radioactive relatives because of his staunch support of moderation and self-controlled radiation. The destroyed safety shield Evie made is letting space rays rain down on the city. I can't stand this rampant violence in the streets. And where are our police?"

Tavia agreed and voiced both of their thoughts. "And what's become of Evie? I wonder what's going on with her. I'm beginning to worry. She usually follows through with her commitments and really seemed excited about helping us."

"Yeah, and she usually brings Liz," said Carl joining up with them. He had missed the meeting at Heidi's, but wanted to escort them to Gilda's then continue on with them.

"Something is weird ever since we were summoned to Evie's world. I can't imagine how it happened. I saw letters, symbols and numbers floating in the air as we were sucked into their world. It was amazing to become human size. What a strange feeling. I felt as if I'd inflated with empty space like a hot air balloon. It wasn't a bad feeling, but I felt I was floating in stuffy cotton," confessed Gilda.

"Yes, as a matter of fact," piped in Heidi, "I felt less energized, like my fires had all burned out."

"Well, I'm worried about her more than the weird feelings. I really respect and like Evie. Wish we could figure out the Formula to go to her, find out where she is. Heidi thought she saw Evie come out of Beryl's Palace the other day. Sure enough, Beryl just told me Evie had paid her a visit," Tavia trailed off as they approached Gilda's Palace.

Approaching Gilda's palace a mob scene made them reluctant to go through the gate. Radioactive rays shot into the crowd in front. "They are storming my Palace!" Gilda screamed. She dashed through the crowd to stand on her balcony. "The Radioactives are taking it over!"

Tavia, Heidi and Carl floated up to join her on her balcony. Marauding Radioactive soldiers grabbed Gilda. One handed her a hand written letter from Beryl. They forced her to read it aloud to the crowd below:

"My Dear Gilda, The Radioactive Party requires your Financial Services. We will be your welcomed guests at your palace through the campaign process accepting gratefully your renown financial and fund raising services. You may of course rest or continue with your own Campaign for Mayoral position though you will be confined to your Palace. Your supporters and Party Officials are free to visit at their own risk. Our soldiers will be protecting you 24/7. I will visit you frequently for meetings. If you are not in agreement with this arrangement, you risk the safety of your friends, family and supporters. Congratulations from Beryl Beryllium, Radioactive Party Mayoral Candidate."

Tavia shouted, "They are taking over and making you a hostage. This is unprecedented and unacceptable. Order them to leave, Gilda!"

The sight of soldiers dragging away her family members with threatening bolts of radioactivity, forced Gilda to agree with the proclamation. She would sacrifice herself as a supposed "Financial Planner/ Fund Raiser", a Hostage.

With golden tears in her eyes she told her friends to fly off from the balcony to safety. "I'll be all right. I can still work on our Atom City Party. But I now must withdraw my bid for Mayor. Tavia, you must take the baton as long as I am a hostage. If we can still gather support, I will serve as your Co-Mayor."

She turned to face her supporters gathered below, surrounded by the soldiers. No more Gilda lounging indolently on her chaise. In her tight gold lame dress, Gilda barked orders to the crowd of energized aids. Her supporters rallied to her call to action. Gilda stood on her balcony and shouted down to the crowd in a confident, impassioned voice:

"We will continue to work as long and as hard as we can. No need to stop our work. Keep making those posters and packing campaign buttons in boxes to bring to rallies. Octavia Oxygen will be the new candidate for the Atom City Party. She will run the campaign from the outside. She will handle publicity. I hope Heidi Hydrogen and Carl Carbon will continue to help also. I thank you citizens of Atom City for rallying to support the peaceful coexistence of every ElemMate." Turning to her friends inside she urged, "Now go! Before the soldiers take you hostage too…and take some flyers."

The soldiers attempted to restrain the friends. Carl, Heidi and Tavia leaped from the balcony into the radioactive tainted air. They headed east toward the Oxygen neighborhood. Sirens wailed. An alarm sounded. ElemMates with microphones down in the street urged crowds of ElemMates toward shelters in the Lead neighborhood four blocks east.

"Heidi, do you want to go back to your family? I better check in on mine," shouted Tavia.

"No, my family is in good standing with Beryl and can stand up to her soldiers. It's closer if I go to yours and Carl's neighborhoods.

Now Carl, Heidi and Tavia floated their way north east through the war torn city toward the relatively safer Oxygen neighborhood. Below Tavia squinted her eyes through the smog thinking she saw Evie and Liz entering her Neighborhood. Sure enough flying lower they spotted the two girls near Tavia's apartment. It looked like Liz dragged a stumbling Evie by the hand. They swooped down to the girls.

"You chose a bad time to visit," said Tavia noticing Evie's pale white pallor and agitated behavior.

Evie leaned heavily on Liz fighting the stampeding crowds and thick smoke filled air.

"I gotta fix things. I've lost it all. I have no powers. Used them badly. Need your help," ranted Evie out of breath.

"What's going on with you?" Tavia put her arm around her. "You look sick. Is that a hospital gown you're wearing? We've been so worried about you. We actually hoped for your help. Things are dire here."

Liz said, "Listen, Evie's very, very sick. She absorbed way too much radioactive material and all kinds of other toxins. Her mind snapped. She went a bit crazy. I think she poisoned her boyfriend. Could be from the Garden, or from the Primordial River or, no offence, just being here. I found her in the street unconscious. She's been in a coma in the hospital. The doctors are studying the evium in her to see if it's good for her or bad. Today she woke up, insisted on escaping from the hospital to come here. She dragged me to the Park and attempted to say the Formula. She kept calling you guys. She has no powers. No Formula. We actually hiked here from Marblehead.

Not sure why I haven't suffered. But, whoa, it does look pretty bad around here. What the heck is going on? We noticed it from Terra Mountain, on the trail from home," said Liz distraught.

Octavia and Carl exchanged worried looks. "Maybe she can get checked out at our hospital. Dr. Plutonium has been swamped by the crisis. You know the stadium has been closed for months now, since the fans rioted. The mayhem spread throughout the City. ElemMates are edgy. We are seeing brawling and fighting. This is almost a civil war," said Octavia.

This was a revelation for the Liz. Like a tourist in a resort town, she had not looked beneath the glossy surface.

Evie moaned. "Oh, no, this is also probably all my fault! I caused all of this. I'll do anything to fix this. Yes, let me help! I promise to buck up. Quit feeling sorry for myself."

"Well, maybe solving the problems here will help everyone. It's a start," Tavia suggested.

Heidi related their plan. "We're going to canvas the city to gather support from any more moderate Radioactives who will join us. We're heading to Dr. Plutonium's Estate to plead for endorsement and maybe his connections for supporters. He's our best bet."

Because Evie couldn't even float, Heidi, Carl and Tavia held
her to glide down south. However Evie's pallor had worsened so
they landed at the north bank of the Primordial River.

The water had not been this rough last time. Liz shouted over
the River's waves crashing on the beach. "I think we need to stop
for a break? Aren't we near the Bismuth Café? I think Evie needs
some refreshment. I'm starving too."

"Yes, it's right over the dunes. They serve exotic life delicacies
fresh from the River," said Carl trying to cheer up the white faced
Evie and her ravenous friend. With an arm around each girl
he led the group back up the beach to a café on the boardwalk
overlooking the river marina. Settled on colorful bismuth seats
at a table with a pink linen tablecloth, Mr. Bismuth greeted them
all and served his specialty, hot soothing pink drink. The main
course was a steaming stew with strange looking sea creatures
marinating in a lemon oil sauce. Liz nibbled. Carl wiped a crumb
off her chin. "You certainly are a brave eater, especially after
Evie's near poisoning last time."

Liz shrugged and continued chewing. "I trust the chef. Evie,
come on this stuff is great, taste like squid and shrimp." Liz
hoped some warm food would revive her friend.

Evie sat in a trance.

"OK. Everyone," said Liz pushing the plate away. "Fill us in."

The ElemMates caught them up on their attempts to recruit
moderate Radioactives, how Beryl coerced the Sodiums into
her service, how Beryl's soldiers had just taken Gilda hostage in
her own palace and forced her to abdicate her candidacy. Gilda
named Tavia to run for mayor or Co-Mayor in her place.

"Oh, how selfish, I've been. I got a taste of reality when I visited Beryl. I was into my own ordeal. Had blinders on, I admit. I did try to talk sense to some Radioactives, " said Evie glumly picking at her food. "I have never once asked how your lives are when we're not here. We had dramatic adventures together, but I am just learning about your everyday life."

"Yes, in all of Atom City History there's never been such turmoil," said Carl usually unfazed.

"Well," said Heidi, seeing Evie had regained some energy. "Should we get on with our campaign canvassing? We can head west from here on Riverside and cover downtown first. Maybe later the river won't be so rough."

The group walked into the busy City Center with its huge double domed mall and tall skyscrapers. Despite Atom City's bad state, the mall was crowded. They approached everyone: ElemMates loaded down with packages, store proprietors, ElemMates lounging in the cafes. Some were afraid to even listen. Some took the fliers and fearfully scuttled away. A few took the flyers and joined The Atom City Party.

Suddenly an argument at a Food Court table erupted. Two Strontium brothers divided by politics, faced off. Usually very responsible pyrotechnic workers, they soon came to blows. Green and Blue glowing electrons spattered the other customers.

Tavia, the mediator, stepped in. "Guys, guys, please. Let's not argue. You are endangering everyone. Maybe we can help you to the Hospital Spa for some calming treatments…" Zap! Tavia lay stunned on the ground.

"You stay out of our affairs, Tavia Air Brain!" yelled one of the green glowing Strontiums ready to aim another radioactive bolt at the fallen ElemMate.

Carl rose to defend his friend. "Hey, cut it out! My friend was just trying to help. You two better control yourselves." Now both Strontium brothers turned on Carl. "And who is this giving orders? We said to stay out of our business." Zap! Zap! Rays struck Carl from both radioactive ElemMates. Carl collapsed to the ground. Customers screamed and rushed from the fight. The two resumed slugging each other. Liz dashed to her wounded friends, knelt and stroked Carl's lifeless hand. Evie went to Tavia's aid while Heidi tried to usher the mall crowd out of harm's way.

Seeing Tavia was ok, Evie revived and sprang into action to stop the two brothers and their destructive, spreading rays. Quickly she found she could generate her crystal Evium fibers and wove them into a concentrated force shield. She plunged between the two radioactive brothers, knocking them down, tamping down their rays. With her reinforced Evium shield spread wide, she covered them, completely smothering their rays. Exhausted she collapsed onto the pavement.

"What's going on here?" Dr. Plutonium's voice cut through the commotion. He had heard about the melee and arrived with city police and emergency trucks. He rushed over to examine Evie, then Tavia and Carl. He ordered an ambulance to escort the three to the hospital. Liz and Heidi joined them in the truck. The city police surrounded the Strontium brothers.

"OK, boys, up on your feet," ordered Plutarch in his most authoritative Mayoral voice to the glowering Strontiums. "You two will be escorted to the Hospital under police arrest where you will be thoroughly de-radiated. Then you will be brought to the court house where your behavior will be dealt with."

Still Mayor of Atom City until the election, Dr. Plutonium faced the crowded plaza. "We all must live in this city in peace. For if we fail, the universe fails. I know I myself am a highly radioactive element. Yet I work hard to control my impulses. I am no better than many of you who also must control year deadly radioactive and toxic properties. Those Strontium boys come from a fine family. I've heard the family has divided political leanings. Nonetheless, rarely has this behavior occurred. Indeed there is something in the air. The earth is changing. Perhaps with human influence we have been altered, even mutating into dangerous monsters. Are our deadly radiation properties becoming too strong for us to control ourselves? Are too many of us influenced by the human world? Maybe. Yet we must, must try to control ourselves."

In the ER Tavia and Carl's bruises rapidly healed with anti-radiation machines and some soothing lotions.

Evie needed more attention. A special cleansing machine allowed her to bask in a glass dome. It was a relief compared to the contraption at the Marblehead Hospital, which tethered her to the machine with needles. Instead of days, it took minutes. The doctor advised her she was not completely cured. More cleansing sessions were needed. She would also have to muster her health, her energy and mind to retrieve her full powers.

Leaving the Health Center, Evie saw Beryl accompanying the handcuffed Strontiums to the courthouse. That scent of Beryl's poison dessert perfume lingered, leaving good and bad memories.

Their delayed trip to muster voters resumed. They headed southwest from Radon Hospital along Riverside Drive through Proton Park and across the Eastern Bridge. They hoped to find Plutarch back at his estate by the time they arrived.

"I thought this place never changed, and the laws of nature were set and everyone obeyed them. So what's going on?" asked

Evie.

"There's always change. It may not be noticeable at first. Step back, let great chunks of time pass and there it is. Perhaps the Mayor is right. Humans are influencing us and the whole world, making change more rapid and unpredictable," said Tavia.

"All I can say is something has got to be done about all this radiation before it's too late," put in Liz. She walked supporting Carl. He let her, although he was fine. Both ElemMates were completely healed.

"Maybe we can meet and work together like we did with the Ozone Hole to get rid of some of those radioactive dump sites," Evie suggested.

"I hope Plutarch will help us and endorse us at least going door to door in his neighborhood," said Heidi.

On this side of the river the scenic mansions and museums set on landscaped sprawling lawns, buoyed their spirits.

From Plutarch's gate they walked up his long driveway bordered by lawns stretching toward an elegant, modern concrete home. On a patio in front Plutarch Plutonium sat reading on a lounge chair.

Evie couldn't keep her secret any longer. "Oh, what have my powers unleashed? I didn't think ahead to all the details, nor considered everyone's lives. I poisoned the world instead of healing it." Evie burst forth... "And now I did a terrible thing. I purposely poisoned Paul. I need to save him," she cried mournfully.

Plutarch frowned. "Extreme stress makes evium brittle, fragile and shatter easily. But you are young. You were thrown into a strange world and given powers you couldn't handle. Your body has been bombarded both physically and emotionally. While your actions to Paul were done in the heat of passion, you must save him. We are your friends and will support you. Your hospital and ours helped remove most of the toxins and radiation from your cells. I know you will make things right."

Her friends' vote of confidence boosted her confidence. "I am determined to try. I feel my powers returning." She felt a tingling course through her body. As her evium crystals regrew to their proper size, she watched her electrons regain their sparks and begin to orbit at atomic speed.

Plutarch served them bubbling grape juice and some yellow cake. "Don't worry, these snacks are safely un-radiated, now let's talk," he said.

"Time to make our plans. Remember you all worked as a great team to close the Ozone Hole and plant the Gardens in the desert."

Evie' added, "Yeah, we overdid the Garden. The scientists are perplexed and amazed by all the new plants. They found many of them produce very potent, toxic and radioactive chemicals that are making everyone sick. The Garden is killing everything."

The Mayor paced the room. "There is a build up of poison making every day more deadly. Besides the other pollutants, radioactive waste is growing at an alarming rate. This is the root cause of today's crisis. The Radioactives are my family and my friends. I don't want them destroyed, only turned from their de-structive ways to use their energy constructively." Dr. Plutonium's usually calm voice choked with emotion.

"Of course," the group chorused. "Where and how should we begin? " Liz asked ready for a new deed to perform.

"Very close to home," he said, "Just south of the city."

Heidi piped up. "I have the feeling there are other moderate Radioactives who don't agree with the Radioactives Party. At the meeting so many are on board including the Strontiums. Would you support us in knocking on some of your neighbor's doors, seeing if they want to help solve some problems?"

What a relief. Plutarch agreed to accompany them to gather support both for the Atom City Party and the Radioactive Clean Up. ElemMates at each family neighborhood they visited were enthusiastic about supporting the Gilda-Tavia ticket and joining in the Clean Up.

Everywhere they went they inspired followers ready to reverse the radioactive poisons. Soon Evie and her friends led an army of billions.

Chapter 21
Radioactive Rescue

"So where are we going, exactly" Liz asked. "Guess we're up for a surprise location," said Evie all pumped and ready.

They mustered their army at the extreme edge of Atom City's southern border.

"There are so many places full of toxic dumps. Some deep under the ground, others just fill barrels in parking lots. Some are radioactive waste sites. Many old factories have been dumping wastes into the rivers. You can see mutated fish, no fish or no life at all. People and ElemMates get sick," Plutarch explained loud enough for everyone to hear. "We start close to home, right here near Atom City and Marblehead."

Evie knew about Chernobyl in Belarus. She had heard of sites in China, India and out west in Nevada where nuclear reactor wastes were stored. But she hadn't thought of the poisons in her own back yard.

She definitely didn't want to see any mutations. Her troops followed the trail in broad daylight camouflaged by their atomic size. Dark gray clouds began to cover the sunny skies. Mobs of the Carbons' relatives confronted them. They saw factories spewing toxic smoke. By the time they reached the first site they were having trouble breathing.

"No offense to you, Carl, but your friends and relatives coming out of these factories are toxic," choked Evie.

Carl Carbon choked also, "No offense taken, my family has gone haywire, just like the radioactive ElemMates."

This site had all kinds of dangerous toxins. Carbons, Mercurys, Leads, Cadmiums and countless other ElemMate families rampaged the factory. Rescuing soldiers quickly surrounded these unruly cousins. As they advanced, the soldiers cajoled and finally convinced the wild ElemMates to calm down and restrain their impulses. All it took were a few words to give their cousins an excuse to stop running amok. Evie covered everyone with her soothing fabric.

Healed ElemMates joined their now trillions strong army. They would need these numbers for the next daunting task: a local nuclear waste storage site. Evie had heard of these places way out in deserts or buried under mountains. But here it was a few miles from her house. Shocking. She was determined to clean that up.

The site lay hidden deep in the forest a short flight from the factories.

Warning signs and barbed razor wire marked their destination. Neither plants nor animals grew here. Their atomic size allowed them to pass right through the padlocked gate. They trooped down newly built steps. Bright fluorescent lights shed harsh light. Thousands of neatly stacked steel canisters faced them at the bottom.

"Looks like everything is ship shape," said Carl.

Voices came from the canisters in a low hum. "Hello, hello," called Plutarch knocking on a humming canister. "What's going on? Are you ok?"

"We have been fine. Calmly sequestered. Until recently. We

think the canister is weakening. We are afraid it may break," came worried Plutonium and Uranium voices from inside.

Heidi and Tavia took a walk around. "Look!" they shouted in unison. "Over there. Look at the water!" Sure enough a small crack in the cavern wall leaked water onto the floor forming a pool around some of the canisters.

"Water must have been here for awhile. See at how it rusted the canisters." Tavia showed them the white and red powder and tiny holes in the containers. Green glowing ooze dripped out into the water then flowed into a crack in the floor. On closer look they saw millions of Plutonium and Uranium ElemMates flailing helplessly in the thick liquid.

"Quick, Troops, we need some Plutoniums and Uraniums to help. Go into the canister and try to calm everyone down. Tell them to stay where they are in the canisters, and not get caught in the ooze. We need most of you others to follow the escaped ones stuck in the water seeping into the floor. Looks like many radio-active ElemMates have already fled the canister. We have to stop them before they leach into the water supply and contaminate the ground water, the land and everything it touches," said Tavia assuming commander role.

Heidi volunteered to lead the water brigade. She and Tavia talked a freewheeling Hydrogen loosened from the radioactive water into joining them as a water molecule. Together they solicited more Hydrogens and Oxygen water molecules to detach from the Radioactives and track down their toxic brethren.

Meanwhile Tavia knew if she and her family bonded with Heidi's family and Phosphorous ElemMates, they could remove the rust to reseal the containers. They immediately got to work.

Plutarch volunteered to stay in the canisters until everyone there was calm and cured. He gave first aid to the many victims with sheared off electrons and ripped opened hearts bleeding infected radioactivity. That done, with the canisters secured, they followed their army and the escaped radioactive ElemMates into the oozing crack.

In moments they caught up to the first of the escaped toxic ElemMates. The Plutoniums and Uraniums dove courageously into the goo to rescue their brethren. Like the other victims in the canister most had split apart and lost electrons making them unstable, toxic and radioactive.

Evie and the other rescuers wrapped their arms around the sickened ElemMates. Everyone worked to gather stray electrons, replace the right number to each ElemMate in the correct order, and get them orbiting correctly. The frenzied, aggressive ones who had taken on too many electrons required restraint and quick surgery to remove the overload. Particles were returned to wounded hearts.

At every sickened ElemMate, Evie sprang into action. She stretched her healing evium cloth over them to complete their healing.

Onward they pressed through the glowing labyrinth beneath the earth. They wound in and out of dark alleys, came to dead ends and rode around in circles with their army of healthy Elem-Mates growing behind them. As restored ElemMates joined the troop, the rescue work went quicker.

Suddenly an explosion stopped everyone in their tracks.

Chapter 22
Horror Deep Below

A gigantic crack split the ground. Mustard yellow light glowed from it. Then a shower of sparks shot out.

Everyone screamed. Forces coming from the gash in the earth rolled and dipped everyone on a huge roller coaster. Another thunderous crack ripped the earth's wound wider. Tongues of flaming lava erupted green, glowing radiation rays.

"That's where we're supposed to go?" shrieked Evie over noise.

"This looks like the ground zero, the center of it all," said Carl floating next to Evie. "We had better brace ourselves and get to it. It won't be a pretty sight in there."

The group stood on a narrow ledge just out of the lava's reach. They could glimpse into the crevice. Glowing mustard-green shapes gyrated against orange molten rock. Odd off key voices assaulted their ears.

"Okay everyone we're going in, now jump." Tavia commanded.

They landed on a wide ledge of rocks above the lava flow so hot they could barely stand. Plutarch led them down rocky steps following the lava river. The group wound deeper and deeper into the burning world. Hot red stepping-stones forced them to hover above them.

Suddenly the lava flared up into a contorted flame then materialized into a grotesque figure. Its head topped by huge horns howled putrid breath at them. "Hoho, where have you been? I have been waiting for you," it said, spitting yellow saliva at them, burning when it hit. Its red body flickered. Only its eye and visible heart remained steady. Both purple organs pulsed rhythmically sending sparks at each beat. The monster's eyes hypnotized the girls, forcing them to drift closer to the deep burning pit yawning nearby.

"Stop!" Heidi yelled pushing them back from the edge of the abyss, blocking their fixed stares into the monster's eyes. "Hey, you two out of your minds? You really must look sharp in this place including looking into the monster's eyes. No joke."

Both girls blinked and shook themselves out of their stupor. "Thanks, Heidi, didn't know I could get hypnotized so easily. This place is what I've heard hell looks like…" mumbled Liz, fearfully.

"Oh, my, it's those paintings of Hell and a scene from a horror movie… only this is real!" Evie gasped backing up as snakes crawled out of the pit toward them. Hundreds more slithered up the walls. The steps disappeared under molten lava. She shook with fear. Taking a breath Evie closed her eyes chanting "Control yourself, control your evium, Evie. I am evium." Her fear decreased. Her strength returned. "Come, let's go," she commanded. The steps reappeared. The snakes disappeared. The group continued down the stairs.

They finally reached a place where the steps widened into a great stone floor. Black columns supported a stalactite-covered ceiling. Cracks between the stones glowed orange.

"Welcome, friends," said the deep voice. This time the girls knew to avoid looking into the monster's eyes. The huge pulsing monster now sat on a throne of blue fire. Huge mustard-yellow and silver ElemMates stood guard around it. They cast eerie green reflections on the walls. Thousands of loose electrons ricocheting wildly lit up the room. Fragmented ElemMates bodies lay scattered everywhere.

Evie stepped toward the throne. "Who are you?" she said defiantly, careful not to look at its eyes.

"Ah, you are a smart one, my pretty little rainbow. Guess my name. I am the forces of the universe mixed with mankind's mistakes. You think I am a mere piece of poisonous gas and flame. Look again!" Its body began to change from oranges to the blues of the throne then glowed neon green and violet. Its sparks became gigantic spinning balls of fire. Showers of them pelted the visitors. "I am so much more than you can see. My invisible rays lay waste and mutate the earth. Look around at my creations. Welcome to my home." Thousands of vibrating rays shot from its body. "You can call my Ray, or you can call me Gamma, or you can call me what you will." Its menacing laughter disharmonized with the sad and angry voices they could hear throughout the cavern.

The monster's body grew to illuminate the whole immense cavern. What had seemed to be cave stalactites were really huge radioactive ElemMates shooting constant streams of radiation in every direction. Now they could see movement advancing toward them from the far side of the room. The singing voices grew louder coming from a mass of living creatures. As they paraded closer they could recognize animals mutated into the most horrible forms. Frogs with half a head, an octopus with fifteen legs and lizards with one eye crawled miserably past.

What looked like two majestic horses pranced nearer. Mutated into a horse with huge wings on its back, the other a horn centered on its forehead. "Yes", the monster said, "Some mutations are good, the so called improvement of the species, the survival of the fittest."

A slight movement in the corner suddenly caught the visitors' attention. A naked, pink creature with whiskers twitching crawled into this otherworldly horror. Instantly the monster sent a flaming tentacle toward it.

"No!" screamed Liz. "Leave it alone!" She fearlessly ran to scoop up the tiny mole rat into her arms. The small creature flamed for a second then collapsed into ash and Liz, badly burned, fell to the floor unconscious.

Evie dashed to her side weeping. "This is no dream! Oh, why did I drag her into this? My Adventures! Damn! I've murdered my best friend! It's all my fault. Oh, oh, what should I do? What will I tell them? Now I've killed two people!" cried the hysterical Evie.

"Now hush, we can help," soothed Tavia embracing the sobbing girl. "We will all help," she said with authority and turned to face the watching crowd.

Carl knelt by Liz's side. Quietly sobbing, he picked up her hand, kissed it and pressed it against his cheek. "Come on, Liz, breathe for me, girl," he whispered tenderly in her ear.

After a few minutes Evie noticed the silence around her. No creatures moaned nor sang the sad tunes that had filled the cavern. The crackle of radiation had ceased. Everyone seemed joined together in this tragedy. The monster waited in silence. Evie wiped her tears and stood up.

She turned to the giant radioactive ElemMates guarding the monster. "You have to stop these senseless destructive waves. You have to try to control them, to harness them for constructive things. There is so much you can do. We humans and ElemMates all created this monster. Let's look it in the eye and take back the power it took from us. We must destroy it."

While the monster continued its silence, the huge ElemMates' deep voices murmured amongst themselves. Evie turned back toward the unconscious Liz thinking out loud. "I must take control, ME. I have my own great powers. I must remember I am Evium." She quickly wove her soft evium blanket to cover the dark haired girl.

Everyone waited.

"Oh, come now, she's dead. Once dead always dead," boomed the monster.

Evie and the ElemMates turned toward the monster to bravely stare it right in the eye resisting its hypnotic powers. The trillions of followers and beings in the cavern heeding Evie's pleas turned as one to resist the monster. The stare seemed to last an eternity until the monster blinked.

Keeping up her stare deep into the monster's eyes, Evie wove her dress into a solid, thick shield. She countered the forces the monster sent out, flew over its head, dropped the cloth over it and pulled it tightly around. It struggled to send its strongest bolts at her. Tighter she wrapped the cloth smothering the beast's fire, forcing its rays back upon itself. The shape underneath the cloth shrank, becoming smaller and smaller. The heat and force of the monster's rays decreased.

"You cannot succeed. You will never destroy me. There are more parts of me all over the world." Although the monster's words were strong and threatening, its voice became weaker and weaker along with its shape inside the cloth.

The crowd cheered, "The monster is dead!"

Then a movement of the other cloth over their fallen friend rustled.

Carl rushed over pulling away the cloth. "Look, everyone, she's breathing!" he shouted.

Sure enough color had returned to Liz's cheeks. Indeed all her wounds had completely disappeared. Her eyes fluttered opened. Liz struggled to her feet full of life. Everyone cheered.

Evie hugged her friend wrapped in the life giving cloth and had an idea. She focused on the evium blanket, re-wove it, stretched and enlarged it until it could cover all the mutated creatures. Then flying up to the ceiling she dropped the weightless crystal fabric over them.

"You have the power now to do the right thing," Evie proclaimed to the huge radioactive ElemMates. "You pulled your dangerous particles, rays and waves back into your bodies and made yourselves whole and stable. This cloth will heal you, too," she told them flinging more fabric over them. Little by little the radioactivity diminished until the room went softly dark. The only light came from healthy ElemMates' correctly orbiting electrons.

The terrible singing stopped. The cloth had soothed the mutated creatures' pain and healed their wounds.

When a shaft of soft gray dawn pierced the deep cavern everyone realized the monster was completely gone. The crowd cheered and followed Evie and her friends up the long stone stairway to freedom.

Mild morning sunshine and sheltering blue sky welcomed everyone back to the surface.

Joyful healthy ElemMates danced and spun into the fresh air.

ElemMates concocted their special nutritious green sugar

crystals for the healing, hungry creatures and children. Evium coverlets were tucked around each child for a final healing. In a few minutes healthy children and animals happily laughed and played, then scampered off to their homes.

The oozing toxic water ran clear. On either side lush green grass was just giving up its dew. Willow trees dipped their feathery branches to the water. Honeybees humming among wild flowers replaced the crackling electrical hum of the cavern. Everyone took deep breaths of fresh air. Off in the distance cows munched on clean, sweet grass.

"We're just in time. It looks like we stopped the radiation before it did too much damage," said Evie bending down to examine the grass on the riverbank.

"I don't know, Evie," Liz said kneeling down next to her. "True, the blades growing from the water look okay. But what about the life in the water? Look closely at this seemingly healthy plant. With our heightened vision we can see both good cells and also really mutated ones. Maybe those cows over there are eating huge mouthfuls of this tainted grass. I wonder what it's doing to them? Maybe the toxins have already begun their destruction."

The restored Plutonium and Uranium ElemMates knew what to do. Quietly they infiltrated the streams and fields. They gently approached any still damaged radioactive cousin, surrounded each, and gave them the aid they needed. Evie shot yards of evium cloth into the air. The light coverlet covered everything with its healing film. Each newly restored ElemMate gladly joined their army to help.

Cured Plutonium and Uranium ElemMates chose to resettle in Atoms City or have more space deep in the earth.

"Ah, now we can breathe easy," sighed Evie as she waded

along the edge of the truly clean stream back toward Atom City.

The rest of the army chose to float above the surface. The sun felt warm on everyone's skin. Lilies grew in the tall new shoots of green grass.

"Well, I think we've all done a great job here. Let's head back to Atom City," said Heidi proudly slapping Evie on the back.

"I must do one more thing if I may," said Tavia seriously. She climbed to the top of a hill, silenced the huge crowd of healthy Radioactive ElemMates milling around below. She raised her arms for silence. The crowd turned immediately to listen.

"I want to thank you, to congratulate all of you for your restoration to full health. You are now strong enough to control your own radioactive urges and live peacefully together. I thank everyone who worked so hard to aid your fellow ElemMates in time of need. You should be proud of your ability to join together to save so many. Still, we are not finished. We must all continue to control ourselves and help others. Many more sites exist and more are created every day. Use your power well. Now, everyone: Back to Atom City! Let's fix our city!" With that call to action the crowd burst into cheers.

Carl said urgently, "And on the double. We left Gilda hostage with the Radioactives. With our moderate Radioactives allies, we can free Gilda and perhaps win the election."

"Yes, we've got to get home, too." said Evie. "We've cleaned up so much. I hope it made both Atom City and Sparks Park Garden safe again.

And now I've got to try to save Paul!"

Chapter 23
Atom City Celebration

The victorious army marched to Atom City in high spirits assuming their successes carried over to curing all the city's problems. Sure enough when they entered the city from the Eastern Parkland they felt less tension in the streets. There was no evidence of wild gangs of Radioactive ElemMates.

Tavia expected a great welcome home. She was all geared up for cheering crowds to welcome them.

Instead the City was quiet. Where was everyone? Signs and billboards supporting Beryl's campaign still proclaimed her violent slogans. Beryl was still the Radioactive Party Candidate promising "Radioactive Freedom!" and "Power to the Powerful". Her fliers littered the streets.

In contrast no sign of Gilda's campaign. Most of their moderate Radioactives troops dispersed exhausted to their homes. The six friends and some of their followers rushed west toward Gilda's castle to liberate her. They didn't know what to expect. They hoped despite her House Arrest, Gilda continued her political efforts running a busy campaign.

At first glance Gilda's bustling castle headquarters looked normal. On closer look they were dumbfounded by the changes. Instead of serious minded Atom City supporters standing up to their Radioactives Guards, they found ElemMates from both parties in bathing suits frolicking in Gilda's pool and lazing in the sun. There were no desks, computers nor one piece of campaign promotion in sight.

Exhausted, Tavia was short tempered. "What is going on here?"

Gilda and Beryl reclined on golden chaise lounges while ElemMates of every color and size tended their nails, hair and make-up. Gilda beaded gems onto golden wires creating a necklace so long it jumbled all around her and hung to the floor. Beryl read a book.

"This is how I'm running Beryl's and our campaign at once," Gilda laughed demurely. "I invite everyone to parties. Treat them right. Then they spread the word. Look around. I've got a representative from just about every ElemMate neighborhood. They've all signed my book." She reached under the chaise for a jewel encrusted gold book. Indeed, inside she had names of the leaders of every ElemMate family; every square in the city was noted.

"But who are they going to vote for? Is everyone just taking advantage of your parties? Don't you think you are being a bit naïve?" protested Tavia sternly.

"Well, isn't that up to them? I've shown I can do good things for the city. Beryl and I bring everyone together and make sure they work together happily and productively," Gilda responded.

Evie said resigned, "I guess it sounds like the way it should be, ideally. Yet have you looked outside? Have your heard the whispers and rumors? The Radioactive Party is still bruising for a fight. The city is plastered with their messages."

"Well, Evie and Heidi, didn't you say you were going to help? Do publicity? Tavia, I thought you'd be my campaign manager. Before you left me a hostage you reassured me you'd solve the problem. You announced you would be running as the Atom City candidate. Then you and my closest friends leave me hostage in my own castle to go off into who knows where cleaning up other peoples' messes," Gilda said, revealing her tough, sharp side. "I approached Mayor Plutarch long ago to endorse me, but he was so busy at the hospital with all his ailing family members. He forgot he is still Mayor of Atom City. Then he too took off with you to save the world. Truth is, this project is more than I can handle. I need a running mate, a Campaign Manager. Tavia, you dropped the ball in the city and took on the world. I know you also have your job here at the paper. So who is going to run Atom City? Beryl is here and willing. She's had a great change of heart."

Tavia could see the tension in Gilda's face. Her friends had deserted poor Gilda. Tavia hugged her. "Of course I'm in. I said I'd run for office. Perhaps as a pair we can get things moving again. Hey, Beryl, is it true you want to join us and make this city better? Give everyone enough freedom and enough self control to keep things safe and make everyone happy."

"Hmm," the reformed Beryl considered seriously. "I am having fun here. Truth is I really like socializing and doing my scientific research better than the nitty gritty of running a city. It looks to me like everyone's angry fires are gone. Seems the citizens are tired of fighting. You guys must have done a terrific job out there cleaning up the poisons and radiation, healing the Earth. I've come to see everyone can change, even me."

Gilda said, "Beryl and I have been working on compromises and reconciliations. Thought we'd offer Radioactives more opportunities to release their pent up energy. We invited everyone here to hash out issues. It's an ongoing process. It can't be solved in a day."

"But tomorrow is Election Day," Carl pointed out.

"Guess we'll just see who shows up and how the votes go, then," said Gilda.

"And I'm still the Radioactives Party Candidate. I'm going to see this to the end." Beryl raised her fist in a fighter's challenge and flounced out the door back to her palace followed by her guards.

The following morning Liz and Evie awoke in Atom City. The mood at Gilda's Election Headquarters was subdued for an Election Day. No one knew what to feel: tension, anticipation, fear, or excitement. So no one said anything.

Gilda huddled with the girls, Tavia, Heidi and Carl in her private "War Room" study."

"Did Plutarch finally officially endorse you, Gilda? asked Heidi. "After all I would think he would support his own party, despite the divided loyalties."

"No he hasn't been here since his return. No message sent by any media either."

Plutarch Plutonium's sudden appearance at the Golds' Palace campaign headquarters re-ignited the excitement. Gilda and Tavia emerged with Liz, Heidi, and Carl for final rallying speeches. Plutarch agreed with the Bipartisan angle his Party was taking. The city would officially be reunited in peace.

Tradition dictated the voting takes place on Terra Mountain, a neutral area where the candidates can address the whole city.

So the processional began. As the crowd surged northward, ElemMates from each neighborhood joined in. First came the moderate Atom City Party supporters from the North Central city. The crackle of excited ElemMate electrons spread out in waves to further neighborhoods. By the time the procession reached the entrance to the mountain trail, ElemMates from the whole north, east and central neighborhoods had gathered. When the front of the parade began the long winding trail up the mountain, ElemMates from the west side territory merged. Next Downtown streamed in: the businesses, the factories, the Mall, Darm Stadium, Bismuth Café and museums. ElemMates who had been intimidated into joining the Radioactive Party trudged, floated and flew up the path. Finally the Southern Radioactives, some from the army that had just fought together to conquer radioactive monsters, save wounded fellow Radioactives and clean up the injured Earth marched up the rear.

Evie, Liz, Carl, Gilda, Tavia and Plutarch reached the summit first. Beryl and her closest supporters flew in landing lightly next to Gilda.

Plutarch raised his arms sending welcoming rays to illuminate the zillions gathered to vote. The votes were cast in Atom City's time honored tradition: Each ElemMate shot one of their electrons into the sky where they amassed into specific areas for each candidate. As the incumbent Mayor, Plutarch designated the eastern sky for the Atom City Party and the western for the Radioactive Party. The voting continued through the day. Finally as the sun began to set, Plutarch sent the signal for the voting to end.

The purple evening sky filled with the twinkling sparks of zillions of electrons. The outcome of this election needed no tallying of votes. There in the sky to the west was a tiny mass barely showing dully against the setting sun. To the east in contrast the whole darkening sky filled with a solid canopy of sparkling electrons.

A great cheer rose from the citizens of Atom City. Beryl

laughed and hugged Gilda, Tavia and Evie.

Beryl stepped forward to give her concession speech. "I congratulate Gilda Gold and Octavia Oxygen as Co-Mayors of Atom City. Not only are Gilda and Octavia compassionate leaders, but they also know how to work together to gather the best talent and resources to get things done. I promise to join with them to contribute what I can to help Atom City thrive. If I may add, I am glad I was the one who brought Evie Sparks to our city. My selfish aim was to learn all I could about the human world and use that power for myself to control Atom City. Now I see how Evie, despite her very human faults, has used her powers to bring not only ElemMates back together, but humans as well."

"Thank you for your kind words, Beryl," said Gilda facing Beryl and the crowd. Gilda radiated a warm glow to include everyone. "There are indeed many places for such a brilliant scientist as you in Atom City. We will certainly take you up on your offer."

Octavia stood firm her blue windblown hair framing her face. She turned to the crowd. "And thank you ElemMates of Atom City for your support. We will indeed work hard with all of you to make this city what you want it to be. Now our city celebrates a new era of peace and community."

The crowd roared.

Tavia motioned for quiet to continue. "There will be parties laid out all over the city. But before you go, I also want to honor Evie for her contributions to the city. She has worked for all of us and has become an ElemMate, an ElemMate that keeps growing and finding new strengths and powers. So it is time Evie had a place of her own in our city. Her neighborhood will be built in a presently unoccupied area of the park on the north bank of the

Primordial River just east of Radon Hospital. Evie will build it as we all do of her own element, evium, and plant her Eviea flowers. I'm sure she will welcome help as she is the sole inhabitant of her neighborhood. And Liz, we also thank you for your help and support. You are always welcome in Atom City."

Evie couldn't believe this gift, this honor. With tears of joy in her eyes she said, "Thank you Gilda and Tavia." Then turning to face her friends and the crowd she addressed the audience. "I thank all of you ElemMates who have befriended me, and all of you I will make friends with in the future. Yes, I welcome all possible help. As Tavia pointed out, I don't have trillions like me to fill the neighborhood, so I hope you will keep me company there." Turning toward Liz, Evie clasped her hands saying, "Liz, of course I hope you join me and stay as long as you like. I do have some ideas. Now I invite everyone to a post election party in my new neighborhood!"

The crowd remained respectfully quiet for a few seconds, and then burst into applause.

In an orderly fashion citizens of Atom City made their way back down the mountain stopping at parties at neighborhoods throughout the city. Evie's friends gathered on her new piece of land. The moon sparkled over the Primordial River. Gems and flowers glittered in all the city's gardens. The Bismuth's, now Evie's close neighbor, supplied refreshments from their café. The Xenon and Neo Clubs set up a light show. Zincs and Coppers brought their brass instruments for some wild music.

Finally the moon began to sink toward the horizon.

"Oh, dear. I've been having such fun. I've got to get back to save Paul," Evie gasped realized the passing time. "There's no more time to waste. I've got to act. I swear I'm going to concentrate all my powers to curing Paul. I'll use all my powers to fix what I wrecked."

"One consolation," she thought to herself, remembering she still had two containers in the pouch around her neck. "I didn't give him all the lethal poison and still may have the cures."

After heartfelt goodbyes, Evie took Liz's hand and thought the Formula thinking of home and Paul.

Chapter 24
Healing

The girls opened their eyes to rough waters and a blazing sunset. Each went straight to their homes to reassure their families they were fine. Evie's mother grabbed her and hugged her tight.

"My god. You're here. My baby's home! You disappeared from the hospital without a trace... For four days we've had everyone looking for you. You were so sick. The doctors were afraid the toxins had permanently destroyed many of your organs. I can't believe Liz went too. That she let you leave the hospital." Then May pulled back to look at her daughter. "But you look better. Where on earth were you?"

"Mom, how is Paul?" looking at her mother with tears in her eyes. "Is he ok?"

Her mother shook her head sadly. "No, he's been in a coma and his vitals are fading. No one knows what happened to him. No doctor knows if it's a virus, bacteria or toxin.

"Mom, I've got to get over there now. Could you drive me? You know it's all my fault. Now I've got to try to fix it."

"What do you mean it's your fault? This has nothing to do with you. You weren't even there."

"Yes, Mom, I poisoned him with the eviea flower. As you probably guessed, I too feel pretty upset about what I've done. Yes, Mom, I did do it to him. I remembered what we knew about the eviae flowers. One of the ElemMates, a kind of magician scientist gave me more tips. I was pissed off and jealous and lovesick over him. My mind just went to pieces. What with the stress of everything else, I snapped. Obviously my exposure to toxic minerals and plants made me pretty sick also. But I've tried to make ammends and clear myself of those horrible toxins."

Her mother sat down heavily in the chair. "Deep down I kind of suspected what you've told me. The stress of everything has been too much for a child your age. I admit Dad and I have not been there for you, because we too are so wrapped up into all these events you initiated. We saw you sinking into depression and exhaustion making yourself sick. I was hoping you wouldn't turn to a desperate act."

"Yes, yes. All true. Can we talk all about it later though? Now could you please drive me to the hospital. I must help him before it's too late. We can talk in the car," said Evie impatiently.

Her Dad arrived home as they were leaving and joined them in the car. He listened quietly as Dr. Sparks continued. "I had a feeling you'd use the flowers, too. You and I worked together from the beginning on the chemistry of those flowers. Because I suspected you were involved somehow, I felt I needed to help. Besides that he's an innocent kid, your special friend and I am a plant toxin specialist. I gave the doctors some of the eviae flower extract as an antidote, which they are administering to him in a weak form intravenously. They are willing to try anything at this point. Nothing, however has worked. Paul has not stirred from his coma since he collapsed. The medical team has little hope."

The hospital waiting room was empty. "It looks like the epidemic is subsiding. The hospital has been packed all the last couple of weeks. Turned out many of the exotic plants and minerals in the garden were radioactive or toxic. They quarantined some areas and are doing a massive cleanup. Inexplicably the hazard cleared up almost instantly yesterday right before they were going to dig up the whole garden. Everyone is perplexed, but relieved," sighed her mother.

"Oh, I'm so glad. Liz and I and the ElemMates also attempted a massive cleanup. Glad it worked. Anyway, do you guys mind waiting here?" asked Evie apprehensive about what she must do and if she could succeed.

Her mother embraced her. "We have been so worried about you. You know you are still ill. You are still poisoned. Please promise after this you will stay here and let them take care of you?"

"Okay, I'll let the doctors do what they think best. I should go in," she said arriving at Paul's hospital room. Then suddenly she collapsed into her mother's arms sobbing. "Oh, Mom, I'm so, so sorry."

"I know, honey," soothed her Mom without malice. "And now I know you can cure him. You will succeed. Go in now. It is a horrible affliction you gave him; now you will be strong and take it away."

Evie tiptoed into the darkened hospital room. Even in the dark the sight of him made her recoil. The creature's grotesque body hung ghoul-like from the ceiling. His distorted bones and organs had to be suspended from a traction stand to relieve the painful pressure on the huge organs. Wires and tubes connected him to bags of blood, saline and medications. The low hum of life sustaining machines serenaded the mercifully unconscious boy.

Evie forced herself to look at her vile creation. More disgusting than any movie alien, trunk-like nose held up by wires extended up four feet dripping copious amounts of green mucus.

The rest of his face was massive rolls of oily red flesh that hid his eyes deep in its folds and extended down his neck and underneath the white sheet. Tufts of auburn fur covered his head, the immense curved horns and his pointed ears. More hair sprouted out from between each fleshy roll of his neck. The long rat-like tail emerged from under the sheet dragging on the floor. She was glad the sheet covered the rest of him.

"I'll give it all I've got," she said to herself pulling open the pouch she still wore around her neck. Through the window blinds a slash of moonlight fell across the bed. She clasped the pouch containing the healing pills made from the blossoms and leaves. Maybe there was a chance, she hoped fervently.

Glancing up Evie realized the moon was full. She still had the vial with the pollen, 'a love potion when applied under a full moon'. Banish that thought! Certainly not the time for that.

The blue-topped vial with the pills was still intact in the pouch hanging from her neck. Hoping her antidote worked better than her mother's, Evie emptied the tiny balls into her hand. With the other hand she searched among the creaturer's slimy skin folds for the mouth. In the dim hospital light, her fingers moved folds of rubbery flesh beneath the elephantine snout. Scales coating the slimy flesh cut her as she probed. Finally Evie found the mouth guarded by long yellow teeth. The rotten decaying smell of his breath not only nauseated her, but also reminded her the boy was close to death. With her fingertips she carefully pried open the pointed teeth and pushed the spheres into the afflicted boy's mouth. As the last one went in, the strong muscled jaw snapped shut, just missing biting off her fingers. She held the folds of skin tightly shut hoping he would swallow them. Then she sat on the empty chair to wait.

An hour went by with no change. Evie was beginning to despair. She even stroked the beast's face and matted fur.

She realized how much she needed her Atom City friends. She easily recited The Formula, thinking of the ElemMates, visualizing them here in the hospital room. She would bring them to her world as Beryl did on the mountain. No one appeared. She was on her own.

Evie remembered her Formula's tones when she and Beryl danced. Singing to herself, Evie began the spinning Bonding Dance, the ElemMates' bonding dance. With eyes closed she sang and spun faster and faster. Evie felt her evium crystals grow, her electrons orbited faster and brighter. Her evium fibers stretched from her body causing a jeweled fabric to fill the room.

Slowly she stopped spinning. The silky cloth was the same cloth she had used to heal Liz and the radiated creatures. She floated up toward the ceiling pulling the healing coverlet with her, then let it flutter down onto the unconscious boy.

Looking down upon the scene, she suddenly noticed it was crowded with familiar faces. Enlarged to human size, the ElemMates had come. Relieved and grateful Evie let herself float down into her friends' embraces.

Everyone helped. Tavia surrounded the boy with fresh oxygen. Heidi pressed against his body to draw out poisonous acids. A whole crowd of ElemMates joined them. Quickly they bonded to create healthy new proteins, which his unconscious body absorbed. The Sodiums added their life giving salts to the bags hanging around his bed. Dr. Plutarch helped leech out the radioactive substances. Even Beryl lent her support destroying some of the terrible growths. Electrons orbiting the ElemMates sped up increasing positive electronic vibrations until the room pulsed with bright healing energy.

After everyone had done all they could, they stood together around the bed watching and waiting. Evie lifted the silken evium coverlet and saw no change. Perhaps her blanket wrapped him too loosely. Maybe the cloth needs to soak into his body. Evie began to rub the evium covering rapidly, heating it to its melting point. It soon turned into multi-colored marbleized goo, then instantly disappeared leaving only a colorful slick coating over the monstrous body. The horror she had caused lay exposed for all to see.

With tears in her eyes Evie touched his face. The melted crystals had indeed done their work. They had softened the flesh turning it doughy. Like the putty used for actor's makeup, it easily came off when she pinched and pulled it. It was very unpleasant work, but with growing excitement Evie peeled away the beast's whole face like a mask to reveal the human face underneath. First the huge trunk was flung away so it dangled freely on the traction hook and his thin nose remained. The smooth forehead, cheekbones and brows arched over long lashed eyelids emerged. His parted lips exposed even white teeth. A sigh of relief filled the room.

Evie set to work to complete the job. Octavia volunteered to help pull off the fur, but it did not budge. Others tried with the same results. Only Evie's hand could un-sculpt her folly and remove the hideous hide.

As soon as it was gone, the body underneath sprang back to its original human form. Massive haunches shrank to muscular shoulders, arms and legs. The backbone straightened. The monitor showed strong, regular vital signs.

When Paul's eyes fluttered open, Evie again fell under their deep brown power. She impulsively reached for the last tiny vial in her pouch, the pollen love potion. The full moon made his skin polished white marble. She sprinkled a bit on her hand and reached for his. When a cloud covered the moon, she came to her senses and brushed the powder off thinking, "I will use potions only for good, for healing, for creating. And I will love only in its own good time, not forced by magic or chemistry." Paul's eyes closed again, and he slept peacefully.

The room filled with everyone's sighs of relief.

"Oh, Evie," said Tavia giving her a hug. "We were so worried about you. Thank goodness your Formula could bring us here. We didn't realize the enormity of what you had done and what you needed to do to undo it."

"I thought coming to Atom City, cleaning up the toxic waste and helping promote peace among your citizens, I could redeem myself. It did help me clear some of the poisons from my body and mind to regain my powers. I needed to go through those tasks to be capable of healing Paul."

Beryl apologized. "Evie, I wanted you to learn from me, not to commit black magic. I brought you to Atom City in the first place to learn from you. We are all scientists out to learn all we can about the world. I saw your hurt and anger, but I thought you were feeling strong and determined when you left."

"Well, I couldn't have done any of this without all of your support: finding my powers, healing the earth, myself and Paul. Thanks everyone. I apologize for also ignoring your needs. I could have done more to help with the campaign. I'm so glad the election resolved Atom City's crisis. After all, Atom City's peaceful relations among its citizens are part of its beauty. I'll be back to help more, and take care of my little plot of evium. And don't worry Carl, I'll bring Liz." Evie said smiling. "Now I'll send you all safely home".

Evie recited The Formula to herself, thinking the ElemMates back to Atom City.

As Evie's electrons slowed and dimmed, her friends disappeared, and her evium crystals absorbed into her skin.

She gazed at the peacefully sleeping youth until he called out for his mother in his sleep.

Evie turned to leave the room. She cast one last glance at the boy curled up under the blanket. "I'll go get your mom. See you later, Paul. I still haven't given up nor forgotten our trip to the stars."

Far down the long hospital corridor Evie spotted her parents and ran into their embrace. Liz had arrived with soft drinks sloshing in her hands. Evie told a nurse she thought the boy in room 18 seemed much better and was asking for his mother.

True to her word, she let her parents immediately check her into the hospital. She submitted to all the tests. Let them take her blood twice a day for the four days they kept her. Although her blood was not as full of toxins as her first stay in the hospital, they still needed to hook her up to a special machine to clean the rest out.

Tests showed one unknown mineral. It seemed non-toxic, and boosted the immune system. Dr. Sparks told them Evie had been exposed to it when she discovered it at the Blast Site. More investigations were being done on it.

On her last day the nurse handed her a slip of paper. "From the cute boy down the hall. I think he wants you to visit him."

"Oh, glad you got the note," Paul said propped up with pillows in the hospital bed. His skin was still very pale, but he sure looked good to Evie. "Thanks for stopping in. My Mom says you really helped make me better. I sure don't know what happened to me. Did you get my other note? I apologized for neglecting you. Should have included you with my friend from California. I didn't know how to handle it. After the astronomy camp, which was crazy busy, I went to hang out with my family and old friends. Guess I just wanted to be back in my old life for a bit. She's an old friend of the family. I've known her all my life." He said reaching out his hand for hers.

"I was so hurt and jealous. I guess I should have been cooler. But I couldn't find you. I missed you so much," Evie confessed letting him see her hurt. "And now you and your California girl will be long distance lovers, I assume."

Paul pulled her closer. "Only you are into star gazing, climbing cliffs, swimming and making weird sculptures. I hope we can be together again."

Evie leaned over the bed into his arms. Her electrons picked up speed as they kissed.

Chapter 25
The Festival

"Boy, the news must be really popping with the story of our cleanup," said Evie on her release from the hospital.

"No," her mother informed her, loathe to bring her daughter's spirits down. "It will probably take awhile to be discovered. Remember, those sites are kept well hidden underground. Nonetheless everyone is aware the Garden is no longer toxic and everyone is healthy.

It took awhile for the news to pick up stories about drastically reduced water, air and earth pollution and radiation contamination.

By mid-August and fully recuperated, Evie rallied her club to make the Science Festival happen. This was going to be a big one, a last hurrah of summer before school began. They had been working on this since May, thought everything was good to go, yet by two weeks before the Festival there was still so much to do. Every day was a whirlwind of things to check and arrange. The caterers, exhibit designers and suppliers they had booked went way beyond their usual services for them. They were all happy to help these kids make it a successful two-day event.

They sent out last minute publicity everywhere, and in every media. The media ate it all up. They were riding the crest of a hot worldwide new trend of Science Festivals revved up with cool music and amusement events. They benefited from the momentum from a recent hit Boston Science Festival. It helped that theirs was organized by kids.

Everyone in town helped prepare the now non-toxic Park and Garden. Wrought iron solar powered street lamps lit paved paths through the wild foliage. Club members thought it would be cool to make a maze out of the low shrubbery and bushes bordering Sparks Park. The Center stage was set up near Evie's now forty foot high glittering gem sculpture and the rocky cliffs. Rows of tents and booths curved out from it leaving a grassy space in the center for the audience. A tent right of the stage gave performers a place to prepare and rest.

To the left a spacious tent for all the KISC groups from all over the country would exhibit projects, experiments and each club's news. Plenty of chairs and refreshments made it a good place to meet each other and hang out. Their Marblehead chapter space at the entrance welcomed and checked all the groups in.

Lots of organizations contributed refreshments. Mixed among booths exhibiting new Science ideas, inventions and technologies were science oriented food, craft, product and game booths. And of course they had planned for tight security and crowd control.

According to the schedule the Marblehead KISC would officially open the Festival at noon from the stage. They would thank donors, the town and the vendors, describe some performances and activities, introduce some local chapters and finally introduce the first band. Two members would always be at their table in the KISC tent. Others would be strolling hosts taking in the festivities and giving out information about events, exhibits, vendors and food. At 7:30 the evening band would take the stage. That schedule followed for both days. After Paul's Jazz band finished Sunday evening, Evie would give the final closing of the Festivities. She was going to wear the dress Paul gave her. Clean up began at 10:00 p.m. sharp.

Parents, volunteers and teachers continued their support. Ms. Melillo put aside her work to help full time. During a quiet moment a week before the fair the girls presented their Atom City gift to her. "We wanted to give you this to thank you for everything. We found it mixed in with some of the sand you said we could take. Looks pretty and a bit weird like a spiked seashell, we thought," Evie explained nervously, hoping their teacher believed the little lie.

Ms. Melillo touched by their gesture said, "This is beautiful and so thoughtful. Thank you, thank you. You two are a gift to me. You both amaze me. Of course I hope you will continue to work with me when school starts though you will no longer be my students. We'll study this new sample. There's so much to do."

Early the Saturday morning of the Festival Evie slept on her trundle bed with Liz sprawled asleep across the big bed.

Evie's mother knocked on the door.

"Girls, it's eight o'clock. Don't you need to get up for the KISC Festival today?"

That got Evie out of bed in an instant. "Liz, come on. This is big day. Good luck to us."

Donning KISC T-shirts and grabbing a quick bite, her Mom handed her the birthday dress wrapped in cleaner's plastic to keep in the Performer's Tent. They and their army of club members, volunteers, parents and town workers had everything ready by noon when people began trickling in.

Soon other club chapters arrived to set up their tables in the

KISC tent. Most groups had brought Science Fair Projects. Liz first up at the Welcome Desk showed the Salem Club members to their spot next to theirs.

Liz jabbed Evie in the waist with her finger whispering. "Evie, check out that guy in the Salem Chapter." The dark skinned boy with chiseled features and curly black hair flashed a dazzling smile at Liz.

He boldly strode over to the girls. "Hi. I'm Carlton Carbonne. Glad we're getting our Chapters together. We're so close to you. We should think of doing things together." His eyes twinkled like diamonds.

Liz gazed back into his eyes. "Is your last name really Carbonne?"

"Funny you should ask. Our family is from Italy. Long line of miners. Ended up owning some mines there. Our family is still in the mining business. I'm really into studying minerals. Hey, do you want to see my Science Fair Project? Really cool stuff." He noticed Liz's display. "Hoo, boy. This yours? You did carbon studies!"

That was it. The two became inseparable. Both girls agreed Carlton's resemblance to Carl uncanny.

High noon on a gorgeous, warm late summer day brought thousands of peaceful excited fans of all ages. After checking out the KISC projects and introducing herself, Evie ushered the KISC members out onto the stage for the official opening of the Kids in Science Club Festival.

Then the Festival swung into full speed. Liz with Carlton manned the Welcome Desk. Evie and Paul were the first strolling hosts of the Festival. Every booth thrilled Evie with exciting, creative scientific ideas. They gawked at displays of electronics, science equipment, New Age crafts, jewelry, crystals, clothes and accessories. Magicians, musicians and theater groups performed amongst the crowd .

Down one aisle they spotted Evie's Mom at a plant seller's booth. She was deep in conversation with the owner. Strange, Evie thought, the seller's green tinted complexion and red hair reminded her of Nyla Nitrogen.

Paul dragged her away toward another booth. "Look, Evie, here's the booth for the store where I got your dress. I noticed the store wasn't in town anymore."

"Oh, this stuff is beautiful." She examined finely beaded dresses and blouses hanging on the racks. The booth also sold hand crafted gold jewelry set with emeralds. Evie did a double take when the owner turned to greet them. Beryl?

Ignoring the question the booth owner explained her work. "I do all the beading myself. My jewelry is a joint venture with a goldsmith. I admit some of the gold pieces aren't really all gold, just alloys, and mixes with other metals. I like to experiment. Ah, but here's my gold artist." Her partner turned toward them. Wide eyed Evie stared at… Gilda?

Paul bought Evie some hooped earrings with a tiny emerald in each.

"Gilda? Beryl?" she asked tentatively.

"Mmm?" both responded smiling neither denying nor asserting anything. "Come see us soon. We've moved to the next town over, in Salem. Cheaper rents there."

Flabbergasted by these coincidences seeing Carl, Nyla, Beryl, Gilda look-alikes, Evie said nothing.

"Come on, Evie. Look over there. It's one of those spa tents. You can get whiffs of pure Oxygen and a massage for ten dollars. Let's do it! I read breathing pure oxygen for ten minutes is refreshing," said Paul already focused on the next activity. The tent had four back massage chairs. The Masseuse, who settled them in and attached their oxygen masks to the tank for what was advertised as "A Breath of Real Fresh Air", had definite bluish tints in her complexion. Her wavy hair was dyed different shades of blue. Her dress, a layered, flowing pale blue tulle was trimmed in frothy lace.

Evie relaxed with closed eyes to enjoy it. The Masseuse bent over her whispering in her ear as Evie breathed the oxygen. "You, got it, Evie, we're all here. We're very proud of you." Evie shook her head in disbelief. The woman turned her back to work on Paul.

A figment of her imagination or not, it made her feel good.

"Paul, thanks so much for these earrings. Sorry I was a bit distracted at the jewelry booth. You've been so good to me. I really love my birthday dress, too. You know I'm wearing it for the final closing of the Festival."

"You're welcome," he said taking her hand.

"Well, I got you a gift, too. Actually it's something special I found at the original Blast site," said Evie. The microscopic gift from Atom City had grown to several inches around. She had wrapped the tiny box in star spangled blue paper. This morning she had tucked the gift in her pants pocket.

"Oh, stolen goods, eh…" he said opening the box. The star glowed and flashed its own light like a pulsing heartbeat. Entranced, he stared at it. "…Oh, wow, awesome…". He pulled her to him and kissed her. She didn't mention there might be more to the little specimen than he thought.

Sunday the final evening's last band got the crowd revved up. The audience danced to the beat and sang along with their hit songs. Colored LEDs and video imagery splashed a phenomenal multi-media show behind the band. Evie changed into her Birthday dress in the empty performers' tent.

As the last notes faded Evie joined the band members on stage. Everyone sang the final encore. She rocked to the music waving her arms high in the air. A heady sense of peace, joy and accomplishment filled her. She took the mic to thank everyone for a fabulous weekend.

A tremendous rush of joy filled her. Evium crystals formed under the beaded dress, her fibers twisted into the cotton dress and blossomed into a full multi-colored gem gown flowing to fill the stage. The audience oohed as the fibers stretched and spread creating a floating shimmering cloth glinting under the spotlights. The LED light show ended leaving the stage dark save a spotlight on Evie and her gown. Hundreds of tiny bursts of light brighter than the fabric gems flashed and spun around her. Now her amazing light show of a dress expanded, rippled down the stage stairs to the grassy arena and swirled around everyone's ankles. The silent band and audience watched her lights and fabric burn brighter in the dark.

The astounded audience gasped when Evie floated up above the stage lifting the glittering fabric upward until it hovered over them, a canopy of a million stars. Evie felt her body and mind surge with power. As she floated, the numbers and signs of The Formula multiplied filling the air. Her evium fibers continued to grow. Visions of the Garden in the Sahara and Atom City filled her mind in swirls of color.

Suddenly an ear-splitting crack erupted from Evie's towering sculpture behind the stage. It crumbled and toppled over the cliff into the ocean below. Evie in her illuminated silken parachute floated back to the stage. The audience roared. When her light went dark so did the park. The crowd sat in stunned silence.

A moment later the floodlights went on. Evie stood in her original spot clad in her beaded birthday dress. Only Liz noticed Evie's over-bright eyes and white flushed skin. The crowd stood for a thunderous ovation. Slowly the applause faded.

Evie held up her hands for silence. "Thanks again everyone for coming. Hope you enjoyed the Festival." Then she ducked behind the curtain to the performer's tent.

House lights told the crowd the show was over. People began drifting toward the exits, speaking quietly, preparing to depart, not believing what they had witnessed, but filled with wellbeing.

Liz took over with the cleanup crew. She took the mic and announced exit instructions. "Thanks again, everyone, for making this a top notch Rave. KISC will be organizing many more of these parties. Everyone is welcome to join in. Have a great evening."

Before they left the site Evie and Liz walked to the rocky bluff to pay homage to Evie's crumbled masterpiece. Shards that had not washed into the sea had embedded themselves into the rocks.

No one was tired when they arrived home at midnight. Evie's parents hovered around her over tea.

Evie handed them her gifts.

"I can tell you guys, there's more to these little trifles than meets the eye. Compliments from the Atom City Museum Souvenir Shop."

May's jeweled flower unfurled its petals before her eyes, sending a light perfume.

"Oh Evie this is beautiful…and something I'm going to have to study. Thank you." Her mom said.

"The Souvenir Shop, eh." Dad laughed as he opened his. The tiny ring had twisted higher into a spiral. He took it out and caressed the smooth curves with awe. "The Spiral of Life, shows growth to a higher level. Thank you, Evie." He kissed her forehead. "And what an exciting, exhausting spiral you've had."

"Yeah, what a year it's been. But I think I've come through for the better, definitely spiraled upward," said Evie "I fell into these strange, exciting adventures as a frustrated little girl. I did big headline superhero, earth-saving deeds. I was a superwoman with a swollen head and too big a job for my age. Then those world problems took a back seat to my personal problems: my own jealousies, mind games, stress, heartbreak and I guess, physical illness. I'm glad I got through it… so far.

Dad, you have it right. Growing up is a series of tests and a journey. I followed tortuous paths, fulfilled quests, made mistakes, destroyed and saved.

Now I know I'm strong enough to grow more, Mom. I have so many ideas. There's so much to think about. I want to do it all. I don't know if I'm really a scientist. My art makes me so happy. Guess I'm still a kid. I want to have fun. But I can't do it on my own. I really need you guys. I need everyone."

In a rare occurrence these last few months, her Mom tucked Evie in and sat down on the edge of her bed. Dad leaned on the headboard.

Her mother kissed her. "You are so smart, my Love. Dad and I are so proud of you. We will support you in all your dreams. You are a wonderful artist and scientist and a whole lot more.

You've already done lots of building, creating and fixing. Don't worry, we won't let you forget you are our child and not let you grow up too fast. We'll make sure your life is full of fun and joy."

"Oh, don't worry about me growing up too fast. I think I'm still the shortest kid in my class," Evie chuckled sleepily.

"Oh, you silly. Go to sleep," Dad said kissing her.

"Mom, Dad, it was such a thrill. Today I floated over the crowd. I turned into evium out there."

Alone in the dark, images flashed before her. She saw herself on Terra Mountain made an honorary Atom City citizen, the ElemMate Evium with powerful properties. There she was negotiating peace at the Ozone Hole. With her friends she'd created the beautiful Garden in the Sahara and in Marblehead. Hadn't she and her friends led an army of trillions to bring peace to Atom City? ...And started a national science club in her own town.

She thought about her next visit to Atom City and her plans for her own piece of land there.

So, bottom line, is Atom City all in her imagination? Course not. Liz had joined her. Atom City is right here in Marblehead just off the cliff side trail. She and Liz walked to Atom City from Sparks Park, and her ElemMate friends were at the Festival.

Of course there's no question atoms are real. Everyone can see them through a microscope. They bond together to make her body. Their electrical sparks fire her memory, senses, knowledge and her imagination. Oh, such possibilities. For sure she could be a scientist and an artist.

Drowsy she closed her eyes. Sparkling colored crystals and Paul filled her dreams.

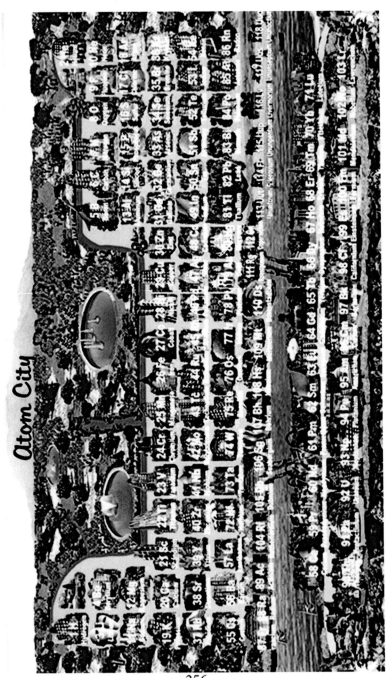

For more about Evie,
the ElemMates and Atom City
go to the ElemMates website:

ElemMates.com.

Meet the ElemMates characters based on
the real chemical elements.
Get to know their personalities and interests.
Learn about the real elements.

Atom City is based on:
the Periodic Table of the Chemical Elements Chart.
See each ElemMates home.
Visit Atom City destinations: Parks, Theaters, Mall,
Museums, Spas, Zoo, Hospital, Town Hall, Cafes.

Create, Engineer, Design things and do projects
for the ElemMates, Atom City and the real world.
Write new stories about the characters.

Join STEAM based Kids in Science Club.
Do real experiments.
Form KISC Chapters with "How To" Documents.
Links to Science, Tech, Club and Arts sites.
Find card games, craft and activity ideas.

See the Blog for Real, Science, Events and Atom City News.
Post comments.

Leslie Wallant

Evie & the ElemMates

259